WHEN EAGLES CALL

When Eagles Call

Susan Dobbie

RONSDALE PRESS

WHEN EAGLES CALL
Copyright © 2003 Susan Dobbie

RONSDALE PRESS
3350 West 21st Avenue
Vancouver, B.C., Canada
V6S 1G7

Edited by: Ronald B. Hatch
Typesetting: Julie Cochrane in Fairfield Light 11 pt on 16.5
Cover Design: Rand Berthaudin
Printing: AGMV Marquis, Quebec, Canada
Paper: Ancient Forest Friendly Rolland "Enviro" — 100% post-consumer waste,
    totally chlorine-free

Ronsdale Press wishes to thank the Canada Council for the Arts, the Government of Canada through the Book Publishing Industry Development Program (BPIDP), and the Province of British Columbia through the British Columbia Arts Council for their support of its publishing program.

National Library of Canada Cataloguing in Publication Data

Dobbie, Susan, (date)
    When eagles call / Susan Dobbie.

ISBN 1-55380-005-2

I. Title.
PS8557.O21W43 2003   C813'.6   C2003-910024-3
PR9199.4.D62W43 2003

At Ronsdale Press we are committed to protecting the environment. To this end we are working with Markets Initiative (www.oldgrowthfree.com) and printers to phase out our use of paper produced from ancient forests. This book is one step towards that goal.

ACKNOWLEDGEMENTS

When I attended Simon Fraser University in 1989 as a mature student, more than a few young classmates claimed boredom and yawned through Canadian History 101. I was raised in Scotland, where people feel passion for their past, for Bannockburn and Culloden. Other nations share this passion — the English for Waterloo, and the Charge of the Light Brigade; the Americans for the Alamo. Canadians do have the Plains of Abraham, but British Columbia was wilderness then, not yet a province, so the emotional impact for westerners is insignificant. Yet we did have many struggles on our coast that defined us, and it is hoped that this historical novel, based on the Hudson's Bay Company Journals in Langley, offers one such example. Certainly every attempt has been made to remain truthful to the facts and spirit of the time. My thanks to those bored students who sparked in me the idea to write this book, to add a human dimension to dusty facts, to relive the struggles and passions of those early years.

For access to the Fort Langley Journals, my thanks to the Langley Centennial Museum, where I have been privileged to work as a docent for the past ten years.

Special thanks to Dr. Ronald B. Hatch, Director, Ronsdale Press, for his patience and guidance through the writing of this book.

TYPESETTING NOTE

Hawaiian and First Nations' words and phrases are indicated in italics for the first usage, but thereafter they are printed in normal Roman type so as to include them as a natural part of the narrative. Their meaning is explained by the context.

For my family, without whose support this book would not have been written.

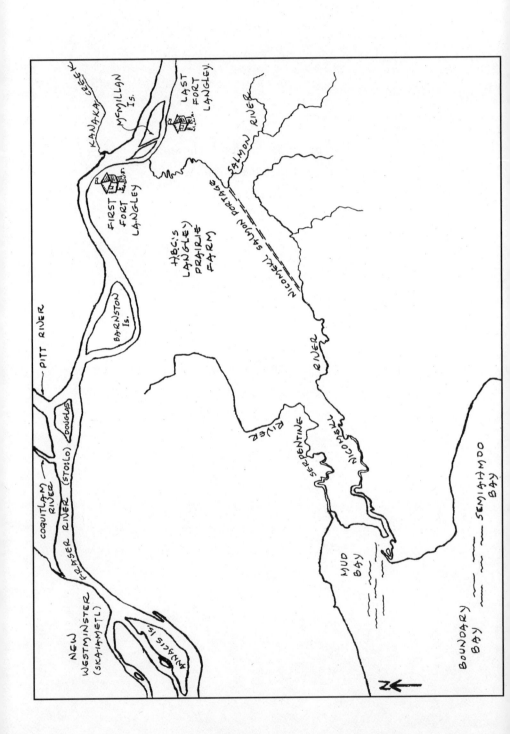

chapter one

HE WOKE WITH a headache, pain arriving in long ocean rollers, like the morning surf pounding the nearby shore. Sprawled across the gnarled roots of the kiawe tree, he fought to lift his head. His brown cheek wore the indentations of the tree's bark. His mouth felt dry from the sand that had found its way into his throat. His eyes hurt from the grit beneath his lashes and he forced them open one at a time, each slit hurting as light caught the iris. He peered skyward, where the tree's great trunk soared like the cathedral pillars in Hopoo's old pictures from the mission. Sunrise had come, poking ribbons of light through the tree's branches, fingering to warm the sand, damp from the cool night air.

He struggled to sit up, then it came to him. Yesterday his mother had married Pikoi. He hadn't gone home after the wedding because he'd drunk too much rum, something he'd never done before, and now regretted. He couldn't remember falling asleep beneath the kiawe. The giant tree had stood sentinel on the beach for longer than people could remember, its aged branches spreading shade farther than the slender young palms, rooted in disarray along the shore. A shadow startled him, cutting suddenly into the sunlight.

"*Aloha* Kimo, you a'right?" It was fat Oolea, moon-faced and rotund, wearing a tapa wrap around his loins, and nothing else. His brown stomach protruded and hung over the wrap, skin taught and shiny as if he'd polished it last night with kukui nut oil. He squatted on his haunches beneath the kiawe. He had the biggest feet of any man Kimo knew, and hands the size of taro leaves. Oolea picked up the gourd wedged in the sand and sniffed.

"You empty this, cousin?" Kimo didn't answer. "Kalama will be fine, Kimo. Pikoi's a decent man. Besides, it rained for them, didn't it?"

"The luau went well enough," Kimo conceded. Yes. His mother had worn a swath of tapa round her still slim body, sarong-like, instead of the modest muu-muu the missionaries encouraged. The white hibiscus behind her ear had emphasized her dark eyes and the gleaming black of her long hair and Kimo thought she had never looked so beautiful. He did not approve the match, but his mother had been lonely. Rain, fine as vapour spray, fell just as Pikoi had danced the *kahiko* for her, and this had eased Kimo's mind, for it guaranteed good fortune. The evening ended with a wedding *melé* from the guests, the soft modulating chant drifting upwards on the perfumed air, reaching for the gods. He wondered which gods, if any, would hear their prayers, the old Hawaiian gods or the *haole* God, brought by the missionaries.

The perfume from the *leis* and *heis* worn by the guests lingered even now on his skin, the delicate fragrance of orchids and plumeria, of hibiscus and ginger at odds with the sour dregs of rum left in the gourd. And in his mouth. He wanted nothing more than a drink of water. Just a mouthful, even. But if he had it, it would sizzle in his throat like spilled water over hot roasting stones.

"You still leaving, Kimo?" Oolea shifted uncomfortably. For months they'd planned to go but now it was time to act, he'd changed his mind. Kimo wasn't surprised. Ordinary things kept the big man happy, his canoe, music and dance, and food, provided there was lots of it. His best friend had been carried along by the force of Kimo's discontent, not his own. "I've let you down," he said dejectedly.

"No, *aikane*, it's no crime to change your mind. I'm still going."

"I'd come if it wasn't for Lani. Have you told your grandfather?"

"Not yet." He'd tell Keaka after he signed the papers. When there was no turning back. It wouldn't be easy. His grandfather wouldn't want him to go. He'd taken him in after his son, Kimo's father, had died eight years ago. It was a day Kimo never forgot, for Keaka had knocked out his own front teeth at the time. Four of them, with a round, smooth white stone from the beach, the size of a coconut. Blood had streamed down his swollen chin, along with scalding salt tears to form a pool of shocking scarlet on the white sand at his feet. Kimo had feared his grandfather would mutilate himself, or gouge his eye out, as custom required before the haoles arrived, but he did neither. And afterwards, he and his mother lived with Keaka's *ohana*, and their extended family. His grandfather had tutored him and sent him to school to learn English.

But this was the time for him to leave, now his mother had married Pikoi. For years he had worked the taro fields of Waikiki, the flat marshy plain five feet above sea level not far from Honolulu's harbour, with the others in the ohana. They would till the day they died, he reckoned, and seek nothing more. But Kimo felt there was more to life than picking someone else's taro. He couldn't remember when the idea first came to him to buy a plot of land, grow his own taro, plant some banana trees, find some measure of independence. He just knew he would, though he hadn't figured out how. Till now. In the old days, before the white men came, land belonged only to the *alii,* but now ordinary men could buy property if they had the means. The key was money, and he knew how to find it. He'd sign up on one of the foreign ships that stopped in Hawaii to stock up on fresh water and food, now the Islands were the midway stop for the great sailing ships that traded in the South China Seas.

After Oolea left, Kimo rose unsteadily and headed for the waterfront. He was glad of the few miles he had to walk, for it would help clear his head. He wished he looked better. His dark blue cotton trousers were creased from his night on the beach, his shirt equally wrinkled from having been rolled into a pillow. He slung his black leather shoes across his left shoulder, to dangle one in front, the other behind. Sand cascaded from the heels. They were the first pair he'd owned. He'd worn them to the wedding but they pinched badly so now he walked barefoot. He'd bought them, not for the wedding, but because he'd heard from men on the wharf that when a *Kanaka* left the Islands, he must have shoes.

Overhead a brilliant yellow sun cast a net of oppressive heat across the entire island, with no hint of any kindly trade wind to cool the air or soothe the skin. With long strides, he made his way west from Waikiki, past the old *heiau,* the temple, then past the grass hut of the haole Campbell. They would tear it down soon to build a Seaman's Mission, so people said. He walked on, stopping only once to greet a friend and drink water from his gourd, and eventually arrived at the long rows of warehouses lining Honolulu's harbour.

Here and there friends called out alohas amid the sailors, passengers, merchants and longshoremen mingling on the wharves conducting their affairs. Hawaii had changed since he was a boy. Now a row of dingy taverns dotted the waterfront beckoning drunken seamen from every part of the globe, and in darkened doorways, prostitutes clotted in pouting groups hawking their services. He walked by, ignoring the winks and finger signals of the docks' soiled women, aware only of where he was headed and why, and of the blue Pacific lapping softly like broth against the wooden pilings beneath his feet. Even as he passed, two men scuffled, cursing, in a shadowed doorway. One was Hawaiian, a brawling troublemaker known on the docks, the other a white, pock-faced seaman off one or other of the sailing ships in the harbour. People ignored them. Fights were commonplace on the docks, for the usual reasons, cards, rum, women. He quickened his pace.

His timing was perfect. Soon men would need written approval from the government to leave, but the new law had not yet been passed so all he needed was his birth certificate. It was an informal paper, one the missionaries had written up for him when he'd entered school. He'd kept it folded in his pocket for days. He hoped the rumours were true, that they chose strong, able-bodied men. If all they wanted was a workhorse, at six foot three inches with his broad back and muscular build, he should qualify.

"Got your papers?" barked the reedy, wire-brush of a man named Pelly, stooping at the desk in the Hudson's Bay recruiting office, a small wooden shack the Company had opened on the harbour front a year ago. The haole's white hair jutted out in thin airy tufts and his round English eyes were the coldest blue Kimo had ever seen. He pulled out his birth certificate and laid it on the table.

"Kimo Maka Kanui. You speak pidgin?"

"And English. I attended the Mission."

The man's bushy eyebrows lifted curiously above steel blue eyes, assessing him carefully. Kimo wished he'd worn the shoes, and stretched himself full height.

"You're a carpenter by trade?"

He nodded, waiting for the man to ask where he'd been trained.

He didn't, releasing Kimo from the lie he'd had to fabricate en route. The man dragged a soiled handkerchief from the pocket of his jacket and wiped off the sweat gathering in rivulets across his brow. Kimo held his breath while the recruiter plucked at the front of his damp shirt. Once white, the stained cotton was now gray and clung to his chest as he wafted it back and forth in a futile effort to create a tiny breeze to cool his overheated skin.

Suddenly Kimo found himself signing a contract, grinning like a split melon, shaking the haole's hand vigorously, mentally congratulating himself. *I've done it! I've done it!*

Just like that, it was settled. He would sail on the next Hudson's Bay Company ship, work in its service in forts on the Pacific Northwest Coast of America, and receive room, board and wages of eighteen pounds a year. The Company would return him, passage paid, to Honolulu at the end of his three-year contract. It had been easier than he thought. Now he'd tell his mother. She'd need time to get used to the idea.

When he approached her that evening, he expected tears of dismay and disapproval over his imminent departure. Her dry eyes confounded him.

"When do you leave?" she asked calmly, as if he were simply moving to the next beach. He swallowed his surprise, felt it stick oddly in his throat. He had not expected such composure.

"Eight weeks."

"She hugged him wordlessly, holding him so close he could hear the steady beating of her heart, but still the tears he expected did not materialize.

"Three years isn't long," he said. "Then I'll be back. Will you be all right?"

"Of course I will. Pikoi will see to that, Kimo." It was a reprimand. His fault. If only he liked the man more, but Pikoi spewed irrational

opinions like wild seed across the ground where they took root and
flourished, in spite of truth or facts offered to the contrary. He was
forever extolling the virtues of life in the old days, before the haoles
came. Kimo would never openly contradict the man his mother
chose to marry, but Pikoi was wrong. Life had been cruelly stratified
in the old Hawaii. The noble alii held great power and wealth, while
the poor remained virtual slaves who had nothing, and could never
hope to have anything. He wished his mother had chosen a wiser
man. Yet Pikoi loved her and for that he was grateful. His mother had
made her choice. Now he'd made his.

He found his *kupuna*, his grandfather, Keaka, dozing in the shade,
back slumped against the gray trunk of a coconut palm. He wore a
tapa loincloth always, though he owned a pair of unbleached cotton
trousers that he'd worn twice, his one concession to the haoles' dress
code. Age had unsteadied his once powerful limbs. His spine curved
slightly now, making his shoulders droop and his chest shrink inward.
As his long legs stretched before him, his shinbones seemed to shine
white through the brown skin pulled taut across them. Kimo touched
the old man's shoulder and he woke with a loud snort that made his
head jolt forward. Kimo moved to steady him. A soft loose cough
rattled up his throat and Kimo felt a pang. He would miss his grandfather most of all.

Keaka waved a gnarled bony forefinger at the pile of coconuts and
the machete lying on the grass mat between them. Wordlessly Kimo
split one of the brown nuts with a blow from the knife and lifted the
neatly split half to the old man's mouth. He drank the white milk
slowly then wiped his soft brown lips with the back of his hand. Fat
beads of milk clung to his large upper lip, like pukas on a string, till a
long pink tongue emerged to sweep them off their perch.

"*Pehea oe, Kimo?*" Words lisped out of his toothless mouth in a
whuff of air, like the shushing of a wave rolling up the beach.

"I'm fine, Kupuna."

"And the long face?"

"Too much rum." Keaka made a disapproving clucking noise in his throat. Kimo decided to plunge right in. "I'm leaving the Islands, Kupuna." The old man said nothing. Kimo thought he hadn't heard. "I'm here to ask for your blessing."

When Keaka remained silent, Kimo said no more. He'd asked. Now he'd have to wait. Hopoo at the Mission would say that he was superstitious for holding on to the old ways like this, but he really wanted the blessing of the family elder. It would bode ill if he left without it. A minute passed. Two.

"Which line, Kimo? One of the East Indian traders?"

"The Hudson's Bay Company. They have a good reputation on the docks."

"Where will they take you?"

"The Pacific Northwest."

"*Aolé!* America? Men speak of dangers there, Kimo, of wild animals and wild people, mountains too high to climb and rivers too deep to cross. And unimaginable cold. Kanakas who go don't always come home. Many have died there."

"Rumours, Kupuna. Many men have gone and come home safely."

"Think well before you do this."

"I signed up this morning."

Keaka closed his eyes and leaned back against the tree. Kimo looked up at the nuts ripening dangerously atop the palm and wondered vaguely which one of his cousins would lop them off for the old man after he was gone. He waited five, ten minutes then rose, swallowing his impatience. His grandfather had fallen asleep. He would have to bide his time and tackle him again later, after he'd grown more used to the idea.

Hopoo, at the Mission, was no easier to deal with than Keaka.

When Kimo told him his plans, his old mentor berated him for lying.

"What do you know about carpentry?" Hopoo never minced words. His deep voice resonated like a Hawaiian drum. Short white hair covered his square-shaped head like moss on a tree. His slanted brown eyes impaled Kimo like a pinned moth and Kimo had the grace to flinch.

"I've fixed canoes. I can use a hammer and saw as well as the next man."

"That's not the same as being a qualified carpenter, and you know it."

"I had no choice."

"There's always a choice, Kimo." The missionary wrapped a worn cape around his shoulders with arthritic slowness and huddled into a stoop. A surge of irritation washed over Kimo. You could never argue with Hopoo, for he always made you feel guilty. Trouble was, he was usually right.

"Well, at least Pikoi will care for your mother. It must be ten years since your father died of the pox."

"Twelve, Hopoo." And it had been measles, not smallpox that killed his father. Thousands had died from the white man's diseases.

"So many have left. The lifeblood of the Islands is draining away. Now you, too, are leaving." Hopoo's head dropped till his chin rested on his chest, and he closed his eyes in prayer. An early convert to Christianity, he'd left the Islands years ago to study for the ministry in America before returning to Honolulu. Now he was part of what Keaka scornfully called "that missionary crowd." Many were truly Christian men, like Hopoo. But others came to Hawaii to provide the bread of life and stayed to gobble the whole damned Island. It was Hopoo's belief in one God and one God only, that troubled Kimo most, for Hawaiians had worshipped many gods, gods who'd made their presence known for centuries, gods who answered their prayers.

How could they suddenly be denied? Many, like Keaka, disdained Hopoo's Christianity, clinging fast to the old gods, while Kimo wavered between the two, trapped by respect and affection for both men.

Don't make this any harder, Hopoo, he pleaded silently to the bent head. As if he'd heard the words, the old missionary opened his eyes.

"Go with God, then, but come back safely when your contract expires. How long before you sail, Kimo?"

"Two months."

"Long enough to learn your family chants. Keaka can teach you, unless you've written them down already?" He hadn't. He should, since he was the only one of his family who knew how to write their new alphabet. Twelve letters, five vowels, seven consonants. Simpler than English. Before, Hawaiians had no written history, just oral tales in the memories of the old ones. It was something he should do as an only son, to keep the family history.

In the following weeks, farewell parties engulfed him as luaus were held in his honour, and several pretty *wahines* cried over his departure. He regretted not ending his relationship with Lili Lihau sooner, though. The girl had the body of a goddess with the mind of a mango. Still, her copious tears shamed him and jolted his conscience, for his leaving commanded a proper show of distress, and Lili, with her flair for drama, obliged, making their parting more intense than he intended. He consoled himself that the lovely Lili would find an accommodating new partner the moment his ship left harbour, and fervently hoped he was right, for he truly wished not to hurt the girl.

Two weeks before he sailed, he revisited Keaka. He found him huddled in the shade, curled up involute like a sleeping snail, fanning himself with a torn banana leaf.

"You learned well at the mission school," he said, as they sat on the tapa mat in the shady lanai of his small grass hut. Yes. He'd learned to read and write in the large thatched roof hut, open at each end for the trade winds to blow through to cool the heat of the day. Soon, they would erect a building, a proper haole missionary school, from stones and coral and he wondered how it would feel to be confined indoors so many hours a day. Keaka had sent him to the missionaries because of their wider knowledge of the outside world. There he'd learned to judge Hawaii from the haoles' perspective, to recognize its ancient cruelties and flaws. Yet, with Keaka's sly prodding, he'd come to view the whites with an equally critical Hawaiian eye and, though he approved of many haole beliefs and admired their power, he found their thin souls wanting. In time he learned to straddle both worlds, but fit neither.

"I've read your signs and laid out offerings to the gods," Keaka said. White bristling eyebrows framed his dark far-seeing eyes. Kimo looked down upon the lined face grinning toothlessly up at him, brown skin wizened in folds deep enough to plant taro and hoped this meant the old man would bless him after all.

"Hopoo thinks I should learn my chants. Will you teach me before I go?"

The old man closed his eyes and mumbled a series of jumbled prayers, making Kimo shift uncomfortably. His nose picked up the faint smell of milk gone sour and he hoped Keaka wouldn't pull out his dusty bag of dry bones. He wondered which "offerings" his grandfather would put out in his name this time, a handful of weeds, or shells, or hair, or fingernail clippings, no doubt.

"For once I agree with that old fool," Keaka sniffed. "To know your chants, that's good. Yes, I'll teach you. Then you'll come back." Kimo said nothing. He was only going for three years. Of course he'd come back, whether the old man made his offerings or not. Keaka waved a skinny hand in the air with a flick of the wrist, as if tossing away an old banana skin.

"We begin," he pronounced solemnly. And they did. Kimo learned his genealogical chants. They were long, and he fought hard to keep his mind on track while Keaka droned on through generations of history, ending when the *Iphigenia Nubiana* arrived and traded guns to Kamehameha, who used them to conquer the Islands. Kimo secretly deemed the chants tedious and unnecessary now he could write, but nevertheless he worked hard, out of respect for the old ways. He promised himself he'd write them down soon. Maybe he'd find time on the ship.

On his last visit to the old man's lanai, Keaka placed in Kimo's broad brown palm a tiny koa wood dolphin strung on a narrow leather thong to wear around his neck for good luck. Keaka's arthritic hands were knotted and twisted and Kimo knew it must have taken many hours to carve and polish the tiny perfect creature. Keaka strained to reach up, stretching his bony legs, thin as chicken's thighs. Kimo had to stoop to accommodate the old man's reach as he placed an open maile leaf lei around Kimo's bronze neck. Sweet smelling and pungent, the leaves trailed down his muscular brown chest, falling below his narrow waistline.

Now, he thought, *it will come.* His heart lurched suddenly, rising into his throat at the thought he might never see the old man again. He loved him and wanted to tell him so, but could not. Instead, he stood motionless as Keaka offered his blessing, chanting a sad farewell melé.

"Mahalo, Kupuna." Kimo kissed the old man. Keaka smiled a wide toothless aloha, hugged him fiercely and assured him of protection because of the many sacrifices made in his name. And with Hopoo's Lord's Prayer echoing in his mind, Kimo drew guilty comfort from Keaka's assurance that the old gods would watch over him as well.

Where he was going, he'd need all the help he could get.

chapter two

THEY'D SAID NOTHING about him having to shoot people! Kimo swallowed hard, forcing the consternation inside to subside slowly. Instinct directed him to appear fearless, like his ancestor warriors, so that his face reflected nothing of his confusion. He bit the folded end of the small paper cartridge and immediately spat it out, grimacing at the bitter taste the specks of black powder left in his mouth. The mix of charcoal, sulphur and saltpetre burned his tongue, and the acrid smell made his nostrils twitch.

"Pull the flint back once, laddie, till it's half-cocked, in the safe position. Then ye won't fire it by accident." The red-haired, freckle-faced Scot leaned so close, the bristles of his beard rubbed against Kimo's neck so that he picked up the man's smell, an odd mix of sweat, smoke and pine needles.

"That's the priming pan on the outside of the barrel, and this here touch hole," McKay prodded the tiny circle with his finger, "connects it with the inside. Now pull the frizzen closed over the pan and lay the butt of the musket on the ground."

Kimo set the butt against his left foot and gingerly poured the packet of gunpowder down the barrel as the lanky Scot handed him a small lead ball. He fumbled, wiped the nervous sweat off his palm, then grasped it tightly in his fist.

"Peel the paper off the cartridge and wrap it round the ball then push it with the ramrod all the way down the barrel. That's it. Tamp it hard, twice. Then pull the flint so it's fully cocked. Now you're ready to fire."

Kimo raised the musket to his right shoulder, took aim at the line of boards propped up against a giant fir three hundred feet across the clearing, drew his breath and pulled the trigger. A fierce, explosive bang resonated in ears, deafening him and knocking him off balance so that he staggered drunkenly. The Scot laughed and laid a hand approvingly on his shoulder.

"You hit the boards. Not bad for the first time."

Stunned, Kimo shook his head to clear the clanging in his ear. When he recovered, he eyed the muzzle curiously. "The flint strikes the steel and . . . ?"

"The spark falls in the pan and the powder in the pan catches fire. It moves along and up the hole and ignites the large charge of powder. That makes the explosion and the shot. You did well, Kanaka, for a first try. It took you fifty-one seconds, start to finish. With a bit of practice, you'll be able to cut the time to half a minute."

A knife was still swifter, Kimo reckoned. Time would have to be on your side for a musket to be your weapon of choice. What enemy would pause for half a minute while you loaded a gun? He made two more attempts and managed to cut six seconds off the time it took to load and fire, but knew he'd need a lot more practice to complete the process as swiftly as the bearded McKay.

When the next man arrived for instruction, Kimo left the clearing and trekked along the footpath to Fort Vancouver. He now knew he was in Oregon Territory, a vast area covering the Columbia and areas of New Caledonia west of the Rockies. He was still trying to unravel the fort's confused history. The American fur trader Astor had built Fort Astoria at the mouth of the river in 1811. In the 1812 war with the British, they renamed it Fort George but it reverted to the Americans in 1818. Both countries then agreed to joint occupation of the Territory, until such time as its future could be negotiated. The fort was moved upstream and renamed Fort Vancouver in 1825. He didn't know why, but guessed at better deepwater moorage facilities for the sailing ships.

It was a fine fort, grander than he'd expected, though he didn't feel at ease around the place yet and now hunger pangs made his stomach gurgle. His limbs felt weighted with lead and his shoulder muscles ached from the strain of cutting logs for the fort's saw pit. A strong whiff of smoked salmon carried on the evening breeze suddenly teased his nostrils, making his saliva glands spurt, and he quickened his steps.

He hadn't yet caught the mood of the place. Six days on dry land and he still felt disoriented, but he thanked the gods for finally stopping the ground from moving beneath his feet. The *Thomasina* had been decent enough as ships go, but six weeks at sea had brought hardships he'd never anticipated. Sleeping below decks in a hammock too small for his bulk proved a nightly challenge. Food was another. Once the ship's fresh fruit and vegetables ran out, the crew ate salt pork and dry biscuits, from which black shiny weevils dropped so routinely that men laid bets on which bug would scuttle across the table's edge fastest. The salt pork was hard as a kukui nut after a good polish. After two weeks at sea, it chipped Kimo's lower left molar.

His forehead turned black and blue from bumping into beams. The ship's low ceilings bore down on him, the cramped sleeping quarters oppressed him, and he could span the length of the decks with a few long strides, which hardly constituted a decent walk. It gave him an odd sense of diminishment, of restraint, of somehow becoming less than he was. Each day he clambered up the rigging, where at least he could reach upwards, if not outwards. There were days when he would make for the ship's rail and gaze at the horizon till he felt quieted, letting the space fill him.

Privacy was non-existent. He prayed for calm seas when the call of nature came, for it meant climbing like a mountain goat onto the leeward channels and stepping carefully along the platforms on the side of the ship, where the crew spread the rigging, to void into the ocean. Or using the wooden structure hanging over the *Thomasina's* bow at the beak head, the "head" of the ship, square boxes with holes cut into them.

The ship's workdays demanded every ounce of energy a body could muster. New tars like Kimo performed the most menial chores, with one day of drudgery following another. When scrubbing and polishing brasses drove him to distraction, he had to remind himself of his goal to keep his frustrations at bay. Only in the evenings could men find time for rest or recreation. The crew would sing songs and fiddle, dance jigs and reels. He played cards with Moku Mu'olelo, a man from Kailua, who slept in the adjacent hammock in the overcrowded fetid quarters below deck, and with Billings, the pasty-faced Englishman who befriended him the day he boarded. The talkative Billings was gaunt, with a face like a white potato, pitted with smallpox scars. His sparrow-like eyes sparkled with keen intelligence though, and he offered advice freely and often. He showed them how to mend sails, and as they sewed, regaled them with tales of life at sea. He'd left England when he was a boy of fourteen, and had sailed to all the world's major ports of call, London, Amsterdam, Boston, Rio, even Canton, and his tales of far-off places stirred in them new wonder about the wide world beyond their islands.

Seven other Kanakas had signed on in Honolulu, all good men but one. His name was Ahuhu. You could tell the man was trouble from the moment he climbed up the rope ladder from the rowboat onto the deck. He exuded an aura of menace that you felt long before you drew close enough to see his face. A line of scar tissue ran from his right ear across the cheekbone to stop where a broken nose had healed, obviously untreated, and lay unnaturally broad and flat. Another line stretched the length of his chin, just below his mouth. Kimo wondered how he'd managed to pass the recruiter. False identity, he guessed, for Ahuhu meant poison-weed in Hawaiian, and no man would bear such a name. Unless, in some twisted way, it amused him to do so. If it was a joke, it was a bad one, but he wasn't the first malefactor to leave on a sailing ship one step ahead of the law.

"Don't cross him," Billings warned Kimo and Moku, "nor turn your back on him either." It proved good advice. Three weeks into their journey, a fight broke out during a poker game below decks when Collins, a slow-witted Welshman, accused Ahuhu of dealing off the bottom of the deck. Collins was small, a thin reed of a man and Ahuhu towered head and shoulders above him. The Islander took pleasure goading him, and struck him to the floor with a fist the size of a coconut. Collins tried to regain his feet, but Ahuhu hit him again, then again. When two crewmen moved to intervene, the irate Collins drew a knife, and the men backed away. The Captain arrived, irritable and sleepy-eyed, with his pea jacket flapping over his night clothes, and called an end to the fight. He ordered the blacksmith to clamp the little man in leg irons and Collins dragged himself around in clanking chains for the rest of the trip, a pathetic sight.

"He brought it on hisself," Billings said when Kimo expressed pity for the man. "No captain will stand for cutting onboard ship. There's jail material in crews, scrappers that take offence at nowt and look for trouble. The Cap'n has to be tougher than they are, or we'd have chaos afore we reached port. Men 'as been lashed for drawing a knife, and keel-hauled even. The Cap'n likes discipline, but he's not cruel like some."

The incident vexed Kimo, though. True, crewmen were a tough lot, hard to control, but discipline at sea was cruel and swift. Men had been drowned by keel-hauling, though few Captains practised this any more, preferring punishment in leg irons, and these were clamped on Collins for the duration of the journey. Ahuhu had cheated and lied. He'd started the fight, not the first he'd provoked since he boarded, but dim-witted Collins paid the price for his violent reaction. The sight and sound of a human being in chains appalled Kimo. Whenever he heard the wretched man dragging himself across the deck, clanking his irons, he had to avert his eyes. From that day forward, he yearned for dry land, though the journey was barely halfway through.

It took six weeks for the *Thomasina* to reach the West Coast and four more days to navigate the dangerous Columbia Bar. Kimo blessed his ignorance, for Billings told him only after they disembarked that ships had gone down crossing the dreaded Bar, and that men had lost their lives in these cold waters. Islanders included. He wondered what the Company did when men drowned or died here. Did they inform your family? He'd heard of men leaving the Islands and not coming back. Their families didn't know if they lived or died, or what their fate had been. He shook his head. It was too late to think dark thoughts. Here he was, safe and sound, on dry land. That was something to celebrate.

THE SHIP'S CREW TREKKED from the dock to the fort, rain puddling at their boots, to drink the traditional welcoming tot of rum. He felt disoriented, but the rum rolling down his throat warmed his insides and he followed the crew into what Billings called The Big House, the large wooden structure in the centre of the fort. He found a space on a wooden plank bench beside a great roaring log fire, as men milled around waiting their assigned sleeping quarters. His nose twitched from the onslaught of odours, of wood smoke from the fire, of rum tots and men's sweat, and the steamy smell of damp woollens and wet leather. Within minutes, he heard his name called out through the hubbub in a clipped, bird-like English accent, followed by Moku's. The two rose in tandem and shouldered their way towards the clerk's desk. The man talked as if he had pebbles in his mouth.

"Kanui? Mu'olelo? We're sending you two north next week. Here are your papers. You board the schooner *Cadboro* when she arrives."

"North? Where?"

"Fort Langley. You can bunk in the village till then. You'll get orders nearer the time."

"Off one stinking ship onto another!" Moku muttered.

Kimo folded the paper the clerk had given him, then slumped on the wooden bench beside Moku. The recruiter in Oahu had said they could be posted anywhere from Sacramento north to Alaska, but they had only just arrived, and disappointment seized him. He was glad he wasn't going alone. Moku was good company, impulsive at times but open-hearted, a fine looking man with wide set eyes and a quick grin. An inch shorter than Kimo, he was so powerfully built and muscular that men eyed him apprehensively at times. If you didn't know him, his size and bulk could intimidate you.

"Where is this place?" Moku said.

"North, somewhere."

"That'll mean colder, right?"

To be sure, sun-loving Hawaiians would prefer to go south, if they had a choice. But they didn't. Moku swore, voicing doubts about his sanity for coming. Kimo rubbed the koa dolphin tied around his neck, deliberately ridding his mind of any sense of disappointment. Nothing good would come from regrets or dark thoughts. He would look on this as another step in the journey, that's all. The dolphin felt warm between his fingers and, as he rubbed the wood softly, he sensed the presence of *Aumakua,* his family's ancestral guardian spirit. Silently he prayed that things would work out, that all would be well.

He rose, crossed the hall and walked through the door to the compound outside. The place had a smell, different from anything he knew, of musk and smoke and unknown green growing things. He surveyed the countryside and his heart turned over. This was a gray place. Cold and dreary, surrounded by tall trees, forbidding and dense. Everything as far as the eye could see was dank and wet. The sky was bleak, without promise and heavy with clouds. The thought arrived like an arrow piercing the heart that this would be a sad place for a Kanaka to die, far from the sun of his Hawaiian home.

The fort felt less forbidding once the rain stopped. A lemony sun struggled to shine in the leaden sky. It looked pale to Hawaiian eyes but promising nevertheless. Kimo, Moku, the loutish Ahuhu and three others moved their belongings from the ship into the fort, which comprised a large cluster of wooden plank houses and sheds, surrounding a central log stockade. They were now officially "servants" of the Hudson's Bay Company, as were the dozens of Islanders living there. Hundreds more worked in the Company's other forts and ships from California to Alaska. He would have liked to work in the sawmills that operated upstream, but they sent him instead to fell and trim logs for the pit. As he eyed the tall stands of timber covering the surrounding hills and mountains, their immensity awed him. It would take generations to cut down such a forest. The trees were so enormous, it would take a whole day to fell just one of them.

The fort's farmland astonished him, stretching for miles, about twelve hundred acres with thousands more acres in grazing sheep. Billings claimed they sheared more than ten thousand a year, and there was even a gristmill for grinding wheat, oats and barley. Men said the place had been raw wilderness just fifteen years before. It was hard to believe, for they grew fruit, peas, root vegetables and squash and kept horses, cattle, pigs, sheep, goats, chickens, turkeys and pigeons. Crops were growing in the huge fields surrounding the fort, and huge quantities of butter and cheese were manufactured. Kimo was impressed. The haoles had converted a forested wilderness into productive farmland. *A land flowing with milk and honey,* old Hopoo would surely have said.

It took them a week to figure out the fort's hierarchy. There were labourers, apprentices, tradesmen, guides, interpreters, a postmaster, clerks and apprentice clerks, traders and the factor, though the categories were loose, and men at the low end flowed from one to the other.

"Appears we're the donkeys," Moku said, when they discovered Islanders were without exception in the lowest "labourer" category. The haole clerks looked after the finances and the *Canadien* trappers handled the boats. The Islanders boasted of being the backbone of the fort's fighting force when battling the natives, which bothered Kimo. Kamehameha and the missionaries had all but eliminated island tribal warfare and historically it was true they were a warrior race. But it didn't take a genius to figure out that being least in the hierarchy meant you were the most expendable. The thought stuck with him, though he tried to dismiss it. Were they the cannon fodder for the Indian wars he was hearing about now for the first time?

The *Thomasina* spent four days in port completing repairs to her deck from insect damage, as well as installing a new mast. Not every port readily provided quality lumber, but it wasn't difficult to find a tall, strong tree in the forests of the Columbia. The day the ship was to weigh anchor, Kimo visited the wharf to say goodbye to his friends remaining on the ship, and to Billings in particular, who'd made life on board more bearable than it would have been otherwise. Odd how he'd bonded with the pale-faced Englishman.

"Thanks for all your help on the ship, Billings."

"Go on with ye! 'Twas nothing, nothing at all. Mind what I told you, lad, the most important thing to remember on land or sea?" Billings squinted up at him.

"Never volunteer for anything."

"Don't forget that, or you'll be in trouble up to your arse before you know it." He extended his knobby hand. Kimo made the haole handshake but it felt too formal for such a friend, so he grabbed Billings around his skinny shoulders and hugged him. The English-man's pasty-white cheeks turned pink as a boiled ham. His arms dangled awkwardly straight to his thighs as Kimo gave him a bear hug, nearly crushing his bones. He coughed and lifted his arm to tap Kimo's back and Kimo got the message. Quickly, before anyone looked in their direction, he ended their embrace.

"Away with ye, now!" Billings said. "I'll look for ye next time I'm in port, though God knows when that'll be. Cheerio, Kanaka, and good luck to ye." One last hand shake, and he rolled away in his sailor's gait, along the wharf to the waiting ship.

When the *Thomasina* finally lifted anchor, it was under a clear blue sky dotted here and there with clouds, but the sun shone through and you could feel a warming breeze. The Hawaiian seamen called loud alohas from the rail, but their shouts were drowned out by the lanky Billings balancing on the yardarm yelling in his nasal, English twang, "Aloha mateys! Cheerio!"

"Aloha!" Kimo called back, waving. The ship shuddered then lifted her sails, commencing her voyage down river towards the broad, brown estuary, rolling to sea with the tide. Moku arrived and stood next to him grinning, clutching a bundle wrapped in brown sackcloth under his arm. It had a large bulge on one side.

"He said to give you this after he left."

"What is it?"

Moku shook it. A gurgling noise rose from the package as an unmistakable aroma pinched Kimo's twitching nostrils.

"The bandit! He must have stolen it from cook's stores!" He visualized the cook's tantrum when he discovered the rum keg gone from the galley and laughed out loud. The two trekked back to their hut in the village, where all the low-ranking men lived. Hawaiians counted for the majority, but Iroquois, French, Scots, and others with Indian wives, all lived in the village beyond the stockade. Only officers and their families lived inside. The village was larger than Kimo first thought, with about forty crowded huts housing hundreds of men, native women, and their children.

It surprised him how many men had made liaisons with the Indian women, only because it was something he hadn't given thought to in Oahu. Some of the women had been given to the fort men by their male relatives as a gesture of friendship. Others had simply been bought, while still others saw opportunity in marrying the fort men and initiated the arrangements.

As far as he could tell, some "country marriages," as they were called, worked well, some worked poorly, and some wives had been known to run away. Still he reckoned this wasn't too different from marriage anywhere else. In old Hawaii, before the haoles came, men used to give their female relatives away too, for the same reasons. To forge political bonds, or family ties that would ensure peace or advancement of some kind or another. Of course, it was frowned upon now and discouraged by the missionaries, but it certainly flourished here. And there were consequences. He wasn't surprised there would be illness at the fort, from wounds from accidents with saws or froes, or from muskets backfiring, which they frequently did, but many men were sick from venereal disease, the "Chinook Love Fever." Maybe the women gave it to the men, for all he knew, but he'd bet his wages it was the other way around, for the haoles had certainly brought diseases to Hawaii, killing thousands. The fort provided treatment for it, and men requiring mercury did so with little apparent shame involved, as if their sickness were as innocuous as the common cold.

The residents were quick to offer Kimo and Moku advice on living at the fort. First was the warning about punishments imposed for breaking Company rules. It jolted them that flogging and imprisonment were commonplace at the fort. They'd thought they'd left that behind on the ship.

"Did you know any of this before you signed on, Kimo?"

"No." The idea unnerved him. He was glad the wretched Ahuhu lived in another shack, and wouldn't be near them to cause them trouble. The others, whose house they shared, appeared friendly and easy-going, and he didn't foresee any problems. "If we do our jobs and mind the rules, we'll have nothing to worry about," he assured Moku. "Just don't think about it."

They tried, but didn't succeed and as night fell and shadows crowded their cramped quarters, they sought consolation in Billings' rum. They shared a recess containing two bunks in one of the village's shacks, where there was little room to store belongings. With nowhere to hide anything, news of the rum travelled swiftly and since Hawaiian tradition called for sharing, the keg sped quickly around the room.

"To dry land!" Moku raised the jug.

"And a safe trip north," Kimo added. He swallowed long and deep then passed the jug to the occupant of the adjacent bunk. As the evening wore on, their apprehensions diminished and courage returned, swelling with each round of rum. When Billings' keg emptied, bottles appeared from trunks and beneath beds. The two weren't used to rum uncut by water and soon entered into the spirit of the party, singing and dancing till the early morning hours. Even as he participated, Kimo realized the men around him drank too much, out of community spirit and merriment of course, but some clearly from regret, from the stress of living in this dangerous wilderness, from homesickness, and others, he supposed, just for the sake of it.

When he rose the following morning, rain threatened. It was in the air, a fine wetness that promised to drizzle but didn't quite as he plodded one unsteady foot in front of another beside Moku on a bleary-eyed trek towards the gate. A wormy anxiety had begun to gnaw at him, that someone might find out he had lied about his carpentry skills. His stomach tensed as he saw by the outer walls, groups of Indians setting up camp. They looked different from the Indians inside the village. They dressed oddly in home-made gray and black and brown blankets, decorated with bands of red and white stripes, and wore reed mats to keep off the rain and strange conical hats perched on their heads. Most of the older Indians sported beards.

"Am I seeing things?" Moku said.

"No. Their heads *are* misshapen. Billings said they flatten them to slope like that, up to the crown, on purpose. They bind the baby's forehead at birth and over time, with pressure, it takes that shape."

"Why, in the name of the gods?"

"It's their idea of beauty."

Kimo found the sloped heads distressingly unattractive, but as he passed the strange group, he wondered what the Indians would think of the empty eye sockets, broken teeth and other disfigurements that death once demanded in old Hawaii, and the bound heads suddenly seemed less abhorrent. He wished the drums in his head would go away.

"Heard anything about the place they're sending us to, Kimo?"

"It's on the Fraser River. They need to relocate a fort. We're closest, so help has to come from here. McKay, the Scot, says it's in a bad location, on a flood plain. So it has to be moved."

"Where, and how far?"

"Two miles upriver."

"There's talk of fighting Indians up there."

"Yes, but from what they say, the Indians by the Langley fort are friendly enough. They call themselves Sto:lo, the River People. McKay says if there's trouble, it'll come from the Lekwiltok tribe. They're at war along the entire coast, with the forts, and with the other tribes as well. He said they hang the heads of dead warriors on poles above the bows of their canoes till they dry out and drop black, like a fig."

"Aolé! Do we have to go? Sounds like it's a good place to stay away from."

"We've no choice. McKay says when the Company says 'Go', you go, no questions asked."

Conversation dwindled as they began their day's work. The two lopped branches and trimmed trees. The day felt cool and Kimo was grateful for the mindless labour. Thankfully, his wretched headache didn't intrude too much. He'd never gone to work hungover before and vowed it wouldn't happen again. They'd depart for Langley soon, and what lay ahead was in the hands of the gods.

He didn't sleep well that night, feeling thick-headed from the rum and exhausted from a day of cutting logs. When he finally did sleep, in his dream Indians surrounded him. With painted faces, they climbed out of a canoe half-beached on shore, one after another, endlessly, far more than any one canoe could possibly hold. They chased him along an expanse of beach, across miles of sand and pebbles and kelp, till finally he tripped over a piece of driftwood and woke abruptly, sweating profusely, still sensing the tang of salt sea air and pungent seaweed of his nightmare.

Thankful he was only dreaming, he turned over, hearing Moku snoring softly in his bunk. Exhaustion finally overcame him and he fell into a deep sleep. He awoke as dawn crept through the Kanaka village. A gray morning mist feathered up from the green tangled undergrowth as he stepped from the door of his shack. The air felt clear and cool. The trees surrounding the fort reached like giant warrior spears, piercing the clouds. A pair of ravens circled overhead, swooping in tandem across the treetops. An omen, he decided. Then McKay appeared, like a lean, gray ghost, striding through the dawn mist towards him.

Their orders had changed. The *Cadboro* wasn't coming after all. The ship was delayed in Sacramento for repairs. They'd have to make the journey north by canoe and portage. In two days time. Through territory rife with hostile Indians.

He had one more day with McKay for musket practice.

chapter three

RAIN AND HIGH WINDS assaulted the northern shores of the Pacific Northwest as fierce spring storms beat down upon the people living along the banks of the Fraser. It had rained for so long that the people had grown dispirited with the unending leaden gray skies. The landscape reeked of dampness and dank. People struggled in vain to keep their homes and clothing dry. The sheer wet weight of things added to the wretchedness, and sickness soon followed the never-ending rainfall. Once in a while, the sun would fight its way through overcast skies, teasing the inhabitants momentarily but then clouds would reappear and rain would descend in sheets, cascading over their heads, percolating through all things again.

Finally, a thin sun emerged and the sky began to pulsate with promise. Light crept in, bringing colour back to the landscape, and people's spirits rose with the temperature. As a warming breeze swept through the mountains and valleys, men and women returned to the routine of life, following the seasons of the land.

Marie Rose Fanon rose early, quietly, so as not to waken the household. The sun spilled narrow beams along the rush mats that covered the floor of the small cedar house in the Kwantlen village on Sqwalets, the island white men called McMillan, across from the Langley fort on the Fraser River. She threw a reed cape hurriedly around her body and crept across the room to peer behind the reed mat divider. Good! Neetlum had gone to work his trap line, so there would be peace in the household for a few days after last night's quarrel.

"Morning, *Naha*," she whispered to her mother as she exited the low doorway, and made her way to the river's edge. The day was cool and clear. Every line, every contour of the mountains stood out sharply in the morning light. The water's freezing temperature barely affected her as she bathed. On her return, she quickened her step as smoke caught at her nostrils. The aroma of oatmeal wafted along the beaten pathway from her home. They ate it regularly now they could trade for it at the fort.

Her mother, Lawi'qum, sat on her haunches tending the thickening meal. She added dried cranberries, stirring with a wooden rod to prevent the meal sticking to the bottom of the pot. The fire below crackled inside a circle of smooth round stones outside the front door. In wet weather, her mother cooked indoors, which made the cedar house reek with smoke even though a hole had been cut in the roof to allow it to escape. The iron pan containing the oatmeal had also been acquired in trade at the nearby fort, in exchange for one of her stepfather's pelts.

Rose ate quickly, for today she planned to visit the fort across the river. Already smoke from the fort's morning fires drifted over the stockade. The Hudson's Bay people had begun their working day.

"May I borrow the canoe? I want to trade baskets at the fort store. I can take your nets at the same time, if you like." Her mother used to weave strong, fine fishing nets out of nettle stalks. She'd split the stems and weave them patiently over time. Now she obtained twine from the store, and the store welcomed the finished nets back in trade. Rose had been visiting the fort more often lately. She hoped to find work there soon, though she spoke of this to no one. It would offer her a measure of independence. She could contribute to their household and reduce the burden her presence placed on Neetlum. And perhaps he would not press her into a marriage she did not want. He could insist and as a Kwantlen woman, she would have to obey. But because she was not his child, and only half-Kwantlen, so far he had not done so, and she was grateful for that. But he was running out of patience, and last night they had argued again.

It had started two moons ago, when her cousin, A'asmax, had married at age thirteen. Rose was sixteen, almost seventeen, old by Indian marriage standards yet she had rejected the last suitor her step-father, Neetlum, put forward. She felt guilty, for the one-room cedar house they shared, parents and four children, was too small to contain them all now. The children had grown in recent years and her continued presence placed a burden on the home, and meant another mouth to feed. Marriage would ease the burden, and bring a fine quantity of goods from the groom to her family.

"What are you trading for?" Her mother's dark eyes widened with curiosity beneath black arching eyebrows in her high, sloped forehead. Her round face showed few lines and her mouth displayed even white teeth.

"Cloth." Rose had been waiting months for fabric to arrive at the trade store. "Or blankets, if they don't have any. Is there anything you need?"

"Your father wants nails. And I'd like a tea kettle but it'll have to wait till he brings in more pelts."

It didn't usually bother Rose when her mother addressed Neetlum as her father, but the taste of last night's quarrel remained on her palate. Indians did not use first names, for this was unspeakably rude, so Neetlum was called "Husband," by her mother and "Father," by her sisters and brother. It would be offensive if she called her step-father by his first name so she buried her resentment this morning with silence.

"Be sure to get home while it's still light because we need to pack for Semiahmoo," her mother said. Rose nodded. She hadn't forgotten, for she had been weaving baskets for months in preparation for the trip south to meet her mother's relatives. She headed for the riverbank and the family's two canoes. Neetlum had built the ten-foot cedar dugout with his brother, for use by both families during the hunting season, but she chose the small two-man craft he used for duck-hunting because it was light and easy to handle. She found it part way down the beach, turned upside down and covered with frayed reed mats to protect it from the weather. The inside of the canoe was painted red, a mix of oolichan oil and ochre, but it had begun to fade and needed repainting. Neetlum hadn't got around to it yet, simply because the outside still looked good, the wood a strong charcoal black from charring with torches when it was made.

The craft was light and small so she lifted it easily and dragged it across the round pebbles to the river's edge. She located the yew paddle she favoured, the one with the rounded blade, because it was perfect for her size and stroke, and loaded her mother's nets and a stack of woven baskets into the small space at her feet. Cedar withes tied the thwarts to the sides of the canoe, passing through holes in thwart and gunwhale. With her stack of baskets and nets, there was barely room for her to squeeze in, and she had to kneel uncomfortably in the small space for the trip across the river.

It was only a short paddle to the south bank of the Fraser River. The sun overhead grew warmer as she stroked, reflecting pinpoints of light on the river. There was little turbulence. An accomplished paddler, Rose made the trip quickly but found the fort's dock already crowded with canoes so she pulled in further downstream, and had no difficulty hauling the craft up onto the beach. She headed for the fort with her stack of baskets. Kwantlen women usually carried bundles from a tump line around the forehead, but today Rose carried hers perched high on her right hip.

She slowed her pace and lowered her baskets to the ground when she came upon an old Indian sitting on a moss-covered log by the side of the trail leading to Fort Langley. The fort's water carrier was separating a wad of tobacco, tamping dark bits into the bowl of a chipped clay pipe with his yellow-stained forefinger. The sun threw spangles of light between the shawl of leaves overhead, reflecting across his shoulders, shining like copper coins.

"Bonjour, Huntas! Are you coming or going?"

"I'm sitting here," the old man answered with a wrinkled grin. "Neither coming nor going, as you can see."

She laughed with him, noting the age lines furrowing their way across his wide forehead. Thinning white hair, once black as night, was pulled tightly back and tied with a piece of frayed twine at the nape of his thick neck. A crosshatch of chicken skin stretched tightly over his scarred cheekbones. His dark eyes were small and sloping. Like cats' eyes, they darted here, there and everywhere. But they were kind, and glittered when he laughed, which was more often than one would expect from someone so harshly treated by life.

She invariably addressed the old Indian respectfully, as an elder, though she did not need to, for he was s'texem, of low status, and not of the Kwantlen tribe. Captured as a child, he had been held in slavery most of his adult life before being sold to a local chief. The Hudson's Bay had ransomed him, and he had worked for the Company ever since.

"I didn't see you last time I visited. I thought perhaps you'd gone south with the Langley Express, to Fort Vancouver." Fort Vancouver, on the Columbia River, was the largest, busiest fort on the Coast, north of Spanish California. It was well established, and more prosperous than the newer Langley fort.

"I stayed out on the trap line. Just came in two days ago."

"Any luck?"

"Three beaver and a bull elk. Plenty food for a while."

"Good hunting!" Her compliment was genuine. It required skill and courage to kill an elk, and Huntas was no longer a young man.

"I might even have enough for a vest," he said, trying not to look pleased with himself, tapping his chest. Rose bit her tongue. In the old days, tough elk skin was used for protection in battle to repel arrows, but what good was it now, when faced with the white man's guns? But the old man would follow the old ways and waste nothing of the animal, making tools from its bones and fastenings from its sinews.

"Three beavers? I'm impressed!"

"Fine skins. Two thirty-five pounders and a young one."

"That'll please them. The *Xwelitem* can never get enough beaver pelts," she said. It was a puzzling thing to the Indians that common beaver pelts were valued so highly by the whites, when there were other more beautiful furs to be had. It amazed her that men would go to such lengths, crossing seas, climbing mountains and navigating treacherous rapids, in the scorching heat of summer and the cold of winter, just to make hats for people who lived in lands far across the sea. What kind of people did that? It seemed preposterous to the Indians but since the Xwelitem wanted beaver pelts so badly, they obliged. To a degree. Rose had long ago figured out that while the whites gained furs, the Indians gained just as much in the form of new tools, new knowledge, new methods.

"Good work! Now your skins will cross the sea to roost on some-one's head."

He gave a short laugh and shrugged. "Who can understand the world of the Xwelitem?"

"So, when are you going south again?"

"To Fort Vancouver? I go when I go. When they tell me."

"I can't imagine what it must be like now," she said, moving to sit beside him on the cedar log. She had lived as a child at the fort, one hundred miles up from the mouth of the Columbia River, but could no longer remember the feel of that grand place, though she dreamed of it often. What confused Rose, and every Indian, was the pact of 1818 between America and Britain to joint occupation of the Oregon Territory. The two white powers had agreed that whoever colonized most and built the most trading stations would assume sovereignty over the Territory. The white men's talk of "sovereignty" perplexed the Indians. This was their ancestral land. They had moved freely back and forth between what the white men called the Oregon Territory and New Caledonia for generations, to hunt and fish and camp. And at times not so freely, for the tribes frequently battled over territory. Now the white men were battling. So far, with words.

"The voyageurs say the Americans are moving in fast."

"Those Canadiens gossip like old women," Huntas said, disdain wrinkling his long, hooked nose.

"But the tribes say the same thing."

He remained unperturbed. Typical, she thought. It was his nature to accept whatever came his way. She wondered if his animal spirits ever bubbled at all, or if he lived perpetually in this accepting, passionless state. Was it the remnants of his slave mentality that made him wait to be told what to do, how to think? As if he'd read her mind, the old Indian shook his head and spoke reflectively, slowly removing the clay pipe from its firm grip between his yellowing teeth.

"One thing is certain, the land won't change beneath our feet or

42

the sky above our heads. If other things change, for good or bad, what a person must do is survive."

To survive was sufficient, she supposed, for a slave.

"How is your mother, Rose?"

His blatant attempt to change the subject amused her. Like Neetlum, he did not approve of her interest in politics, a man's domain.

"Her health is good," her well-bred Kwantlen half replied, but her other half persisted. "Do you think this Territory business will come to a head soon?"

"Why concern yourself with things that may never come to pass?"

"But if they do?"

"Britain will never give up the Oregon Territory. Or the Hudson's Bay Company Fort Vancouver. Why would they? It's such a splendid place."

The fort *was* splendid, the hub for trade on the Coast. A system of canoes, boats and brigades transported furs from small outposts to the fort for loading on ships to Europe. It was the centre of power on the Coast, and it was there that her father had met Huntas, when he sought an interpreter for his marriage to the pretty Nooksack maiden, Lawi'qum.

With a sudden surge of insight, Rose understood that for Huntas, it was inconceivable that politics could alter the destiny of this mighty, powerful Company. Technically free, his heart and soul remained in bondage. The Company would always be his master.

It had been her father's too, till he disappeared. Now the Company both fascinated and repelled her. It had brought her a father and dreams for a wider life, then sent him on a trip from which he'd never returned. She was seven years old, and for months, years after, whenever she sighted voyageurs paddling upriver, she ran to the riverbank hoping desperately to see his face among the crew. She never did and after time, gave up looking.

The old man had fallen silent, puffing intermittently on his pipe.

She eyed him fondly through the drifting smoke. She'd remained close to him over the years, in spite of their difference in status, not only because of his connection with her father, but because he spoke a smattering of French. And maybe, just maybe, because they were both "outsiders," he wholly Indian but a slave and not Kwantlen, and she, only half-Kwantlen.

The old man's eyes rested on her, and she knew he was gauging her appearance the same way he would rate a good beaver pelt. She wore a European style, dark blue calico dress, calf-length, tied neatly at the waist. It was second-hand but clean and the long, full skirt hung in folds from waist to hemline. At home she wore a knee-length fringed skirt of shredded cedar bark, with a cape of woven cattails fastened at the waist, that left her upper body bare. Recently she'd learned to adapt the fort's blankets for capes, and had begun to make European style clothes with cloth acquired in trade. The new clothes would not be half so warm as their winter robes of animal skins, from the bear and the marten, the otter and the lynx, so Rose planned to adapt and combine these with European materials before the next cold season.

Huntas sniffed appreciatively and smiled at the sweet scent of bedstraw plant emanating from her skin. Rose liked to smell clean. The Kwantlen bathed daily in the rivers and oceans around them, which was more than she could say of some people at the fort. Often, too often, she'd have to stand upwind and back a full arm span.

"Neetlum's kill?" Huntas indicated her new moccasins.

"No. Just deerskin I traded for baskets." Most Kwantlen rejected the buckskin favoured by the inland tribes because the leather leaked badly on the wet damp coast and when it did dry out, it grew stiff and hard but her father had liked moccasins, and she did too. It was one of the few things she remembered about him. Sometimes she couldn't recall what his face looked like. But there were days she saw him clearly still. Then her heart seemed to expand with emotion enough to explode in her chest.

Huntas finished scrutinizing her garb then nodded to indicate his approval, which amused her. The difference in their status should have prevented such presumption, but she didn't mind. He cocked his head and leaned towards her, eyes reaming her with curiosity. "Do you still have your books?"

She froze instantly, her mind a-flutter. *Whatever had prompted that?* She'd learned to read at her father's knee, for he insisted she speak French and English as well as Kwantlen. She only had one book left. She kept it in a treasured cedar bentwood box that her Indian grandfather had patiently carved by hand and without nails. It was tattered and worn with faded ink drawings inside, fragmented pieces yellowing and separated at the spine, unreadable after years of damp storage. Remnants of a dream.

"No! Well, one, but the writing's faded." She spoke crisply and raised her chin, signalling an end to their conversation. *Why had he brought that up?* Through the dam she had carefully constructed to contain them, memories broke, strung together like beads on a string. Blue beads. Amazing coloured beads from the Vancouver store that her father gave her when Indians ornaments had all been dark and earthy. Shining brilliantly, sparkling blue, and others in colours of the rainbow. And fine books, one with a red spine. The memory caught her painfully. She saw it in her mind's eye, felt herself turn the printed pages, for years her most treasured possession, read and re-read while her father drilled her in French and English. It was the reading that had set her apart, right from the beginning. Books had made her different, incomplete, somehow. Half this, half that. Wanting. It struck her hardest when he left, when the pain of not belonging skewered her.

"Your father would be proud of you, Rose." Huntas emphasized the "e" on the end of her name, so that it sounded like the English "Rosie."

"Which father?" she retorted sharply. It was rude of her to speak so, but her anger spilled out anyway. Nearly ten years, and she didn't know if he were dead or alive. Rumour said he'd gone east. The Company had traced him as far as the Red River, but there he had vanished. At the time it felt like the end of her world. It wasn't, of course. Her mother had married Neetlum a year later. A good provider and father to the three children Lawi'qum had borne him, he treated Rose decently enough so that she could never fault him for his care in the feeding and clothing of her body. If her soul at times cried out for more, she never acknowledged it and remained grateful for the life she led in the Kwantlen village.

She regretted her sharp words to Huntas the moment she said them, the Indian in her feeling she had dishonoured both men by her ill-tempered response. Thankfully he appeared not to notice.

"What're you taking for trade to the store today?" His dark eyes slanted inquisitively, the left one skewing up sideways like a toppling question mark.

"Baskets. And nets."

"Well, hold out for a good price. Make sure you get what you want."

"Since when did you need to tell an Indian how to trade?" she asked tartly and the old man laughed, then broke into a wheezy cough.

"You shouldn't smoke so much tobacco, Huntas. It's bad for you."

"At my age, I should worry?" It was the answer he always gave. He coughed again and spat noisily on the ground. For effect, Rose suspected, and averted her eyes.

"I'll walk with you to the fort," he said. "Cook will need water for dinner."

Rose waited patiently while he rapped the bowl of his pipe sharply against the tree trunk, then straightened his six-foot skeletal frame above his wide, bowed legs, and towered above her. He lifted her baskets, leaving her only one net to carry, and she nodded her thanks. He wore white men's clothing now, like the other fort men, but his shirt drooped like a tattered flag. He was tall and rangy too, not like the men in the Kwantlen village, who were broad-shouldered and sturdy. Like them though, he sported a small beard and tiny moustache which he trimmed each day with two halves of a clamshell, disdaining the fancy razors from the fort's store. They were keen and sharp, but made too many cuts to his chin. The old man placed his pipe in his pocket and joined her in an unhurried walk along the footpath towards the fort.

"Some day this fort will be as big as Fort Vancouver," he predicted proudly. She doubted that. Fort Vancouver, from all accounts, was a splendid and wonderful place. Fort Langley was far from splendid. It had been built not just as another fur depot but for defence, to control the local tribes. Many remained angry at the intrusion by the whites on their land. "This is where we'll grow the food to feed the Company's northern forts," Huntas said.

"Can't they grow their own?"

"Not enough to keep themselves. It's too cold."

She fell silent as her thoughts returned to the grand fort in the Oregon Territory. The dreadful thought arrived unbidden that when men lost territory, at least in the Indian world, that meant war. Could that happen between the whites over the Territory? What would it mean for the native people then? Suddenly it all seemed like the white man's version of *slahal,* their Indian bone gambling game. But who, she wondered, would be left to pick up the bones?

It was foolish to speak with Huntas about such things. He was s'texem, not privy to the dealings of men of power, either within the Company or within the Indian community. Still, he had been her

47

father's friend and she cared for him. When he spoke of the early days and the hardships the fort's men endured, she understood but felt equal sympathy for the Indians struggling to adjust to the new-comers invading their territory. This struggle was far from over, though peace of a sort reigned along the river, a peace that allowed her, at least for now, to walk with the old water carrier freely and unafraid along the short footpath leading to the Langley fort.

As they walked, she wondered again what had become of her father. For Lawi'qum, his disappearance had been painful. For Rose, their half-white child, it was devastating. Her soul, bruised and abandoned, struggled to come to terms with his leave-taking, and for months she withdrew into a cocoon of private pain. Like some wild thing of the forest she felt trapped, turned inside out, scraped and hung out to dry and the bud of resentment in her heart blossomed into a hard kernel of self-reliance as the years went by.

"How old are you now, Rose?"

"Seventeen next spring." She knew what he implied. But she would choose more wisely than her mother had when she chose the voyageur, Jacques Fanon.

"Your mother made a new life for herself and she's happy. It's best to let old wounds heal."

"Any wounds I had healed long ago," she replied brightly. She lied, with her clever smile and dark intelligent eyes. Large almond shaped Indian eyes, they were, fringed with long thick dark lashes. But she had a European nose, thin and straight, like her father's. And she'd never had her head bound, for he had forbidden it, and some pitied her for this. Rose had a very ordinary straight forehead and knew it. Even with her high Indian cheekbones, she knew she would not be considered beautiful by Kwantlen standards. Sometimes it was nec-essary to face the hard crust of truth. She was different, one of the new part-European, part-Indian, half-breed men and women around Hudson's Bay forts.

Huntas coughed suddenly, then stooped over, stumbling. She took his arm to steady his walk. He raised his right hand, skin dry as beef jerky, to point to the sun dappling through the trees. "Soon it will be noon," he said and she nodded. The sun was their clock, the times of day — sunup, noon, sundown, and night.

The air was fragrant now with the scent of growing things and as they walked the rutted pathway from the river, sunshine glanced off the surface of the water in shafts of sparkling light. The sun's rays sliced through the trees, falling across the dirt path beneath their feet. It was a soft, brown carpet to walk upon, the fine dusty earth covered with leaves of trees and plants grown years before, now dried and powdered and inches thick on the ground.

He was calmer now, and she walked with him, slim, lithe, poised, quiet, too. Her voice, light and clear as running water, soothed him as they moved forward. She spoke French to him, enunciating each word carefully, as if biting into a crisp apple, their conversation a private garden, a special place the two of them shared. Then nostalgia suddenly overcame her with the force of a blow so powerful, it almost stopped her in her tracks. The old man's nearness evoked in her a bittersweet memory of her father, an aching sense of loss and longing, of abandoned dreams and buried hopes. So many ifs . . . if her father had not been white . . . if he had only stayed . . . if . . . if.

Huntas stopped.

"Are you all right, Huntas?"

"*Oui, oui.* How could I not be? I'll be the envy of every young buck at the fort when we walk through that gate!"

"Nonsense," she said, but laughter resurfaced, low and deep, fresh as the water in the Fort Langley well. It was just talk. She'd never get through the gate. Only a handful of Indians, employed by the fort, were allowed entrance. She'd never been inside, even when her father worked there. When Huntas walked through, she took her baskets and joined the line of Indians snaking around the walls waiting to enter the trader's shed built outside. She'd applied for work on previous visits, without success, but maybe this time luck would fall her way. They hired Indian help for the salmon runs, and she'd be back from Semiahmoo before the next run was due. The trader today was new. She didn't recognize his face, but he was tall and soft-spoken, and seemed to have a measure of respect for the Indians trading ahead of her. When she reached his desk, impulse took over. She had nothing to lose. She spoke English and asked for work. He hesitated then replied that he didn't know but would take her name. He lifted his pen and a single sheet of paper from the desk drawer, but as he was about to write, a young clerk tugged at his elbow for advice on some newly arrived pelts. Rose waited, fearing the moment was lost. Then she threw caution to the wind, lifted his pen and wrote *Rose Fanon* in clear black script on the blank page. She stood there till he came back and traded her baskets and nets for blankets, for there was no cloth available. Then he saw the paper and started.

"You wrote this?"

"Yes."

"Do you have family at the fort?" She hesitated. It was an advantage if you did. Women working at the fort were all country wives of the fort employees.

"Not now. But I did."

"I'll pass your name to the Clerk. He decides if and when we need help." But he looked her in the eye and smiled. She flew back to the canoe, oblivious to the weight of the blankets, for her feet hardly touched the ground. Her boldness had paid off. She was not just another Indian trading at the post. Her name was on a list, and she'd put it there herself. She had taken charge at last of some small part of her life.

chapter four

Kimo counted eleven other men at the Fort Vancouver wharf:
four Canadiens, the Iroquois, three Scots, two Cowichan Indians
and Moku. They were an odd mix of light and dark skinned men,
wearing layers of mismatched clothes — woollen sweaters over cotton shirts, wool, deerskin or heavy cotton trousers, and boots, except
for the Iroquois, who wore moccasins that fit to the calf. Kimo felt
hampered by the amount of clothing men needed to wear here, but
they assured him he'd be glad of it soon enough. They wore woollen
tocques or tired-looking, brimmed felt hats, except for the Indians
and the Kanakas. McKay advised him to get a hat, not just to retain
body heat but to keep off the rain. He didn't have the money to buy
one from the store, but boots, clothing and knives could be won or
lost in the men's frequent poker games, so he could only wish for
luck at cards.

The Canadien boatman and the tall Iroquois busied themselves stacking bales and boxes of supplies into a large, twelve-man canoe, along with a large brown leather pouch. A pale watery sun broke through the clouds by the time the two Hawaiians hefted their gear into the canoe. The morning air felt damp with the powerful scent of wet cedar, and a heavy gray mist clung in beaded patches along the riverbank.

"Make sure your patch knife is sharp," McKay said. "You'll need it to service your rifle."

"In other words, *expect trouble,*" Moku whispered to Kimo. They were familiar with the sharp, thin-bladed Hawaiian knives used to gut fish and with wide blade machetes that split open coconuts. The ones issued for this trip were different though, honed sharply to a razor's edge, hunting knives with thin blades for preparing food. Kimo noticed the Cowichans and the Scot also packed long bladed knives, like short swords.

"Fer killing, plain and simple," McKay said, matter-of-factly.

Half-repelled, half-fascinated, Kimo picked one up for a closer look. It was stiff and strong and about a foot long, sharpened along one edge and ground to a long, sharp point.

"It's like a Scottish dirk," McKay said. Whether it was or not, Kimo recognized it for what it was, the ideal blade for delivering slashes and thrusts in battle. He hoped he'd never need to use it. He stashed his gear between the bales jamming the canoe, beside the large leather pouch containing everything they'd need to keep their rifles in order, balls, patches, flints, flint knapper, caps, jag, vent pick, screwdriver, nipple wrench, powder measure, and several already-made charges.

"First rule of the wilderness." McKay pointed at the supplies. "Be prepared."

So this is how it's going to be, Kimo thought. How long would it take living in this wilderness for a man to become like McKay, alert, sharp, on edge? Prepared to kill?

He liked the look of the muskets, all the same. From what he'd heard, they'd need them. The voyageurs bore theirs with flair, across the shoulder, sheathed in fur skin, oiled for protection against the damp, with gun covers open at the butt end and stitched from butt to muzzle. Animal tallow had been worked into the fur hair to make it shed water and sparingly enough to prevent condensation, allowing the leather to breathe. Antler bone powder horns, ornately carved, were slung at their waists. The sensible Scots, he noticed, carried their powder in small, compact square tin boxes attached to their belts.

"Doesn't matter where you keep it." McKay tapped his tin. "As long as you keep yer powder dry. In moist, humid conditions, it'll get soggy and ineffective. Or in a hot spell, it'll completely dry out. But you cannae afford to have damp powder if you're attacked suddenly in the wilderness."

"Some day I'll buy a gun of my own," Moku said, eyeing his issued rifle enviously.

"Just hope you don't have to use it." Kimo threw the last bundle at Moku, who trapped it handily then crammed it into the small cranny of space left in the canoe. They secured the last boxes and waited orders to leave. Kimo inspected the canoe closely. It was a dugout, carved from a single giant cedar, almost thirty-five feet long and nearly five feet wide. It was shovel-nosed, with a thick bottom and thin sides and it looked as if you could stand on the edge of it without falling over.

"A fine canoe for riding and gliding on top of the waves," he said, running his hands approvingly along the wood. It smelled of the outdoors, a strong mix of woodsy scents, of salt, of animal skins, and oil. "What are the poles for?"

"Sometimes a river is narrow or full of vegetation," the boatman replied, "so we switch from paddles to long poles for moving along the edges. Paddles work better than oars for keeping us closer to shore, where the current is less strong."

"*Vite, vite! mangeurs de lard,* the day's a-wasting!" urged Pierre Charles, the voyageur already at his paddle. Men clambered aboard, finding seats in accordance with the Company's canoeing hierarchy. Kimo and Moku were the "mangeurs de lard," pork-eaters in French, the greenhorns. They sat among the packs using short, narrow-bladed paddles. The men in the middle were the "milieux." The two experienced paddlers at the back, the "bouts," handled the long paddles. There was a prow man for rapids, though his skill would not be needed this trip, and McKay, the Scot, would steer.

"It feels good to hold a paddle again," Moku grunted when they finally stroked downstream from Vancouver's wharf. Taut muscles strained their shoulders, chest and upper arms, as they pulled evenly in time with the other men. Work on board ship had involved winding pulleys and hauling ropes, and at the fort, sawing logs every day for the pit had taxed their muscles to the limit but paddling came naturally. Though hard work, it felt good and lifted their spirits.

The journey proved spectacular. Kimo marvelled at the scenery, the soaring mountains, the fast blue water of the Columbia, the myriad greens of the forest. He recognized the clean smell of cedar and pine and saw trees eighteen feet in diameter rising majestically two hundred feet into the air. On the riverbank, wind conjured up little gray fogs and puffs of mist that spilled out onto the water and disappeared.

"Watch out! By the gods! If that isn't the biggest river rat I've ever seen!" Kimo gasped in amazement, twisting his torso so he nearly toppled. He swung wildly with his paddle to repel the dark creature swimming by the side of the canoe. The Scot seated in front of him began to laugh, slowly at first, then in great rumbling belly laughs that he couldn't control, making his feathery eyebrows move up and down like ginger caterpillars. He lifted his hand, made a fist and jerked his thumb back, signalling the other occupants of the canoe to look at the dark swimming object receding rapidly from their canoe. Every man in the boat let out a roar of laughter.

"God's truth, lad! That's no a water rat. It's a beaver! Don't tell me you're a servant o' the Hudson's Bay Company and don't know a beaver when ye see it!"

"I've seen dead ones . . . skins before," Kimo replied defensively.

"Aye, well, ye can tell a beaver by its tail. Listen close, ye'll hear a *Whack! Whack!* when he smacks it. They do that to warn other beavers of danger. But ye'll no hear it now, I'm thinking, since there's no danger here. You cannae tell a beaver from a bison!" He laughed at his own joke.

"He's building a castle underground, out of mud. See the sticks?" The big Iroquois poked the water, swirling it gently till the curious little animal rose out of the water and peered myopically at them. "There's the lodge, over there!" The Iroquois pointed out a large dome-shaped structure of sticks, plastered with mud. "There'll be a colony of them inside. They come in pairs, two parents and two sets of kits, usually."

The animal was more thickset than Kimo expected, with small round ears, short legs and large, webbed hind feet. Its coat was a glossy dark brown and when the animal stopped and sat up in the water, Kimo judged him to be more than three feet long, including a rough scaly tail six inches wide and three quarters of an inch thick, stretching a good twelve inches.

"This one's maybe forty pounds, but they come bigger," the Iroquois explained. "I've seen them four feet long and weighing sixty pounds."

"But if he was full grown, he'd have more sense than to swim near a Bay man," the Scot said, whacking the water noisily with his paddle, causing the beaver to duck swiftly and swim furiously towards his lodge.

The group fell silent and paddled onward. Small groups of Indians appeared here and there, more curious than hostile, as the canoe made its way along the Columbia. The Indians made Kimo nervous, for the tension in the boat was palpable every time they appeared. The men's talk of guns and knives, of killing, made him feel like a wound-up spring, edgy and alert, unable to release the tension building in his chest. He hadn't paddled for a long time and his arm muscles tired sooner than he expected. He squinted across at Moku, at the veins bulging in his temple. He, too, was feeling the strain.

They paddled the Columbia till the afternoon sun disappeared behind a band of gray clouds, till the Canadien called out to them "When we reach the Cowlitz River, we stop. The weather, she doesn't look so good."

The boatman was right. Minutes later rain began to fall in a straight down, cold, sheeting drizzle that quickly turned into a wind-soaked tempest. When they reached the Cowlitz, they hoisted their paddles from the choppy water and let the canoe move forward of its own accord then slowly drift to a stop, crunching on the shingle. Swiftly they jumped out, beached the craft on the pebbled beach and swung their tired limbs to shake off the chilly cramps.

The Canadien indicated a sheltered corner of the beach where giant maples spread umbrella branches densely overhead. He dispatched Kimo and Moku for wood but the driftwood on the beach felt wet so they trekked into the forest's edge, to the underbrush, to find drier branches to light the fire. When they returned, arms loaded, Baker, the oldest man in the party, helped them build a fire while the crew unloaded the canoe.

Baker was a soft spoken Scot, of medium build, with gray hair and tired green eyes. He wore deerskin trousers and two heavy woollen shirts, both brown, one on top of the other. He produced a tinderbox containing dried flowers and seed heads and pinches of tiny bark pieces stripped from dry cedar. He laid them below a small pile of sticks standing on end forming an airy triangle underneath a tripod that would hold their cooking pans. Carefully he added a square of charred cloth about two inches long to the tinder to catch the sparks. He drew a small piece of clean steel, decided which flint to use, then began rubbing it briskly back and forth on the steel. A few moments later, red sparks rose up and sizzled, fizzing out in their feeble attempts to fly skyward in the heavy drizzle. Kimo was intrigued. He had a lot to learn about surviving in the wilderness. He lifted the charred cloth to examine it more closely.

"What is this? It smells."

"It's punk. You cut cloth in two inch squares and cook it in a wee tin box over a fire. You need to make sure it's charred black right through, but no sae much it'll break away in yer hands. And you lay it with yer tinder, tae catch the sparks. It does a fine job. Mind you put it back in the box, before the rain ruins it, lad."

Kimo determined to make himself a tinderbox as soon as he reached the fort. The Scot rubbed flint against steel till the fire took and held. It warmed the men and as the flames rose, so did their spirits. And the rain finally eased. By the time they had scouted the area, laid out the bales and boxes of cargo on the beach underneath their propped-up canoe, bannock biscuits and strips of pork were spitting in fat in pans above the tripod over the fire. During the day the voyageurs had eaten Indian style, chewing on pemmican, a concoction of dried meat flakes pounded to a paste with fat. McKay said it kept for months, sometimes years, when sewn into hide bags. But now the smell of hot food drew every man to the fire, as Baker ladled peas, pork and oatmeal onto tin plates.

One of the voyageurs spotted some squirrels, so many that he offered to skewer and roast them, heads off, over the fire, like corn cobs, but no one took up his offer. Then, as Kimo leaned forward to grasp his tin plate, something whirred past his ear in a swift current of air, catching him off guard so that he jerked backwards. He thought it was a bird, but it flew too fast for any bird he knew. It landed with a solid thunk next to Baker.

"What the . . . ?"

"Take cover!" McKay barked, streaking for the trees.

Kimo froze, eyes riveted on the arrow embedded quivering, half way into Baker's blanket. Another whirr, another arrow, missed his ear by inches. He threw himself to the ground and felt Moku thud beside him. Moments later two shots rang out, fired by McKay and the Iroquois, both already finding shelter behind a large cedar. The others spread themselves flat on the ground behind the boxes and bales. He and Moku hunkered as low as they could behind their blanket bedrolls. The Iroquois took off, disappearing into the trees, followed by McKay seconds later. Baker signalled to the Cowichans and they too melted into the trees.

"Did you see them, Kimo?" Moku whispered.

"No. Nor heard them either." All he'd heard was the nervous thumping of his own heart and birds arguing up in the trees. He didn't like the idea of relying on the flintlock musket. It took so long to load. The thing needed more than a dozen motions to prime and fire. Better to keep your knife sharp and handy, as McKay had said. The Scot returned first, followed by the others.

"Gone," he said. "No sign of them." He retrieved the two arrows from Baker's bedroll and examined them, twirling the shafts and riffling the feathered ends with his forefinger.

"What tribe?" the Iroquois asked.

"No markings. But they're watching us. There must be more of us than of them, or they'd have shot more than two arrows. Pack the canoe. No sense courting trouble. We'll move on before they come back in numbers."

They loaded the canoe and paddled up the Cowlitz, rain sheeting down on their heads, till Charles again called a halt. Baker built another fire, after a struggle with damp kindling, but it finally took and the men huddled around it for warmth after setting up camp. Food never tasted so good. Rum never tasted so good. Kimo didn't know if it was Company policy to provide rum for such trips, but he drank it gladly, and decided it was prudent to ask no questions. A sentry was posted; it was the tall Iroquois, and the rest of the men squatted on the beach after dinner, talking in low voices, growing familiar with each other before bedding down for the night.

As Kimo cocooned himself inside his blanket, he felt a sharp sting on the back of his hand, and another, then another. He rubbed his skin vigorously where a hot itch began to rise. "I'm bit!"

"Mon Dieu, there's swarms of them! Cover your heads!"

The camp suddenly swarmed with insects, landing here, there and everywhere, wherever there was a piece of exposed flesh to feast upon. They arrived in black clouds, biting faces, hands, eyelids and ears as men smacked, cursed and swatted in vain against the hungry onslaught of stinging mosquitoes. Baker produced a tin filled with a gelatinous substance and smeared the smelly compound across his exposed skin.

"Here," he shouted, shoving the tin at Kimo, who quickly smeared himself with the grease and passed it along. The tin of tobacco juice and pennyroyal sped around the men, and the mosquitoes eventually departed, either repelled by the grease or sated with the men's blood.

"Can you sleep, Kimo?" Moku whispered across the dark. Everyone else seemed asleep, breathing heavily under their Hudson's Bay blankets. "I'm bit all over. I've never seen mosquitoes big as mice before!"

"Wheesht!" A Scottish voice, stern and full of irritation, croaked from the direction of the fire. Kimo remained silent. His skin felt taut. He felt disoriented, as if this were all a dream and that he'd wake up in the morning in Oahu. But he knew it was no dream.

Someone farted. Not once, but twice, loud and noisily, like the crack of a rifle, and he jumped a foot. Startled men leapt half out of their blankets reaching for their guns, till recognition set in as the awful gas reached everyone's nostrils. Scorn rained down on the perpetrator.

"For pity's sake, Charles!" roared the fiery McKay at the Canadien, who defended himself with Gallic indignation, shrugging his shoulders. Before any man would settle back to sleep, Charles was ordered to remove himself and his blanket downwind of his companions.

"Zut! An' wake up in the morning wit' my troat cut?"

The men laughed, even McKay, releasing some of the tension that had accumulated since their encounter with the Indians, and Charles was allowed to remain with the men around the fire. Kimo tried to sleep, but couldn't. Each time a spark flew, every time a muffled noise echoed from the forest, his ears pricked up. Small twigs broke softly in the dark under the feet of foraging night things. The wind, sighing as it feathered through the trees, rustled lightly across the leaves. Squirrels and field mice scrabbled through the underbrush until some night predator silenced their scurrying and somewhere nearby, a lone coyote howled. Fatigue finally overcame him and he fell into a dreamless sleep, waking only when Moku thumped him hard on the shoulder at daybreak.

Men were up early, washing their faces at the river's edge. Someone had rebuilt the fire and the toasty smell of food crept into his nostrils from the pan of oatmeal bubbling beside the boiling tea-kettle. Charles sorted bales down by the canoe and one of the night sentries reported hearing voices he identified as Klallams, but saw no one.

They ate, doused the fire, reloaded the canoe and paddled towards Puget Sound. Tensions rose again with each new encounter with Indians. From yards away, Kimo felt McKay's silent energy pulsate at every sighting. Waves of concentration emanated from the man, like antennae, probing for signs of threat or reassurance. There were more Indians about now, appearing even when they disembarked twice to portage.

If he hadn't been so worried about another attack, portaging might have been easier for Kimo. He'd walked long distances before, although never with a ninety pound bale strapped to his back, toting a rifle in his left hand and holding up a section of canoe with the right. These men were tough, seasoned Hudson's Bay men. The small Canadiens carried two ninety pound bales on their powerful backs, boasted of carrying three, and still found time to banter with their companions, so he quickly decided he'd better find the strength and determination to keep up with them.

"Kupuas," Moku whispered, making a face, and Kimo laughed. The small Canadiens were unusually broad across the shoulders, compressed by the enormous weights they carried so that their body proportions appeared almost deformed, gnome-like to the big Kanakas. The Indians and some of the Canadiens wore tump-lines, broad leather straps around their forehead, and carried the weight of their bundles on their head straps. If he ever did this again, he'd try it their way.

They portaged with their canoe and cargo till they reached the Sound, where again they encountered Indians. Every man kept his weapon handy while the Cowichans conferred with them, but after McKay made an ostentatious display of his rifle, the Indians left peaceably. The Bay men climbed back into their canoe and paddled north, following the coast line, making better progress because of the good weather and the calmer water, reaching Semiahmoo Bay ahead of schedule. They decided to camp for the night and move next morning through adjacent Mud Bay to the mouth of the Nicomekl River. The men beached the canoe swiftly and Kimo set about helping organize the camp, unloading bales, turning the canoe on its edge and propping it up with short poles. Again the Iroquois made a sighting.

"Campsite." He pointed north. "Half-mile, mile maybe. A family. One man, two women, two children. Maybe more."

"Day'll give us no trouble when day see der's twelve of us," said Charles.

"With guns," the red-haired Scot added, with a nod to his rifle, "which tend to command a proper degree of respect."

Twenty minutes later, an Indian arrived at the men's camp with a young boy in tow. They did not approach directly from the beach, but appeared suddenly, ghost-like at the edge of the clearing where the stony pebbles took over from the grassy vegetation line. The Indian identified himself as Kwantlen and reported he was camping with his family at Semiahmoo till the next full moon. When each was satisfied there was no danger from the other, they parted company and the Bay men continued to set up their camp.

They needed dry wood for the fire, but there were few branches along the beach, so Kimo went into the woods to search. He wasted no time cutting, for broken branches were strewn plentifully on the ground. Heading back to camp, a small rustling movement in the bushes to his left caught his eye and he stopped, instantly alert.

He tensed, waiting. He didn't move. His imagination ran riot. If it was a brave, a painted warrior, he had his machete. It was sharp, and he was ready to use it. Just one, he could deal with. But what if there were two? Or more? Should he call for help or would that just draw the enemy to his side faster? He swallowed hard and gripped the hilt tightly. Immediately in front of him, a few feet from his left elbow, the branches of a wild hawthorn parted softly and a young Indian woman stepped forward, carrying a woven basket full of salmonberries. She lifted her head, as if testing the wind, like some fawn leaving the shelter of the trees to enter a clearing.

Kimo drew in his breath. The wahine was semi-nude and in the evening light seemed almost Hawaiian, her skin a coppery bronze, her hair long and black, and her dark almond-shaped eyes expressive and intelligent. She wore a skirt of shredded cedar bark that stopped at her kneecaps. And nothing else except a pair of moccasins. Her breasts were small and high, and her skin shone in the sunlight. Black hair scaled down her back, disappearing behind small-boned shoulders. She froze, wide-eyed on the spot when he appeared before her. A flicker of fear reflected in her eyes when she spotted the sharp knife he was holding. She had no weapon that he could see, and he didn't want to frighten her, so he slowly lowered his machete inch by inch, bending his knees to drop it with a gentle thunk onto the ground. He had another knife of course, hidden away. He was no fool. There might be others in the trees.

Her eyes swept from the dropped knife to his face, curiosity replacing the fear in her eyes. She didn't move. Neither did he. He didn't take his eyes off her. He tipped the bundle of branches under his left arm slightly upwards, so she'd know he was collecting wood, and he knew the instant she understood. Then suddenly she retreated, stepping back softly.

"It's all right. Don't be afraid." He spoke on impulse, then instantly cursed himself for such foolishness. She wouldn't understand English, and coming upon him so unexpectedly, she was bound to be frightened. He didn't move, in case his speaking had frightened her even more. She stopped retreating however, and slanted her head to one side as if puzzled, as if she were listening to distant sounds in a seashell.

And then she was gone, vanished, as suddenly as she'd appeared and he was left wondering if he'd dreamt the entire encounter. He didn't move for a few minutes, gathering his thoughts, then he picked up his machete and returned to camp with the wood he'd collected, which was enough to keep the fire stoked for hours.

The men ate and settled down to sleep. For Kimo, it was another wild and restless night. He lay awake, watching the stars, and thought about the sky over Oahu. In the morning when he woke, his fingers, stiff with cold, had molded themselves around Keaka's wooden dolphin. He half-expected to hear its message but his narrowed senses, tuned so intensely to the dangers of this new place, excluded all else and picked up nothing, leaving him vaguely discontent.

After breakfast the men broke camp, reloaded the canoe and set off. Kimo scrunched his big legs under the seat he occupied between McKay in front and the Cowichan behind. The stale smell of twelve active men and the odours from the cargo mingled curiously now, sweat, wet leathers, boxes, bales and bundles, each emitting its own peculiar smell. In front, the tall, keen-eyed Iroquois stood like some majestic bronze statue at the head of the canoe, one foot raised above the other. The man intrigued Kimo. Impressively aristocratic by any standard, he spoke fluent English and some French and several Indian dialects. He could have been alii, royalty, anywhere.

"Your scout is different from the other Indians. Are there many like him here?" he asked McKay.

"Aye. They're all over the country now. Many warriors joined the canoe brigades after the Iroquois Nation lost its power. Sakarata, he's a first rate scout, the best steersman I've come across, bar none, and I've met my share."

Kimo would have asked more but the Iroquois suddenly raised his arm and pointed a long brown index finger towards the curve of the bay where a lone, blanket-clad Indian stood by the water's edge. Kimo suddenly remembered his encounter with the girl.

"I saw a woman last night, picking salmonberries."

The Cowichan eyed him curiously. "Aleela came in your dream?"

"Aleela?"

"Salmonberry woman. She comes in your dream to tell you something."

"No. She was real, this Aleela." He spoke the name slowly, reliving the odd encounter between the woman and himself, and wondered now if that was her cocooned in a blanket by the shore. Suddenly his left calf cramped painfully and he swore under his breath. The muscle, a small knotted stone ball, sent pain radiating down to his ankle and up his thigh, and he forgot everything else. He flexed his leg and pummelled the hard calf briskly, massaging it heavily upwards until the pain slowly eased, bringing blessed relief.

Keaka's wooden dolphin lay warm against his skin and Kimo wondered if the Cowichan wasn't right after all. Maybe he had been dreaming, for he imagined he heard Keaka at his ear chastising him for being idle in the canoe. He bent his body immediately and pulled deep and hard, stretching forward with the paddle to yoke his strength to the others, as they stroked powerfully away from the shores of Semiahmoo Bay.

Their canoe swiftly rounded the corner into Mud Bay. From there, they progressed into the Nicomekl, paddling as far as they were able along the winding, narrow river till the heavy tangles of vegetation growing on both sides challenged their power to keep moving forward.

"You call this a river?" Moku, frustrated, pulled in his paddle. The two Cowichans tried poling through the dense, weedy vegetation, but the boat made little progress.

An Indian family watched their efforts curiously from the bank. A small naked child, about two years old, sat sucking his fat baby fingers on a rush mat beside an elderly wizened grandmother covered in a reed cape. Three younger men and two women appeared by the water's edge. The men were broadly built but short in stature. It was difficult to tell from their eyes or expression if they were hostile or friendly. Indians were still the unknown for Kimo, so he eyed them warily. It seemed to him they were more curious than anything else, and he reckoned they must be harmless, for the tall Scot took his time nonchalantly pressing tobacco into his clay pipe as they paddled along. Still, the rifle, Kimo noted, was clearly visible through the crook of his arm.

Because of the dense weeds in the narrow river, the Canadien boatman decided to halt and make the portage to the Salmon River sooner. So they did, completing this last short portage and performing the tedious task of unloading, toting, then reloading cargo before wearily paddling the canoe along the Salmon River into Langley.

After the men disembarked and unloaded the canoe, Kimo stood on the wharf seeking a sense of the place. The stockade walls looked strong and well enough built but overall the fort was a sad looking thing, smaller than he expected. In the middle of such a vast wilderness as this, he wondered if it would withstand assault. He filled his lungs with air.

Was it only two months ago he'd left Oahu? It seemed longer. Already he had changed somehow. He felt it. It was this place, this strange new world where heightened senses forced an acute awareness of everything and everyone around. He had never felt so much on edge in his life. Everything was bigger than he'd imagined, the trees, the mountains. He and Moku had been slowest to respond when those Indians shot their arrows at the camp. He felt some shame in that. He hadn't seen them, or heard them. He couldn't rid himself of a pervasive sense of menace. One thing was clear. They'd have to be more alert and faster, if they were going to stay alive in this wild place.

As a gray dusk settled like a blanket over the fort, in silent tribute, he faced west and touched the dolphin on the thong around his neck.

chapter five

FOR GENERATIONS THE Kwantlen people had moved from camp to camp, depending on weather and food supplies. Their summer village had been downriver at Skaiametl, renamed New Westminster by the whites, but the tribe had moved to Sqwalets, the island by the fort for protection from the Lekwiltok and other hostile tribes. Here, the Kwantlen built their houses along the riverbank facing the fort, but far enough from the shore to avoid flooding during spring run-off. Neetlum had built their house like the others, in the shape of a shed, with an almost flat roof gently pitched so the rain would run off, and inclining upward from front to rear. They used the roof for drying fish and sometimes for sitting on to view the festivities when the village held a potlatch.

Neetlum had laid the cedar wall planks vertically, one against the other, and anchored them by driving the ends down into the ground. Spaces in the walls were chinked with moss, but not entirely, so that air could circulate and rid the house of smoke from the inside fire. They had two small doorways, a front entrance and a back "escape" route, covered with animal skins.

They lived two doors from Chief Whattlekainem's longhouse, the biggest in the village. Sixty families lived on the island now, their homes strung out in an uneven row along the riverbank, where they could see and be seen from the fort. The longhouse was grand, with many doors, and housed several families. It was a hundred feet long and fifty broad, built over a heavy framework of posts. Planks were laid on top and tied to the framework by cedar withes. Mats and planks covered the packed-earth floors, and fire pits, one for each family, were dug into the floor and contained by stones. Fish drying racks hung suspended across the roof beams, and food storage baskets were placed on high shelves near the roof, where air circulation was good. Rose was glad they lived in their own home, though. There was even less privacy in a longhouse.

Every spring and fall, at the end of the salmon runs, when the work of catching, drying and smoking the fish was over, the family journeyed south. Lawi'qum's family travelled north from the Nooksack lands at the same time and the two groups would rendezvous at Semiahmoo Bay. Sooner or later. The Indians did not live by the white man's clock, but measured time by the moon. Two moons, or more. Distance measures were equally vague, measured in parts of days. Two days' walk, or half a day.

The Kwantlen year followed the earth's cycle. In June, they travelled to hunt, fish and dress hides before the July's summer sockeye run. Fishing, drying, storing and extracting oil lasted through August. September feasts celebrated the close of the sockeye season. October and the onset of winter meant more hunting and gathering. In November and December tribes entertained with lavish gift-giving potlatches, followed in January and February by sacred winter dances.

March saw the spring fish, trout and sturgeon returning to the river. In April the great oolichan runs began, and May brought the return of the spring salmon. Then the cycle would begin all over again.

The day after she visited the fort, Rose's family prepared for their trip to Semiahmoo. She looked forward to the journey and put the fort out of her mind temporarily. Likely there would be no hiring till the next salmon run. With luck, she might be called then to help cut the fish.

Neetlum checked the bundle of woven baskets he had strapped on her back. He was square, typically Kwantlen, stocky in shoulder and hip, with black hair hanging in oiled tresses past his shoulders. His lips drew into a tight knot, as if a cord had been pulled through them. With eyes sharp as flint, he hefted the bundled baskets to and fro between his broad, calloused hands, gauging their weight. They all fit neatly one inside the other, but the pack swung awkwardly.

"Heavy?"

"I'll manage," she said, more concerned about the load her brother Sandich had slung across his shoulder. He was nine, the age when boys liked to boast of their abilities. She bit her tongue and said nothing as he affected an air of indifference at the size and weight of the bundle sagging like a sack of potatoes between his narrow shoulder blades. His black hair was pulled back tight to the scalp, and hung shining at shoulder length. He wore britches Rose had sewed from blankets, cinched at the waist with a deerskin belt whose ends dangled mid-thigh. Her sisters, Snana'y and Wawas'u, in brushed cedar skirts and bare feet, toted small, easy to manage packs. Snana'y was eight, doe-eyed and of a dreamy disposition; Wawas'u at seven, was a quick-smiling imp currently missing four front teeth.

With the weight of each package checked and rechecked, they slipped the bundles off their backs, and fitted them into the family's large dugout. It had room for eight paddlers and storage, but it was old and from a yard away you could smell the salt and sweat and animal kill permeating the cedar.

"If we arrive first, we can start to put up the shelters," Lawi'qum said.

If! Rose couldn't remember the last time their relatives reached Semiahmoo first. She'd wager one of her best baskets they'd be the ones to begin erecting the temporary shelters needed for their time together hunting, fishing, gathering berries and dressing hides. They were lucky, though. Not everyone had the right to hunt or fish at Half-Moon Bay, but Lawi'qum's sister had married a sub-chief of the Semiahmoo tribe and her high status permitted them to do so.

The families traded with each other during these visits. Rose wove fine baskets that Neetlum used to exchange for obsidian for making tools, because the hard stone could not be found along the banks of the Fraser. Now they could acquire ready-made tools from the Langley fort, and other goods such as blankets, nails, knives, pots and pans, which made their lives easier, but the families still traded as they had always done, for baskets, pelts, oil, deerskin and other items.

Fort Vancouver's store on the Columbia was crammed with even more goods, with amazing luxury items, such as ostrich feathers and silk stockings. But that might just be voyageurs' gossip, for Rose had never actually seen any of the fanciful goods they boasted of. Though she'd dearly like to. Her Nooksack relatives now traded at the Columbia store, and last winter, during their family gathering at Semiahmoo, she had approached her mother's brother, Sha:l.

"Uncle, next spring will you bring me some calico from the Vancouver store?"

"If the hunting is poor, I can't promise, Niece, but if the season is good, then yes, I'll bring it."

It was possible to obtain cloth by the fathom, or armspan, at the

Langley fort but it sold out quickly and colour choice was a luxury when it wasn't entirely out of the question. Her uncle made no promises, but Rose spoke with her aunt and arranged to make her baskets if the fabric could be obtained. Now she hoped the cloth would be in one of the bundles brought north by her relatives. She needed it to make a European style dress, one that was new and hers alone. She'd traded for the used dress of rough blue homespun she now owned, from a Canadien whose Indian wife had died.

"Five baskets!" the man had demanded.

"Two," she'd countered. "They're well made."

"Three and it's yours," he'd said, and she took it. She'd washed the death from it several times, patched the seams and altered it to fit. It looked drab, but it served its purpose. The Xwelitem at the fort frowned on nudity. Most Kwantlen covered themselves in the summer now, in deference to the white man's prudishness. Of course, in the winter it was too wet not to cover up, but sometimes summers were long and hot, and men walked naked specially if they were fishing. Bare-breasted women traditionally wore knee-length skirts made of shredded cedar bark, and still did in the privacy of their homes and in places away from the forts, and crafted reed capes to cover their upper bodies.

Years ago though, her father had brought from Vancouver soft cotton fabric, blue like the sky, which her mother had sewn into a dress for her, with fine thread from the store and a shiny metal needle, finer by far than their Indian nettle thread and bone needles. She had fallen in love with the feel of the fabric, light as bird down, and easily washed. She'd worn it long after it was too small and too tight, then it was passed along to another child, ending up a tattered piece of rag. But that was long ago. And now as they paddled the Salmon River, Rose looked forward to the families' get-together, praying her uncle had had a good trapping year.

"Paddles in!" Neetlum suddenly called, signalling a halt to this leg of their trip. They raised the laden craft from the water, rested briefly, then began the arduous overland portage to the Nikomekl River.

"It took us longer last year to come this far," Sandich panted between strides. Rose hadn't the breath to argue, but it didn't seem any shorter to her as she doggedly placed one foot before the other, duck-like, striving to maintain her balance in a steady forward plod. Portaging was always the hardest part of travelling. Slog, rest, then slog again, relentlessly.

Ahead she watched Lawi'qum's shadow seep out from her feet, taking reedy form to her right. Her mother's small back swayed rhythmically in time with Neetlum's stride, shortened now to perfectly match her steps while they supported the weight of the front of the canoe between them. Rose and Sandich balanced the back end while the two girls ran alongside. Wawas'u chatted incessantly, head bobbing, oblivious to the whistle created by her missing teeth.

"We'll break here." Neetlum chose a sheltered spot, familiar from previous trips, where leafy cedars and curly willows grew close to the riverbank. They unloaded what they needed, removing food for their evening meal, blankets and reed mats for the ground. After a meal of dried fish and peas, the family bedded down. Rose and her sisters wrapped up together, heads inside the upturned canoe which lay propped up on its side by a short piece of cedar log, and from which hung rush mats to shelter them from any rain. Her parents slept off to one side with Sandich some yards away, bravely on his own, until some forlorn coyote howled in the night, baying in the moonlit quiet, making him shift quickly beside his sisters under the canoe.

Next morning they canoed the narrow Nicomekl to Mud Bay, then paddled into adjacent Semiahmoo Bay, scanning the length of the beach as they drew near. As Rose expected, they found no signs of their southern family. Delays were inevitable, of course. Almost all trips involved portaging between waterways, adding time to your journey if the wrong place or time was chosen to make it.

The pale ball that was the evening sun squatted above the horizon in a thin smother of cloud as they neared the shore and hoisted their paddles from the water. Then the rain they'd been anticipating all afternoon descended on the beach, in a veil of sleeting drizzle as they hastened, shivering, to heave the dugout onto the shore. Suddenly Sandich drew his breath in with a hiss, as if he'd been scalded. He eased his grip on the canoe and the sudden imbalance prompted everyone to halt. He leaned forward and tapped his father's shoulder urgently.

"Look! There! A canoe coming in!"

"It's big," Neetlum grunted, squinting at the horizon. "Can't see its markings from here. They're heading for the far end of the bay. Everybody take cover, quickly!"

They moved in tandem, like any pack of wilderness animals, wordlessly coordinating their movements toward safety and survival. They scurried to haul the dugout across the shingle, slippery now in the rain, and hid it beneath the brush at the edge of the woods. The women shivered beneath the dripping leaves, from cold and from fear. Rose wrapped her arm around Wawas'u and squeezed Snana'y's trembling hand, willing their fright away. Oddly, she felt anger more than fear. This used to be a peaceful trip, but for the past several years, warrior bands had resurrected old feuds, coveting territory, seizing goods and slaves. The family eyed the incoming canoe's progress from their hiding place in the thicket. It seemed like some spirit craft, appearing one moment then fading from sight, drawing towards them through the gray ribbon of fog sitting on the top of the bay.

"Who are they?" Rose whispered. If the canoe was decorated or carved, Neetlum would be able to tell friend from foe. The young girls crouched at her feet now, arms around each other, holding their breath.

"Can't tell . . . but there are twelve paddlers."

Silent as stone and barely breathing, they remained crouched low in the wet thicket. Rose didn't feel the deep chill or the drizzling rain and when she realized the others didn't either, it came to her how much the will to survive made you focus. Time passed. It felt like forever, but could only have been minutes before Neetlum signalled safety, rising from the thicket like smoke from a fire.

"King George men."

Rose released her hold on her sisters' shoulders. Whites at the forts were King George men. Those on the American ships plying the coast were Boston men.

"We're safe," she assured the girls, as Neetlum slid his rifle back onto his shoulder. The family emerged from their hiding place and set up camp while the Bay men beached their canoe across the bay and did the same, choosing a spot higher on the shingle, where the beach and shrub came together.

"They'll see our smoke," Neetlum said, "and send their scouts. I'll go speak with them, let them know we're here."

"Can I come?" Sandich begged, hoping to escape the chores his mother would assign him. Rose knew well enough what he was up to. He stood tall as her nose now. By summer's end, he'd loom above her. Though nearing manhood, he was still a boy, with features unformed and ears that jutted from his skull like a frightened field mouse. His eyes though, reflected keen intelligence, and his heart was good. She understood his urge to go with Neetlum. He looked up to the Bay men. Muskets, of course. And muskets meant power. For an impressionable young man, irresistible.

"Wife?" Neetlum hesitated.

"He can go, Husband."

The women's campfire refused to start for a time because of the drizzle but finally took, and they boiled up a kettle for tea. When the rain stopped, Rose and her sisters dug for clams while Lawi'qum hunted out pots and a supply of dried salmon for dinner.

"Don't pick them off the beach, *dig* for them," Rose warned the girls, who skipped across the sand looking for the tiny holes the clams drilled. With sticks they scraped through the puddles and when their basket was full, filled it with seawater and rinsed the sand from the clams. Because the tide was low, giant oysters littered the beach in heaps so the girls gathered these quickly too. Lawi'qum would panfry them. Neetlum, though, would eat his raw.

As the girls returned to the fire, Neetlum and Sandich reappeared after meeting with the King George men, and reported all was well. Lawi'qum resumed preparations for dinner while Rose headed to the forest to pick berries for tea. The ones she found at the forest edge felt overripe, too soft to eat, so she worked her way through the bushes till she found what she was looking for, orange-red salmon-berries ideally ripened, hanging in drooping clusters. The berries rained into her palm as she flitted from one branch to another, moving slowly from bush to bush, cautious and silent in all her movements.

A whirring at her ear and a faint brush of air made her pause as a hummingbird streaked by, hovering above the honeysuckle vine that twisted through the berry bush. The bird drank from the long-throat of the trumpet flower, sparkling with the raindrops and pollen dust on the stamens inside. She stood still, not wishing to disturb the tiny flyer, no longer than her thumb. The bronze green of the bird's crown shone in the sunlight above a rufous back. Its gorget gleamed copper-red above a white breast and then the bird whirled and sped away on spirit wings.

Once, when she was twelve, one had come as she sat weaving.

When it flew away and returned a second time, her grandfather said this was her *tamanamis,* her guardian spirit and that day gave Rose the new name *Swansalee,* hummingbird. Now, with the benediction of the warm sun overhead, the Indian in Rose wondered what message her spirit helper had brought for her this day.

Her heart almost stopped beating when a shadow sliced across her path. Monstrously elongated, the shape attached itself to a human form as a man's face appeared suddenly in front of her. Her pulse leapt uncontrollably. She hadn't heard him approach and froze on the spot, for he was one of the biggest men she'd ever set eyes on, a full head and a half taller than her father. His skin was bronze like the Kwantlen, with dark curly hair falling wild to his shoulders, and large eyes, black like obsidian. She guessed instantly that he must be an Owhyhee, for he had a look of the man Peopeo, the carpenter at the fort.

The man seemed as startled as she. His arms were thick as tree trunks. The huge muscles of his left arm bulged with the pile of branches he was carrying. She stared at the machete gleaming in his right hand and stepped back, but he immediately stopped moving. Slowly he lowered his machete to the ground and let it fall on the leafy, fecund underbrush with a soft gentle thunk. He moved his left arm up and down, indicating the branches he had gathered. She realized he was trying to tell her he was only collecting wood, and wished her no harm. She stepped backwards, ready to retreat into the trees and then he had spoken to her in English, fracturing the silence of the woods.

"It's all right."

She understood. Her English had lapsed after her father went away but recent visits to the fort had helped restore what she knew from childhood. His voice held no menace. She stopped retreating and held still, though her heart flapped like a snared bird trying to free itself. He was staring at her as if she were some kind of apparition, but then he spoke again.

"It's all right. Don't be afraid." It was barely a whisper, and still he didn't move.

She hesitated and almost spoke, when it dawned on her that he must be shocked by her presence. Her eyes widened in dismay. The white people at the fort were offended by nudity and she was bare, except for her short cedar skirt. Consternation hit the pit of her stomach, rooted itself and spread upward. She raised her right palm, turned quickly away, and made for the trees. She moved swiftly through the bushes, stumbling where she shouldn't, her breath scalding her, and didn't dare look back through the receding tunnel of greenery. When she finally did turn around, there was no sign of him.

She didn't mention the incident when she returned to her campsite. No harm had been done. She thought of the big Owhyhee later that evening though, as she cleaned and stored the salmonberries. He spoke English. He was young, large and powerful. She recognized that he had tried to calm her fears. Uncommonly strange, yet kind.

In the morning, a vee-wedge of geese gaggled in formation overhead, honking her awake at sunrise. From their sleeping shelter beneath the canoe, she heard the faint scratching sounds of a canoe being hauled across pebbles and knew the King George men were preparing to leave the bay. She rose, wrapped a gray woollen blanket tightly around herself, and walked to the water's edge. The hard round pebbles chilled her toes, as the cool breeze tugged at the blanket flapping around her legs. The canoe was already well away from shore.

"The sun feels warm already. It will be a good day." Sandich stood beside her yawning, rubbing sleep from his eyes with his knuckles.

He walked unflinching into the cold water of the bay, and swam in measured round circles. "Are you coming in?"

"Soon," she replied, and stood watching the craft depart, and pondered that men from far beyond the seas would come to Semiahmoo Bay to pick firewood for the Hudson's Bay Company, all for the sake of fur.

Two nights passed before the family's southern relatives arrived in the bay. Rose counted five canoes paddling to shore, with Lawi'qum's sisters and brothers and their husbands and wives and various offspring, including two fat new babies, who drew the women laughing and clucking around them. The men set to work finishing the shelters Neetlum had started along the beach, and Lawi'qum and Rose joined the women preparing the traditional clambake by the shore. The men dug a pit in the ground, floored it with stones and set a fire above them. When it burned out and the stones were heated through, the women set clams over them and covered them with seaweed to steam till the shells opened. They ate till they were sated, exchanging news late into the night. The leftovers were divided among the families and Rose spent the evening pushing clean sticks through the clams, as many as each stick would hold. They'd dry them in the sun, and store them.

"Time for slahal!" Neetlum shouted, and the men instantly jumped to their feet. Soon roars of laughter echoed across the bay as men played the raucous gambling game. The women didn't laugh so much, for usually games continued for days on end, and could have dire consequences for them. So far in the family, no man had gambled away his wife or his house, but it was common practice so Rose's independent aunts tended to show a little more deference to their husbands while slahal was underway. It was a simple game, where carved bones were hidden under a deerskin cover, and one team had to guess who on the opposing team held the designated bone. The slahal lasted through the first night and stretched into the second, and the third, while the families swam, hunted and fished during the days.

Most of the men owned guns, yet still hunted here in the old ways with bows and arrows, spears, deadfall traps and snares. They trapped a fine white-tailed deer with strong skin ropes when it caught its jagged antlers among the trees, after the men drove the frightened animal through the brush. Neetlum took fish in gill nets made of hide strips and cedar bark and used bone and tooth hooks for jigging. Lawi'qum's family fished with dip-nets, spears and gaffs.

"Niece, I didn't bring you the cloth you wanted," her Uncle Sha:l said, poker-faced the first evening. His aristocratic forehead sloped upward and he looked down his bent nose, eyeing her response. Disappointment wracked her. She'd have to wait many moons now for stock from the Langley fort. Then he laughed and flipped a rolled up mat onto the ground. He flicked open its flap and two partial bolts of cloth rolled across the floor matting to rest at her moccasined toes.

"Two! Thank you, Uncle. They're perfect!" She picked them up, held them close to her heart. One was a blue and white checkered pattern, the other plain white cotton. Ecstatic, she ran her fingers over the cloth, feeling the fabric between her fingers, lifting it up to the sunlight to see through it. It was plain cotton, but to Rose, it was beautiful and gossamer fine.

Well worth the baskets she'd made to trade. She'd picked the cedar roots and grasses last summer and woven them during the long winter evenings. She'd soaked roots and twigs, peeled and split them and cured and dyed different types of grasses. She wove and coiled superbly. Her twined open-weave baskets were in great demand for holding shellfish and roots, and the carry-alls she twilled were so popular, she couldn't keep up with requests for them. She gave Sha:l five baskets in exchange for the fabric, and couldn't wait to return home to start sewing.

She spent the next three weeks at Semiahmoo dressing deer hides. It was a chore she disliked, scraping the insides and rubbing them with animal brains. She hated the feel of the gray pulp between her fingers, and eventually convinced one of her agreeable female cousins to exchange chores with her. She ended up drying venison instead. Cut in thin strips and smoked or sun-dried, the nutritious jerky kept for months. She powdered theirs, added hazelnuts and dry berries with melted fat, and rolled them into balls, then stored them for adding to their morning pans of oatmeal.

At the end of three weeks, her mother promised "Two more days, then we'll head home." But it was three before the last of their southern family left. Bundles had to be repacked and stashed in the canoes, exchanges completed to everyone's satisfaction, debts paid that accumulated during the slahal games, and arrangements made for their next get-together. The dressed hides from the men's hunting forays were rolled and packed, the dried clams and berries shared. Women doused fires while men dismantled shelters. Cheerful and tearful farewells were taken, as the canoes pulled out of Semiahmoo Bay heading south. Their departure rendered the beach suddenly silent.

Only Rose and her family remained, for Neetlum still had two traps to retrieve. He hadn't checked them, the last slahal game having lasted three days. Now he took to the forest as the women scraped and scoured plates and pans in the sand, and returned with his steel traps and two dead beaver. He dumped the beaver on the ground at Sandich's feet, dropped his long knife also and turned away without a word. Sandich preened with pleasure. He grinned, cheeks rounding like new potatoes. This was a momentous day. He ran his thumb along the blade's keen edge. Never before had he been allowed to use his father's long knife.

"Be careful with that," Lawi'qum warned, but Sandich could hardly contain his excitement and immediately set to skinning the beaver, slashing its head and feet off with the long knife, then paring the pelt carefully off the carcass with a small, thin skinning blade. He fought but lost the battle to keep the smile off his face. Rose, happy for him, left him to the task. She was stacking bundles into the canoe when her mother's voice called out, registering a queer note of anxiety that froze her to the spot mid-task.

"Daughter!"

She spun just as Snana'y and Wawas'u clutched at her legs from behind, nearly toppling her over in their fright. Three stocky Indians stood next to Sandich. Two of them, barefoot and bare-chested, wore deerskin britches and held bows in their right hands, sheaves of arrows protruding above their shoulders. The third, heavily bearded and taller by far, wore a cape of tired otter skin pelts slung across his broad shoulders. His stained deerskin britches and moccasins were worn with age and frayed. He held a gun haughtily, loosely, by his side, for all the world a sign he considered the women and children no threat. He slung his arm possessively over Sandich's bony shoulders, Neetlum's knife now dangling from his fingertips. The hair on Rose's neck began to prickle. Sandich stood stiff as a ramrod, face flushed, eyes lowered, ashamed for allowing the removal of his father's precious long knife from his hands.

"What do you want?" Lawi'qum's normally low, modulated voice sounded high and reedy as birdsong. Rose guessed the unnatural tone was for Neetlum's benefit. Please God he'd be close enough to hear.

"Food, to start with."

He spoke Kwantlen poorly. He was not local. There was an air about him, something Rose fought to identify but couldn't. He gripped Sandich by the shoulder in a false, comradely hug. The threat was plain enough, unspoken, suspended in the air like a promise.

Sandich stood sullen and rigid, staring at his feet. A grin curled the man's upper lip crookedly to one side, barely visible through the heavy gray whiskers that covered his face. His hair too was gray, and fell to his shoulders untied. His eyes swept the campsite. He leaned forward straining like a leashed dog.

"Empty your bundle, woman!"

Lawi'qum didn't move.

"Now!" He struck then, sudden as a snake, slapping Lawi'qum loudly on her small, high-boned left cheek. The sound was strangely familiar; the sound Sandich made when he tossed his hide ball against a carcass of hung meat. Rose felt sick. Her mother stood tearless as a red welt began to form on her cheek, from the side of her nose to her left ear. As the silence reeled itself out, the man swung to face Rose and her sisters.

"You!" He kicked the bundle at her feet.

She stepped protectively in front of the two girls. Face devoid of expression, she too stood still and silent. Her mind raced. Fearful possibilities presented themselves. They could be killed, or taken for slaves. The younger ones certainly for slaves, herself and her mother for wives. The man stepped towards her, hauling Sandich with him, and swung his rifle upwards. Their eyes met briefly as she readied for the strike, drawing her head into her shoulders like a snail seeking the shelter of its shell. But she saw then what she'd missed before, and the shock rippled through her, as she raised her shoulders in a protective curl.

CLICK! The clear, sharp cocking of Neetlum's rifle pinged across the beach.

"Drop the gun. Step back! Now!"

Breath rushed out of Rose's lungs in pained relief. Neetlum stood feet apart at the tree line, gun pointing directly at the group's leader, his right eye sighting along the barrel, half-shuttered.

"Drop it now! And release the boy!" He spoke slowly, spitting out staccato words that sounded themselves like sharp gun shots.

"We do no harm." The man raised his shoulders dismissively, with a fake smile of entreaty.

"You strike my wife and claim no harm?" Contempt dripped from Neetlum's tongue.

"Release the boy! And drop the gun!"

The man hesitated then let the knife slip from his fingers, but not his gun. He suddenly threw his arm around Sandich's throat and hauled him roughly against his chest. Instantly the boy exploded, transforming himself into a biting, squirming, flailing mass of bony arms and legs. Seconds later, he had freed himself and then he lunged swiftly to retrieve his father's long knife. He wheeled, dignity restored, inches taller. Rose waited now for the challenge that must come.

"What do you want?" Neetlum demanded, his voice hard-edged.

"Some food, that's all. We thought to share yours."

They had arrows and a gun. Food was abundant in this place if you spent the energy to seek it. Something was amiss.

"He's Xwelitem, Father!" Rose found her voice. The white man had blue eyes but looked as Indian as his companions. He could only be a voyageur gone native or a deserter from one of the Company forts.

"Find your own food, before the King George men find you," Neetlum said.

"They won't. The Express passed through a week ago," the Gray Beard replied.

"They left their scouts," Neetlum retorted. They didn't always, but often enough that the tribes knew of their presence in the area. She realized then what Neetlum had figured out. These men hadn't hunted for fear the Company scouts would find them.

"They rendezvous here this very day on their way back from the Cowlitz. You know what happens to runaways, Gray Beard. If they catch you, you'll be flogged and chained and jailed for desertion." Neetlum paused. "And when they hear my shot, it will bring them even quicker."

The three exchanged nervous glances, fighting doubt. No one spoke, no one moved. Neetlum realigned his gun barrel directly at the leader's chest.

"Drop your weapon and leave *now!*" he ordered hoarsely, "or the beach crabs will feast on your entrails."

The man stood still. Silence fell like a rotten cedar. No one moved. Rose's mind raced. The two with bows and arrows looked dull as the weather but if Neetlum shot the white, they could still shoot their arrows before he had time to reload.

Sandich stood beside Rose, his father's knife clutched fast in his knuckled fist. She whirled, snatched the knife from his clenched hand and swung it upwards. Up and over she swung with all her might, in a great arc, intending to strike the arm of the man holding the gun with the flat of the blade. He moved instantly to deflect it, but caught the blade's raw edge instead.

"Aaagh!" A muffled scream tore from his mouth. The rifle dropped from his fumbling fingers. Sandich spun, snatching it from the ground almost before it landed. Blood oozed from the man's forearm as he fell onto his knees, clutching the gash on his arm.

The two bow men didn't move, uncertain which one Neetlum would choose to shoot first. The wounded man rose unsteadily to his feet, tugging a piece of pelt from his shoulders to wrap around his bleeding arm. He shuffled forward slowly, eyes ferreting out his gun, now firmly held by Sandich out of reach. He nodded, indicating the return of his weapon.

"No!" Neetlum's voice sounded like cracked ice, for his spirit power had entered him. "Leave now, or I shoot!" He was done with talking. They knew it and fled, all three, swift as running deer, away from the camp into the cover of the trees.

The women sagged with nervous relief and Neetlum began to sing. Softly at first, then louder. Eyes closed, he swayed back and forth dancing on the beach shingle.

"Ha' ha ha' a/he'a he'a!
Ha' ha ha' a/he'a he'a!"

Sandich and Lawi'qum joined in celebrating his warrior power. Then Rose stood and danced too, shuffling hip-hop, in wide circles, waving her arms, singing Neetlum's song, and her sisters did too, till their celebration echoed along the beach, lifted by the wind through the treetops, reaching skyward.

Later as they doused the campfire and prepared to leave, Neetlum brushed his hand across Sandich's head, riffling his hair, then turned to his wife.

"It's time our son learned about weapons."

"He's only nine, Husband."

"Old enough."

"He hasn't mastered the bow yet." He'd been practising though, with geese and small birds for the family's food supply.

"Arrows can't fight bullets, Wife. The days of the bow are numbered. Too many braves have access now to guns. No telling what might have happened if I hadn't my gun today." He examined the weapon Sandich held and shook his head. "Rusted half away . . . shameful! A man who treats a weapon so carelessly doesn't deserve one. You and I, Son, must go trapping when we get back."

Sandich beamed. He hoped it would be soon, then they'd trade their pelts at the Langley fort for rifles. Lawi'qum lowered her eyes and said no more. Neetlum turned to Rose.

"You were courageous and quick-thinking to do what you did

today, Daughter." She accepted the compliment with a nod. He was a man of few words, not given to extravagant speech but she knew he was pleased with her. At least for today.

The family gathered their belongings, loaded the canoe and headed home. The sky was overcast, so the sun couldn't fight its way through the clouds, but at least it didn't rain. Only the Nikomekl slowed them down because of weeds choking its winding waters, but the canoe fought its way through vegetation that larger craft couldn't. After the usual hard portage, they reached the Salmon, and paddling through, arrived exhausted back in cloud-covered Fort Langley after nightfall.

Rose unpacked her bundles and ran her hands along the cloth. Now she could make a proper dress, thanks to Uncle Sha:l. And to Neetlum, who had saved them today. His actions had astonished her, for she had forgotten about his warrior power. It had come when she was twelve. She remembered every detail, for she'd been frightened at the time. It made him so sick that Lawi'qum had called the Medicine Man. The Shaman had come in a cedar bark headdress shaking his rattle of scallop shells and danced around Neetlum. He divined that Neetlum's grandfather's tamanamis had entered him, bringing his warrior power and he called the family to come and beat drums and poles to help him receive his power, and after a few days, Neetlum grew strong and his sickness went away.

Rose's Catholic father had not believed in Indian spirit power, of course, but she had witnessed the unexplainable too often not to respect it. Because of it, they were alive today. And maybe, just maybe, because she'd found the courage to strike back too. She had acted on instinct when she grabbed the knife from Sandich to strike their attacker. Just as she had acted on instinct when she lifted the trader's pen to write her name. She didn't know when it first came to her that she'd have to do more than wait for life to happen if she wanted to achieve something, that she'd have to take action to direct her own fate. Well, she'd done it. Now she would find work at the Langley fort. She could feel it in her bones. The new trader knew her name. It was on his list. She'd put it there herself. When she finished making a proper dress, she'd be ready.

For what, she didn't quite know but her spirit was prompting her. She knew, she *knew*, her fate was tied to the fort across the river.

chapter six

"Hurry, we'll be late." Sandich tugged at Rose's elbow. They'd been home a week, and normal routine had taken over their lives. Now he could barely contain his excitement, for the *Beaver,* the Hudson Bay Company's "Big Canoe," was due to arrive in Fort Langley any minute. The steamship first appeared on the coast in 1836 and its appearance every few months intrigued the Kwantlen.

"They say the *Beaver* outruns all the Yankee traders along the coast."

"Don't believe all you hear," Rose replied. He picked up such gossip from the fort's voyageurs who frequented the village. They could tell tall tales if they found a willing listener, and Sandich was always that. Excited gasps erupted when the ship steamed into view, as curling puffs of smoke laddered skyward from its stack.

"Six men cut steady for two days to supply enough wood for it to run for just one day," Sandich informed Rose importantly. "It weighs 109 tons."

"And just what is a ton?" she asked. His face turned red to the tips of his ears and he laughed. Of course he had no idea, any more than she did. She eyed the grand ship as it steamed slowly towards them blowing smoke, churning up the river's muddy waters with its giant circulating paddles. It was a sight to behold. And as the Kwantlen watched the ship slowly dock, a group of fort employees arrived on the wharf on the other side of the river to unload its cargo.

Kimo and Moku were among them. Three weeks ago they had arrived at this same Fort Langley dock. The Kanaka, Peopeo, had greeted them with aloha and informed them that James Murray Yale was Chief Clerk, that he'd recently taken over from Factor Archibald McDonald. Then he'd escorted them across the stockade to meet the big chief in charge of this outpost on the edge of nowhere.

When he set eyes on the Chief Clerk, Kimo felt dismayed, as if he'd been struck by surf, as if some maverick Waimea wave had crashed over him, leaving him breathless in its wake. Mr. Yale was a small, insignificant little man, no more than five feet tall. Mousy brown hair, neatly barbered, sat above a small oval face that was entirely nondescript, except for his eyes. Steel gray, these looked keen and intelligent. But the slight little man didn't even reach Kimo's shoulders. In Hawaii, this could never be. A *moi* would be tall, strong, powerfully built. It seemed unnatural that someone so unprepossessing could be in charge of the destiny of other men, and in such a dangerous wilderness as this. The canoe trip north had been bad enough, but to end up in this tired, run-down fort in the middle of nowhere under the command of such a mouse of a man! Neither he nor Moku slept a wink that night. Next day Peopeo laughed at their discomfort.

"Trust me, he's bigger than he looks," he said, which made no sense to either of them, but he didn't elaborate. Kimo couldn't fight his disappointment. The fort was so small, so insignificant compared to Fort Vancouver on the Columbia. And when the men who'd brought them returned there in a few days, that would leave a contingent of seventeen here, eight Kanakas, eight other men and Mr. Yale. He understood others would be coming soon but he rubbed Keaka's dolphin at his neck, for reassurance. It didn't particularly help. Daylight had confirmed his suspicions of the previous night. The fort comprised a small area of forty by forty-five yards, with two bastions, and a gallery that was four feet wide all round. Twenty-five men from the Columbia had built it in 1827. Inside stood a three-room building to house the men, a two-room log house, a store, two other small buildings, and a big house with four large windows in the front with a cellar and attic, and another small building with rooms and a kitchen. There was also a food storage shed.

Peopeo told them they'd be working soon on building the new stockade the Company wanted built upriver. He was tall and broad, in his thirties, typically Hawaiian, with black hair hanging loose to his shoulders, and dark, quick-smiling eyes. His muscles were well-developed, the kind that come from years of hard physical labour. What struck Kimo was how at ease the man seemed to be in these surroundings.

As the newest arrivals, he and Moku were assigned to the pit. Peopeo escorted them to a large square hole in the ground, where cut logs were piled up ready to be squared and planed for their eventual purpose. He and Como, another Kanaka, had built the cradles and pulleys above the pit hole for grabbing the logs. The logs were then placed across the pit and cut lengthwise by two men using long, heavy, double-handed saws.

"One works above, the other below. You choose, or we can toss for it."

"Toss," they replied in unison. Peopeo threw a wooden Hudson's Bay token high in the air where it spun then fell with a dull plop into the dust, beaver side up. Moku won.

"I'd stand topside if I were you," Peopeo advised him.

"I'll cut from below, then," Kimo said. He removed his shirt and flexed the muscles across his broad shoulders, then loosened his biceps. Moku, shorter than Kimo but equally powerful across the chest and shoulders, opened and closed his nostrils convulsively, sniffing the pile of logs suspiciously. His brown eyes widened in surprise.

"*Aolé!* They're new! Unseasoned."

"It'll take us all day to cut them, then. We'd better get started!"

Moku pushed on the down stroke from above the pit and pulled up on the way back. Kimo, below, did the reverse. He found it easy at first but the non-stop push-and-pull soon turned painful, with sawdust drizzling down his head and shoulders, choking him. After a while the dust seemed to take on a will of its own and grew malevolent. It collected in his ears and stuck to the damp clumps of hair on his sweating scalp. It burned his eyeballs. It crawled through his lips, invading his mouth, making him gag and cough and spit, and crept up his nostrils, making him sneeze. He nearly choked from the smell, from the dust that penetrated the pores of his body, making him itch all over. Profanities he'd never used before emerged now, profuse and unbidden. Moku, when he grew tired of listening, eventually took pity on him.

"Enough, man! I'll spell you below. Just stop complaining!"

He did, and they took turns for the rest of the day, and the next, and the next, till fatigue engulfed them utterly. Their muscles screamed at day's end, then they wearily cleaned their tools in preparation for more of the same next morning. They had to oil the blade of the crosscut saw to make sure it was rust free and when they sharpened the teeth of its cutting edge, it reminded Kimo of the sharks circling the reef in Oahu. The wooden handles at each end bounced with the blade humming and twanging when they carried it to the smithy after work.

The sawpit consumed them, became their existence. At night, they tended their swollen palms, opening blisters, bursting the bubbles and pressing hard to release the fluid contents, which eventually disappeared to be replaced by thick, hard calluses. It didn't take long for them to figure out why they were so busy. The old fort really did need moving. But it would take weeks, perhaps longer, to fell the trees, cut and shape the wood needed to build another fort, though they were planning to dismantle parts of the old fort in sections and reuse some of the lumber. The new site was clearly superior, high on the riverbank, away from flooding and would be easier to defend.

When the *Beaver* arrived, every employee was sent to help unload its cargo. Kimo had never set eyes on a steamship before, and was awestruck. The *Beaver* had a sailing ship hull, about a hundred feet long, and a twenty-foot beam — wider where a giant paddle wheel was mounted. Between its two masts and fore and aft rigs, a large central smokestack poked skyward. The deck was open, with rooms and berths below. Boilers sat aft of two engines below, amidship, producing the steam. No one could have boarded the *Beaver* uninvited, for five nine-pound brass cannon were mounted on deck, and boarding nets hung from the bulwarks to fend off intruders. Sails Kimo understood, but steam power? He'd never imagined a ship would be invented that could sail independently, beyond the whims of tides and winds.

"She sailed from England to Hawaii before coming here," McKay told them, "and just switched to steam power when the weather got bad. Then they fit her paddlewheels in Fort Vancouver, and the *Beaver's* been plying the coast ever since. For sure she'll never run out of timber here for the fuel she needs. Before she arrived, many a ship came to grief in these waters. The *William and Ann* sank with her crew and cargo at the mouth of the Columbia in 1829. The brig *Isabella* was wrecked after grounding on the Columbia Bar in 1830. The wind drove the sloop *Vancouver* ashore on Queen Charlotte's Island in 1834 and the Indians seized it. A lot of men have died in these waters, Kanaka, your people included."

Kimo wondered if their souls had found their way home to Hawaii yet, or if they were lost, still drifting deep in the cold alien sea. He'd never wish to die at sea. He'd rather take an arrow, a musket ball, or even a blade. And the thought arrived that in this wild place, he just might get his wish.

Every man on the dock agreed the steam engine was a fine invention, but most felt it would never replace sails for long distance voyaging. At any rate, the *Beaver* drew every man's admiration, white and Indian. The fort's men, pleased with the arrival of mail and new supplies, waited with more than usual good humour to unload its cargo.

As it churned slowly to a halt, the sun came from behind a heavy mat of clouds and shone thinly. Kimo helped remove boxes and a crate of chickens and secured four agitated Clydesdales, frightened and whuffling, into giant leather and rope harnesses to lift them safely onto the riverbank.

When they finished unloading the ship's cargo, Kimo and Moku made their way back to the fort, where they had begun dismantling timbers for possible re-use at the new location. Taking the fort apart piece by piece would be neither easy nor quick.

Their days alternated between dismantling timbers and labouring in the sawpit. They had stockpiled a huge supply of squared logs before Peopeo assigned them to cut pickets instead, and they welcomed the change of pace. Once free of the pit, life improved considerably. Fort food compared favourably to the meals they'd eaten onboard ship, mostly salmon, supplemented by berries, venison and sometimes sturgeon. They had the Kwantlen women to thank for drying the salmon, of course. The fort's men had tried a dozen different ways to cure the fish, but nothing worked till the women showed them how. Peopeo told them that kinship now tied the fort to the Kwantlen.

"We'd never have got by here in the early days without them," he said. "Almost all of us married local women — Mr. McDonald himself, Como, me, most of the voyageurs, and Mr. Yale too. I wouldn't be without my Kwantlen wife. Our worry now is that the Indians don't trade with us like they used to, because the Boston ships along the coast sell them goods cheaper than we do. We'll have to come up with a solution, and soon."

Kimo adjusted to fort life as time passed, as the unfamiliar gradually grew familiar. The long days were tiring but they had food, not plenty but sufficient, and workers found time to talk with one another in the evenings. When he spotted a man sitting on the hut steps writing a letter while it was still light, to save the candles, he decided he'd better write home himself soon. He hoped his mother was happy with Pikoi. His letter would go by Langley Express to the Cowlitz Portage, where Indian runners carried the mail to Fort Vancouver. There it would wait for the next ship to Hawaii. It would be months before his letter would arrive and many more before he would receive a reply. If he ever did, since no one in his family could write, but Oolea or maybe Hopoo at the Mission, might reply.

He crossed the stockade, searching for Moku. It was a soft, mellow evening and the Indians outside the fort were preparing to return to the Kwantlen village. The fort men unwound at the end of the day in their own different ways. Two labourers perched on kegs beside the cooperage, smoking clay pipes. Someone clattered in the rear of the blacksmith shop, whistling a tune. Near the gate, he found Moku arguing the merits of different fishing nets with one of the voyageurs. He joined their discussion, for he wanted to make a wooden mold to fashion a U-shaped halibut hook. He admired how the Kwantlen used these to haul up great quantities of the big fish.

Suddenly a loud shriek jerked everyone to their feet.

"Indian attack! Lekwiltok along the river!"

Kimo's head swivelled towards the sentry in the bastion lookout above, just yards away. Had he heard right? Something caught inside his chest. Men bolted across the compound, while sentries continued to scream warnings across the stockade.

"War canoes!" the sentry screamed again. Kimo had no time to register fear, in spite of the volcanic heaving in his chest, and the briefest moment of uncertainty.

"Muskets!" Moku was already on his feet, yelling.

"Right! Let's go!" Hearts pounding, they raced to join the men scrambling over the compound to locate weapons, while the sentry continued to shout hoarse warnings. McKay nearly knocked him over sprinting for the sheds where they stored the powder kegs. He ran to help. They heaved the small heavy kegs onto their shoulders and reeled back to the walls of the stockade, where men anxiously waited to load pouches and muskets with black powder. Then he ran for the ladder to climb up the side of the stockade with Moku fast on his heels.

"They're loading the cannon," Moku gasped in his ear. He looked up at the mighty swivel guns protecting the stockade's four walls. He'd never seen a cannon put to use before. The muskets they'd been issued in Fort Vancouver had never been fired on their journey north. Today they would be. He found himself squeezing the gun barrel so tightly, its shape indented the brown skin of his palm. The smooth brass plate with the dragon serpent, symbol of the Hudson's

Bay muskets, felt slick and warm under his fingers, forcing him to wipe his sweating palm. He clambered up the ladder, and hunkered down beside Moku.

"Ready?" Moku nodded then rose to peer over the top of the stockade.

"Here they come!" Voice hoarse, he pointed down river. Lekwiltok war canoes, streamed upriver in their direction. The braves' faces were streaked with red and white and black paint, and they had powdered their heads with white down, projecting a fearsome sight to the watching men. The distant din grew to a roar as the paddlers beat their way forward against the current, drawing ever closer to the fort. Shrieking war whoops and screams rose from the water, echoing frightfully across the stockade as the braves slashed furiously through the waves towards them.

"Judas priest, they're travelling fast!" McKay's low voice broke the silence of the men along the ramparts.

Kimo ordered himself to breathe slowly. Thirty men in each canoe. Thirty canoes in sight, more round the bend of the river. He felt sick. His stomach knotted itself into a ball. Blood pounded in his ears and sweat broke out across his forehead. His fingernails dug into his palms, throbbing painfully with the pressure from his nails. He shifted, rechecking his rifle.

Peopeo had warned them about Lekwiltok attacks on the Chilliwack settlements further upriver, but it seemed unreal in the telling. Now, reality hit home, as the warriors headed for the friendly Kwantlen village. The fort had to defend its allies. If the Lekwiltok reached the vastly outnumbered Kwantlen, slaughter was inevitable. Kimo turned and saw Mr. Yale stride from man to man along the ramparts, saying a word or two before passing on, issuing crisp orders to his gunners with an air of brisk confidence.

"Ready!"

Kimo touched the koa wood dolphin at his neck. If Keaka's bones read true, he'd come out of this alive. He took a deep breath. He would defend this fort. He was here to do a job, and like it or not, this was part of it. The men by his side stood firm, muskets ready. He saw no trace of panic. Each man's face was set with purpose. Yet there was a smell of something powerful settling around them, and he suddenly knew what it was, the odour of fear. The fort's gunners remained at the ready, tense, awaiting orders.

As soon as the warriors paddled into range, the signal was given. A hoarse voice called out "Fire!" Kimo took careful aim and fired at the closest canoe. A hole in its hull would impede their progress more than shooting one man, he figured. He didn't know if he hit or missed, but the canoe didn't stop. He struggled to reload his musket and when he looked up, one canoe had made shore already and Lekwiltoks were racing furiously towards them.

Was it possible they would die here today, guarding this fort? He didn't know if he said the words or if Moku said them, but the two stared at each other over their rifles.

"Kimo, if we don't make it . . ." Moku began, but Kimo cut him off.

"We will," he whispered fiercely. They spoke softly to each other in Hawaiian and as they turned back to their rifles, Kimo felt strangely removed, as if he were someone else, for a terrible calm came over him. And guilt, for no man should feel calm in the midst of killing.

He took his right hand from the musket for a split second to touch the dolphin at his neck. The breeze making whitecaps along the river lifted off the water, rustled through the trees, then reached him, riffling his long hair in black tufts. He felt his skin cool, and suddenly Keaka came on the wind, so gently he almost missed him. A split second, and he was gone. The dolphin at Kimo's neck felt warm, and as its heat passed through his fingers, he rose and did what he must do — fire, reload, fire, reload. Moku was on his feet, firing and reloading too.

Fiercely focused on his musket, Kimo did not hear the order to fire the cannon. But suddenly a terrible wave of explosions swept from the rampart walls, momentarily silencing all musket fire. Almost instantaneously the river erupted in a blinding rush of spray, of torn canoes, of bodies flung skyward to fall moments later like so many matches into the river. Even before the last canoes could turn and run, the cannons fired again with devastating effect. In the maelstrom below him, Kimo saw dead bodies surfacing, floating amid planks, upended canoes and bits of hulls poking skyward, drawn along by the river's current.

He licked his lips, cracked now and bitter from biting the ends off the paper cartridges. His rifle arm throbbed from ramming the rod. He'd been so nervous, he'd spilled powder, mere trickles but still enough sometimes to flash and jolt him before the ball was even rammed home. He stood up and leaned on the musket. It was over. He could hardly believe it. He had to shade his eyes from the sun before he could see clearly. And then he wished he hadn't, for braves dotted the water from one side of the river to the other. Brown bodies, lifeless as floating logs, swirled with the current then vanished. Braves who struggled to shore found no refuge there, for the irate Kwantlen, had arrived from their village wielding stone mauls, eager to take revenge on their invaders.

It was the first time Kimo had aimed a weapon at a human being with intent to kill and he didn't like the feeling. Bile rose in his throat at the sight of the bodies littering the riverbank. He realized he was holding his breath, and exhaled painfully. His nose twitched from the acrid smell of smoke hovering overhead. He needed to draw a breath, but the air tasted harsh and scraped the tissue in his throat and lungs. He turned to find Moku curled up on his haunches, head low, sweating, leaning on his musket butt gasping for breath. He rose to his feet unsteadily, wiping sweat from his eyes.

"My stomach's heaving. Do you think that's the end of them?"

"I hope so, Moku."

Below, blood, wounded men and beaten flesh combined to make the landscape unreal. Moku's brown skin looked pale and gray, like crumpled paper, and blow-back from the black powder had sprayed his chin purple with dust.

Kimo felt the day would be seared into his brain forever. War was no glorious affair, in spite of how braggart warriors boasted, be they Hawaiian, haole, or Indian. Ugly and cruel. The dead lost everything, life, liberty, dignity, loved ones. But if you must fight, then you must win. The alternative, the unthinkable, lay before his eyes, and that was not to be borne. He climbed down from the ramparts and walked slowly along the riverbank. The smoke had begun to settle. He felt removed from what happened, as if someone else inhabited his skin. What had taken place here was an affront to decent sensibilities, a place of brutality and obscene acts. The smells of death rose up to meet him, the dreadful stink of battle, of fear and, permeating everything, the fetor of blood.

It was then he spotted the girl by the fort's walls and he stopped in his tracks. The woman's face was misshapen from the efforts to control her revulsion. Or maybe it was grief, because she had the look of that sorrowing madonna hovering over her bleeding son in Hopoo's old picture at the mission. Her hair fell forward, along the line that ran from the top of her forehead to the corner of her mouth, and he saw then that it was the woman from Semiahmoo. She was dressed differently, but there was no doubt. It was Aleela, the Salmonberry Woman.

Rose had been trading at the fort for a kettle for her mother when she'd heard the sentry scream his warning, and she'd run like a terrified bird into the shelter of the trees that surrounded the fort's east side. Women hauling babies had stumbled along with her, wailing loudly as the sounds of gunfire and war whoops followed them into the woods. She'd crouched in a thicket with a young mother and two terrified young children. They waited and waited, hearts pounding; it felt like forever. The boy and girl remained silent, with that strange compliance endowed upon children by serious occasions. Eventually the noise of battle died down and the smell of smoke faded and soft whispered sounds reached their ears.

"It's over. You can come out now. They've gone."

But no one around her dared move. She knew why. Apart from the battle, the forest itself could trick you. You could see things that were not there. Lights shining where none existed. Spirits. The raven, the trickster, could lead you on. He could become a living thing, and make anything happen. Leaves would rustle, speaking with the voices of the dead. Her father claimed such things untrue, but every Indian believed these woods were haunted. Eventually she moved, and the mother rose too, and crept away silently with her children.

She had lost her mother's kettle. Her skirt hem swanned down in an uneven loop, ragged where it had caught on a branch. She found the kettle snagged on a hawthorn bush, shining brightly. She chastised herself, for if the Lekwiltoks had pursued them into the forest, it would have been a beacon to show them the way.

When she reached the fort's walls, bodies lay strewn along the riverbank. She froze in fright. Her heart felt strangely enlarged pumping in her chest. She stepped on something red and withdrew her foot instantly from the small mound, stifling a scream at the sight of a dead brave's head. The warrior's brown legs and arms were covered with red paint. Black painted eyebrows in two broad stripes like crescent moons defined his eyes. His long black hair, oiled and covered with white powdery down, was streaked with blood. She vomited.

She needed to reach the riverbank and find her canoe, if it was still there to find. Exhaustion caused her to stumble, stricken by the sight of the blood and bodies along the shore. When she raised her head, she saw the man, the big Kanaka, musket slung across his left shoulder, walking through the debris in her direction.

"You're the girl from Semiahmoo," he said. "Are you all right?"

She shook like a torn leaf in the wind. He didn't expect a reply. He'd spoken English only because he addressed every non-Kanaka at the fort that way. It had been automatic, just something to say, but she astounded him.

"Yes. Yes, I'm all right." But her voice wavered.

"You don't look it." She looked pinched, like an over-wound spring. He struggled with the fact that this was the woman he'd encountered at Semiahmoo, and that she spoke English. "What are you doing here?"

"I was trading at the fort when the alarm sounded. I couldn't get to my canoe in time."

He turned towards the riverbank. Broken canoes, wood fragmented like eggshells, bits of paddles and crushed planks were scattered along the water's edge, interspersed with bodies. "You shouldn't be here. Is your canoe still around?"

"I don't know."

"Let's go." He took her by the elbow and led her through the dead and dying, towards the river, carving its oblivious way through the channel of the earth, like the blood of those men braceleting the shore, flowing from sundered veins into the dirt. He found her canoe. Incredibly, it was intact. He rolled it into the river for her, held the kettle while she climbed in and leaned over to hand her the paddle.

"Drink some rum when you get home, if you have any. It'll settle your nerves."

She wanted to say something. The moment cried out for it, but words eluded her. She fought for control and drew a deep breath. Lifting her head, straightening her drooping shoulders, she dipped her paddle into the water and rested it there while she composed herself.

"I need to thank you, but I don't know your name."

"Kimo Maka Kanui. Kanaka will do."

"I'm Rose Fanon." Her lips curved in a hint of a smile, half-shy and grateful, before fatigue returned to claim her eyes and the sombre events of the day again took possession of her expression. "Thank you, Kanaka Kimo." She pulled away with a resigned, sad smile.

He watched her paddle her canoe deftly home towards Sqwalets, growing smaller through the purple of the dusk that preceded sunset. When he returned to the fort's walls, shocked men walked about in silence inspecting the tangled mass of bodies on the ground. A burial detail was quickly ordered, and a clean up crew assigned. He hoped he'd never be part of another battle like this. But truthfully, he was relieved the fort had big guns, for they could have been slaughtered otherwise. He tried to make sense of the day's grisly events, as he helped clean up the fort environs and asked Peopeo what quarrel the Lekwiltoks from the north had with the Kwantlen.

"None in particular. The tribes are forever fighting over territory. They relocate frequently to hunt and fish, changing boundaries to suit climate changes and wars. But many Sto:lo died of smallpox after the haoles came, just as happened in Hawaii. And with tribes weak and low in numbers, it's easy for stronger tribes to raid them. The Lekwiltok from the north coast, they are strong in number. They come to plunder, to abduct women and children for slaves. But we, too, had our island wars till Kamehamea united us. The haoles are no different. It's the same wherever you live. It ends only when one side gains superior weapons and imposes peace. I think our big guns delivered that message to the Lekwiltoks today. Mr. Yale did what he had to do."

Kimo had to agree. Mr. Yale had taken charge today, issuing orders, maintaining control. Not all men could remain as steady under fire, and against such odds.

"He knows the land and these people, and how they think," Peopeo said. "Knowing your enemy is the key to surviving in a place like this."

A place like this. How long would it take, Kimo wondered, for a man to know this place like Mr. Yale and Peopeo, to really understand these people? Would this be the last battle he'd have to fight? Or just the first of many?

chapter seven

LAWI'QUM PEERED ANXIOUSLY around the bearskins covering the doorway when Rose reached home and drew her quickly inside. "Are you all right, Daughter? We saw the battle, heard the fort guns."

"Yes. I hid in the forest till it was over." She shivered and Lawi'qum wound a length of wool blanket around her shoulders.

"Sit down. We'll have some tea." Her mother spoke gently, sighting tears pooling in Rose's eyes. "Here, I'll take the kettle."

She had forgotten about it. She clutched it still, staring at it stupidly. Her mother pried it from her fingers and set it down by the firestones. Rose caught sight of her reflection in the kettle's shiny surface. Her nose and mouth appeared elongated and her forehead fat and wide, distorted by the curve of the kettle. It seemed fitting, for that was how she felt, pulled and stretched out of shape. She couldn't rid her mind of the sight of the dead bodies littering the riverbank. Her sisters plied her with questions, but Rose would not discuss in front of Snana'y and Wawas'u the carnage that had taken place.

"I hope they're all dead!" Sandich said with more relish than Rose wanted to hear. "I wish I could've been there!"

"No you don't!" she reprimanded him. But he was only a boy whose foolish enthusiasm overcame sense, so she ran her fingers through his thatch of black hair fondly. He instantly shrugged off her hand, scowling. She read his thought the moment it arrived. When he became a brave, she'd have to stop treating him like a child.

Neetlum returned hours later, flushed with victory. He too had gone into the woods then returned with the Kwantlen men to punish the Lekwiltok. Satisfaction clung to him like a wet cloak. He flit from fact to fact, like some insect biting at fruit, supplying endless details of the battle. Rose expected the entire episode would be completely retooled before bedtime, so she retired early to her small platform bed. It seemed as if the entire village had gone to bed early, excepting the elders who gathered in the long house to dissect the day's activities. The tale would be told and retold around campfires, of a thousand Lekwiltok braves being defeated by a handful of whites — and their big guns. It would give pause to tribes opposing the fort, and the Lekwiltok would not soon invade the River People again. Chief Whattlekainum had been wise when he'd moved the tribe to Sqwalets.

Across the river, the fort's occupants stretched out, exhausted, on their small rope beds. Kimo's thin pallet felt lumpy and when he rose to pound it flat, a strong smell of powdered green leaves leaked from the ticking. He whacked it soundly again and turned it over. He'd have to replace the stuffing. He'd cut some tree branches, cedar or hemlock. Fresh, they made a decent, sweet-smelling filling. In the morning, though. Right now he needed to sleep. Moku as usual, wanted to talk. He always did last thing at night before falling asleep suddenly, like a snuffed out candle.

The two whispered across the dark of the hut, reviewing the day's battle, reliving details of the raid and their intense relief when the terror ended. The wooden dolphin felt warm against Kimo's throat. He touched it, rose from his pallet and padded across the wooden floor. He drew open the door and stood on the step breathing in the cool night air, searching the sky. He sighted the moon through a gap in the broken clouds overhead, its pale white light streaming earthward, and he raised his arms to pray, chanting softly in Hawaiian, ending with a tribute to his grandfather. He had sensed his kupuna's presence during the battle. It had made him strong so that he'd swallowed his fear. It was un-Christian, he knew, and Hopoo would not approve, but he felt sure his grandfather had been at his side today — as sure as he was of the sun rising tomorrow.

"Mahalo nui, Kupuna," he whispered, then called on the soft winds, the winds *kolonahe,* to carry his chant across the sea. When he returned to his pallet, silence filled the small shack and he thought Moku had finally fallen asleep. He was mistaken.

"Peopeo says I've to move stock at the store tomorrow," Moku said, turning in his bunk and propping himself up with his elbow. "Do you need anything?"

"It'll have to wait," he said. He wanted to buy a new shirt. He couldn't wait to discard the one he'd come in, for the fabric was so thin, you could shoot peas through it. He had two, wearing one while the other went through its weekly wash. He hadn't saved enough money yet, for clothing was expensive at the store. Boots and shoes, too. He was lucky he had the shoes he'd bought for his mother's wedding, and after a tip from Billings that he'd need them, he'd won boots in a poker game on the *Thomasina.* Some men ended their contracts with little to show for their hard work after running up bills at what they nicknamed the store, the *aienui,* the big debt.

It was always busy, for the Indians traded there as well as the fort employees, lining up with skins before the door even opened in the morning. If he didn't know what a beaver looked like before he arrived, he knew now, for everything in the store was valued according to the "made-beaver," one good-quality adult animal pelt. Two otter skins were equivalent to one made-beaver, a moose skin two made-beavers. For a dozen made-beavers, you could buy a flintlock rifle. A single made-beaver could be traded for a brass kettle, two pounds of tobacco or a couple of dozen strong fishhooks. Blanket prices varied according to the black stripes along the edges that denoted how many made-beaver pelts a particular blanket was worth. Blankets were a favourite of the Indians, who cut them to make capes and leggings.

"One thing about the store," Moku rambled on, nerves refusing to let him settle. "You find out from the Indians what's going on, which ships are working the coast, what tribes are on the move."

"And you can't believe half of it," Kimo said. He didn't mean they lied; rather, like the Hawaiians, they dramatized events for effect. Verbal truth didn't interest them so much as the essence of a thing. He understood their circumlocution, for it provided colour and perspective, and deepened understanding. It was the haoles who struggled with the Indian manner of conversing, since they tended to speak factually, with the cold edge of a scalpel, paring away colour and texture.

"Some of it's true," Moku countered. "I heard from Antoine that Mr. Yale's getting married soon to a woman from the village." He caught Kimo off guard with that item of fort gossip. Kimo was vaguely disconcerted, not that he was entitled to have any opinion whatsoever on the subject but Mr. Yale had been married before. It was one thing to marry an Indian once, out of convenience or necessity, or for political reasons, or even for real affection, but to marry again? Did the Chief Clerk plan to spend the rest of his life here in the Pacific

Northwest, or would this "country marriage" be just another temporary liaison?

The business of country wives was complicated. A few men stayed here with their Indian wives after their contracts expired, but most didn't. When it was time to leave, they left. Some others returned to their homeland but came back, unable to adjust to living within the restraints of their former lives. There was no doubt that after time, this place could do things to a man's mind.

If Antoine told Moku this news, it must be true. He frequented the village often because he was seeing a good deal of one particular Kwantlen maiden himself, and he gathered news like a dog does fleas. It was Antoine who told them about Yale's former wife, Chief Whattlekainum's daughter, when they'd asked about the little half-Indian child, Eliza, living with Mr. Yale. The child's mother had run away when Eliza was a baby, but the man she ran off with had been her husband before she married Mr. Yale.

"Probably didn't have a choice," Moku said. "Indian women don't have much say when it comes to marriage. At any rate, it didn't seem to bother Mr. Yale that she ran away."

Kimo found that hard to believe. Likely Mr. Yale's pride just wouldn't let him show it. Surely Chief Whattlekainum must have lost face, though. In Hawaii, a chief would have to make some sort of restitution to the injured party if his daughter did such a shameful thing. Then it came to him. If Yale played poker, he couldn't wish for a better hand. He held the King now. And his daughter, little Eliza, Whattlekainum's granddaughter, was the Ace. Yale's bed might be cold at night, but he could sleep soundly knowing the Kwantlen would never betray the fort.

"It'll be a grand affair, his new wedding, by the sounds of it." Moku yawned and fell back into his bunk, at last ready to close his eyes. It was late before Kimo fell asleep on his lumpy pallet. Every time he gentled down to sleep, he rose like some float in the water, his mind taken up with the day's battle, with the indomitable Mr. Yale and his Kwantlen bride-to-be, and with Aleela, the Salmonberry Woman.

AFTER THE TUMULT OF the raid, it felt unreal to Kimo that the morning after should be this calm, this ordinary, as if the death day before had never happened. Now, two frantic red hens ran through his legs, gabbling fiercely. Flapping wings, they soared upwards then descended hysterically to scrabble in the dirt beside him. The wood of the coop was split where the hens had beaked a crack open and he had been ordered to fix it.

He tore out the old planks and tried to replace them but the restless hens pecked him so much, he lost control and swung at them with a plank. Moku, returning from the store, laughed at his outburst. He grabbed first one by the neck and then the other and swiped them under his armpits. He made it look easy.

"Got you!" he roared, and dropped the angry hens among the quiet chickens at the far end of the coop. When the nervous hens refused to settle, the fort's rooster flew from his perch, a storm of feathers, corn-coloured legs and eyes as black as buttons of coal. His head bobbed and his ruff rose up on end, and he lit into the clucking hens in a fury, striking at them with his legs. Kimo thought he'd surely trample them to death but they fled, clucking maniacally into the cover of a blackberry bush that bloomed in the corner of the pen.

"You have to show them who's boss," Moku said, but Kimo had already decided he only liked chickens cooked, on a plate. They left the coop together when he'd finished his task. In the distance, the dense forest of cottonwood, cedar and alder had been turned into cow pasture, turning pale green now from the new shoots pushing their way through the gray ground. Kimo dropped low to hunker on his knees and fingered the dark alluvial soil. He lifted it to his nostrils and sniffed deeply. It smelled strong and sweet.

"Good for growing things, Moku."

"It'll never grow taro or bananas, though."

"No. But it'll grow plenty, all the same. If only the sun would shine more." They'd planted bushels of potatoes in some of the cleared fields, and when the tiny white balls formed, he'd plucked some off the roots with his fingers. He'd brushed off the brown soil and dropped the buttons into his mouth whole. Nothing had tasted so sweet.

It was supposed to be summer but it felt cool to the Hawaiians, and the sky remained gray. He longed for the warmth of Oahu. The days did eventually grow warmer, lighter, sunnier as the weeks went by. The stands of cedar surrounding the fort seemed less forbidding now. Kimo had learned to appreciate their splendour, and their usefulness. The Indians wove the roots and withes into baskets. They pounded cedar bark and shredded it for clothing, and twisted it into twine for making nets and fishing lines. They lashed hooks onto fishing poles and arrowheads onto wooden handles with strong woven twine. They used the cedar to make planks, to build houses, canoes, paddles and bent boxes. These boxes were ingenious and required steaming to shape them to a square, entirely without nails. Some were truly works of art, polished and sanded to a fine sheen with the rough textured skin of the dogfish. They didn't need to steam them now, because they could acquire nails from the Company store. The Indians wasted nothing, even using the tree's branches to place in the Fraser for salmon to lay their eggs on as they swam upstream. The eggs could be harvested simply by pulling the branches out of the water. Kimo thought the whole process remarkable.

When Mr. Yale's wedding took place, a grand celebration of feasting and dance was held at the village. Everyone attended. Food was plentiful, smoked salmon, shellfish, wild game of every sort, platters of berries and bannocks, and kegs and kettles filled with hot rum and tea. The crowd of Indians from along the river was so vast, Kimo could not find Rose Fanon at the gathering. He hadn't intended to look for her, but found his eyes roaming the throngs of people, seeking out girls who looked like her from a distance but weren't, and was oddly disappointed.

After the grand ceremony, life returned to normal, and work continued as before, commanding his attention so that he almost forgot about the girl. At night, Indians from various tribes still canoed past the fort under the sentries' watchful eyes. They'd have goods piled high, as if they were moving to a new location, or they'd pass with bound slaves taken in raids upriver. When two men fell sick, one with a cut thumb, the other with the colic, Kimo had to work in the pit again. He was growing used to working outdoors in different weather conditions, and though he didn't like it, the wet, cold and damp didn't seem to affect him as badly as it did other Kanakas, who were frequently sidelined from illness of one kind or another.

He noticed as the weeks passed that Mr. Yale didn't live with his new wife, but only dropped by for a weekly visit to her small house in the village, though of course, no one presumed to comment upon it. It shocked him though. This would never happen in a Hawaiian ohana.

Work progressed slowly on the new fort. Much of what they dismantled from the old fort was unusable, but they'd had to dismantle it anyway. Every piece of wood — for houses, walkways, storage sheds, beds, tables, chairs, the stockade and the bastions — needed to be hand-felled and hand-cut, by the fort's Kanakas. Building took place around their other chores — felling trees to clear the land, planting potatoes, burning stumps, cutting the dense, tangly brush, digging trenches, making boxes and barrels, storing and baling fur, helping the boatmen and doing whatever else required physical labour. Chores were endless. Men had no trouble sleeping nights, for they fell into bed in exhausted stupors.

A Kanaka named Pali, who'd married a Kwantlen woman two years before, joined Kimo and Moku cutting and stockpiling staves for the palisade and fences. He was a powerfully built man, tall, about thirty years old, with a ready smile. A blue tattoo stretched across his cheekbones, a thin line of dots and dashes below large brown eyes. Peopeo had ordered them to cut pine staves for barrels, near a small lake upriver, the one named Work, after a former fort clerk. Other places along the river had been given English names too, after fort clerks — Barnston Island and Annance's Island, and a mountain named Manson — which Kimo felt to be presumptuous, since they had perfectly good Indian names. The haoles had done the same thing in Hawaii. But whatever its true name, Work Lake was their destination. They left the fort, more than a little nervous, after breakfast. Anything could happen outside the fort walls. The previous week, an Indian had come in with his father's body. He'd found it downstream, decapitated and dismembered in retaliation for some transgression against another tribe. Canoes frequently passed the fort with the heads of their enemies stuck on poles. So the Kanakas had reason to feel anxious when venturing any distance from the fort walls. They canoed to the lake without incident, however, and spent the day cutting their way through a stand of white pine. Then as the sun began its slow move to the west, they heard a noise in the bushes.

"Down!" Kimo hissed. He reached quietly for his Company musket and quickly began loading. Crouched low, he listened intently. It wasn't his imagination, for he heard it again, not far off, the sound of small twigs breaking softly underfoot. Moku and Pali set their machetes and pickets aside and silently reached for their muskets. Kimo briefly touched the wooden dolphin at his neck. Moments later, Moku nodded towards the small clearing at the eastern edge of the grove where they'd been piling up their pickets.

"Yieeaaah!" A loud scream rent the air as four Indian braves appeared at the edge of the trees. One carried a three-foot long torch and waved it wildly. They were all young and half-naked, with identical dark brown fur coverings and bare feet. Long black hair streamed down their backs but they wore no war paint — a sign, Kimo thought, that this might be an impulse attack more than a planned one. They talked nervously among themselves, shuffling from one foot to another, as if unsure of their next move.

"They're going to torch the place!" Moku whispered, and even as he spoke the flaming torch soared and flew, sparks streaming, arcing high into the air. It landed with a thud, rolling a bare five feet from where they crouched, next to the pile of staves they'd newly cut for transport to the fort. Kimo held his gun at full cock, against his shoulder. He raised the sights to centre on the first man's chest, lowered it to the man's abdomen, then to his knees.

"They're not armed!" He bit his lip. He didn't want to shoot an unarmed man.

"They'll have knives, though," Moku cautioned.

"So do we." Kimo dropped the rifle and turned to his companions. "Ready?" Moku and Pali nodded.

"Now!" The three surged towards the Indian youths. Suddenly a woman's voice called out peremptorily across the clearing, ringing out sharply. The Kanakas halted in their tracks, dumbfounded, as the voice spoke crisply in Kwantlen to the braves. The braves also halted, the leader's expression a mix of confusion, anger and uncertainty.

Two Indian girls stepped out of the shade of the trees. The younger one remained shadowed beneath the branches, eyes lowered and silent, but the older dropped the basket she was carrying. She hastened half running, half walking, diagonally across the clearing, all the while chastising the young men. She wore European style dress. Her hands raised the blue skirts slightly on each side so that she strode unhindered across the clearing in deerskin moccasins. The woman's back was angled away from the Hawaiians, but as she raised her arms in a contemptuous, throwaway gesture, Kimo's spine began to tingle. It was the Salmonberry Woman again, the one called Rose Fanon.

Kimo had no idea what form her reprimand took. He just knew it was one, from the tone of her voice, the way she held her head and stood with one hand on her hip, the other pointing at the young men and then at the firebrand they had thrown beside the picket pile. The fire had crept through the grass and reached the picket pile, and now small licks of flame were taking hold at the base. The staves would burn quickly once the fire took hold. The leader of the group, a surly brave, challenged the girl but she would have none of it. He knew she'd won when the young man lowered his eyes, his face a picture of embarrassment and anger. She took another step forward and spoke sharply again, tossing her head derisively. Finally the brave uttered what sounded like an oath or possibly a threat, and raised his fist. It was an empty gesture though, for he suddenly turned with his companions and loped away, leaving the Hawaiians staring in amazement.

A split second later the three Bay men streaked into action, racing to douse the fire, beating at the flames with their boots, suffocating them with dry leaves scooped from the ground, and with blankets. Moku hurriedly shovelled armfuls of dirt onto the fire while Kimo and Pali raced back and forth from the riverbank with buckets of water to toss on the flames. When the flames were finally doused, half the smoking pile remained intact, though it would take hours to replace what they'd lost.

The two girls remained at the edge of the clearing watching the men stamp out the fire. Rose quietly laid a cautionary hand on the young girl, who was about seven or eight years old, with the look of a frightened rabbit, ready to run at any moment. She had bare feet, and the shredded cedar skirt tied about her waist fell just above her knees.

"*Klahowya!*" Pali called out in greeting. He had learned some Kwantlen from his native wife over the years and spoke to the girls. Rose replied, pointing to the long green stems piled up in the baskets they carried. The young one lowered her head and would not raise her eyes as she held her sister's hand tightly.

Rose wore the blue homespun dress torn the day of the Lekwiltok battle. It was the plainest of dresses, but it now sported a small white shawl collar that made a sharp contrast against the bronze of her skin and the mane of dark hair flowing down her back. Pali turned to Kimo quizzically.

"They're here picking nettles to make twine. She says she knows you."

"Yes. She's from the village." He was aware of Moku's jaw falling open like a flabbergasted cod.

"Hello, Owhyhee."

"Hello. How are you?" He felt awkward. It seemed absurd to be so formal. He didn't know what to call her. "I haven't seen you around the fort lately."

"Nor I you."

"We've been busy in the pit, and cutting pickets. We came here for the pinewood. For storage barrels."

Moku and Pali moved away some yards and lit their pipes, but he felt their eyes on him through the screen of smoke they were puffing up for his benefit. Rose Fanon was pretty and limber as a willow switch but he felt at a loss for words in her presence. The young girl took Rose's basket ostensibly to pick nettles some yards away. Her eyes flickered their way every few seconds, but she too discreetly gave them privacy to talk.

"Thanks for your help. If you hadn't turned up, it could've been a bad situation for us. The fire could have spread."

"The tall one is my cousin's cousin, Txwelatsa. He's not bad or a troublemaker, just young and foolish."

"Thanks anyway." Kimo understood and even sympathised. White men cast a long shadow and living in that shadow wasn't easy. It was true in Hawaii. It was true here. He was no scholar, but Kimo knew that when whites move in, they become the new alii, and natives come to feel inferior. This breeds sickness in the soul, for a man must hold his head high, for himself, for his ancestors and for his children. Take his worth away, his world fragments. Resentment is inevitable in response to the imposing presence of the white traders, and if that were going to be expressed, it would be by the young men, with more courage than sense.

He wondered about asking the girl out but felt awkward. Relationships were fluid and easy in Hawaii, but she was Indian, and they had their own customs. He wanted to do the right thing. Maybe he had to ask her father's permission. He knew so little about them. He'd have to ask around.

Rose too, felt full of uncertainty. What a strange day it had been, coming upon Txwelatsa and his friends setting fire to the woods. He was seventeen, a good brave but foolhardy and quarrelsome when his blood was running high, and his friends were not the best. She was glad she'd been able to divert them, for in truth, she thought the big Owhyhees would easily have overcome the resentful teenage braves. She understood their diminished pride, and would not have wished Txwelatsa hurt for his brave folly. The big Owhyhee was smiling at her. He wore an air of kindness, and that she liked.

"I must go," she said, waving to her sister to join her. The girl was slightly sullen, and eyed Kimo suspiciously but Rose spoke to her softly in Kwantlen, and took her hand. And as suddenly as they had appeared, the girls disappeared into the forest, soft and silent as does.

"You know this woman?" Moku asked the instant the girls departed.

"From Semiahmoo, when I was collecting wood for the fire. I scared her half to death and she took off. Then we met again after the Lekwiltok attack."

"How did she get those braves to leave?"

"The big one's a relative, a cousin's cousin, or something."

"They want to stop us building the new fort," Pali said. "Lucky the girls turned up."

Kimo and Moku loaded their canoe with the pickets to take back to the fort. They were carefully separating the good ones from the charred when Pali suddenly called on them.

"Kimo! Moku! Look up. Over there."

High in the air, a pair of bald eagles flew in wide acrobatic circles above the cedars. The birds were magnificent. Kimo had seen nothing like them in Oahu. They were about two and a half feet long, with wingspans about seven to eight feet across, though it was hard to tell from where he watched. They were blackish-brown on the back and breast, white on their heads and necks and tails. He'd never seen such powerful birds or the spectacle they were creating before his eyes. They flew towards each other at high speed, purposefully like great ships cleaving the swells, so that he thought they were battling. Their tail feathers spread wide and moved back and forth and up and down as they soared. Then they collided, grasping each other's talons, and swung around and around, soaring above the cedars in glorious swooping arcs across the sky. It took his breath away. And floating from the sky it came, a single feather borne on the wind, fluttering down and down to settle gently on the ground at his feet.

"What does it mean?" Moku said in a hushed voice.

It was an omen. Kimo felt it in the marrow of his bones. Hopoo might scoff, say he was mistaken, but he wasn't. It had been a long time since he'd felt such certainty. Something momentous was about to happen. He felt its approach, not too close but on its way, like a wing beat, coming on the wind.

"This is the season when eagles mate," Pali said. "The Indians believe a lone eagle feather holds great power. When you hold it, you must speak the truth."

Kimo bent and picked the feather up, and riffled its edge with his thumb. It felt soft yet strong. He would keep it. The spectacle in the sky was an awesome dance of nature. Birds, animals, trees, everything here was so different from what he was used to. He concentrated hard on his surroundings. Cedars grew everywhere, and alder and cottonwood trees. Berry bushes that he hadn't seen in Hawaii grew here in abundance too. Thimbleberries and salmonberries, salal berries, blueberries, currants, elderberries. Even wild strawberries. This wilderness might actually be a place of abundance for the people who lived here. Fish filled the river, deer wandered the forest, and roots and berries flourished everywhere. Yes, Langley might be a pretty good place to live, if you were Indian.

He admired Rose for standing her ground before those braves. The girl showed courage. He sniffed. He'd been aware all day of the woodsy scent of wet cedar but now the air was filled with the reek of smoking salmon from upriver. Suddenly he felt hungry. His mouth watered and his stomach rumbled audibly. His thoughts returned to the girl again. *Rose Fanon.* The name didn't sound remotely

Kwantlen. Maybe she was half white. He knew now that this was not unusual around Company forts. He'd ask around. He'd been surprised when that brave backed down in front of her. In a land where women were bought and sold and traded as property, how had she found the courage to reprimand a brave? An angry brave, at that. If he'd been cruel, or felt shamed in front of his friends, she could have been in deep trouble.

Truthfully, he knew little about the native people who lived in these parts. But if his goal was to survive in this wilderness, if he was to spend the entire three years of his contract in this place, he'd better learn. And quickly. He'd start as soon as they got back to the fort. He knew just the man to ask.

Then he thought about the eagles dancing in the sky, and a fine filament, a current moved within him and he felt full again of the sense of something coming. But what? And why?

chapter eight

"*'YAKA YIEM HALO KLIMINAWHIT.'* This is a true story," Huntas began the way of all Indian storytellers. "Life was easy when I was young, Kanaka. The cedar provided whatever we needed for our canoes, houses, our clothing and rope. Bears, deer, elk roamed the forest. We had plenty fish, salmon, oolichan and sturgeon. Life was good in those days."

Perched atop a keg outside the cooperage, with the sun warming his face, the water carrier's voice took on a dreamy sing-song quality. Kimo placed a wad of tobacco in the old man's hand. It always amazed him how the past improved with distance. He suspected Huntas was like Pikoi, romanticising a time that had never existed except in his mind. He'd have you believe that deer pranced from the forest to greet you, that fish leapt from the water straight into your lap.

"We had troubles, of course. People always fight, Kanaka, for territory and power. It is the way of things. In Owhyhee, is it not the same?" He emptied the contents of his chipped pipe onto the ground. As the gray ash drifted over Kimo's boots, his thoughts too, drifted. Yes. Hawaii did have its share of wars in the old days, but after the haoles came, new and different power struggles surfaced. In time, that would be the case here too. But he said nothing of this to the old man.

"Such salmon runs we had then! We paddled the Nicomekl and portaged to the T'salkwakyan." Kimo knew this as the Salmon River.

"Truly in those days, the fish came up to meet us. Aiee! We could walk across the river on their backs." He paused, coughed and spat, then laughed at his own hyperbole, and Kimo laughed with him.

"Tell me about the Sto:lo, the River People."

"They are the Halkomelem, part of the Coast Salish nation. There are many, more than twenty tribes, each with its own chief, its own rules. The Kwantlen, Musqueam, Katzie and people downriver speak Halkomelem. The Sumas, Chilliwacks, Pilalts and Taits, from upriver and the Island tribes, the Nanaimo, Cowichan, they speak the same. But the Squamish and the Sechelt, they speak like the Skagit and all those people from the east shore, south of the river, the Snohomish, Skykomish, Duwamish tribes. The Nooksack have their own tongue, and the Klallams, from west of the Sound. There are many tribes along the Fraser, the Coquitlam, the Tsawassen, the Whonnock and Matsqui, the Nicomen, Scowlitz. Oh, many, many, but the Kwantlen are siam, royal, and are strong. The river is theirs, from where the Katzie live to Skaiametl, and this is good, for they keep the peace."

"Were they always peaceful, or just since Little Yale married the Chief's daughter?" He meant no disrespect, but the Indian bristled.

"*Little?* No! BIG spirit! BIG courage!" He waved his hand towards the big house, and launched into a tale Kimo had heard before from the fort's men — an astonishing account of nine Lekwiltok war canoes carrying two hundred and forty braves trapping a ten-man Langley canoe on its way home from the Cowlitz. Mr. Yale and nine men boldly faced the braves head on, singing and shouting loudly, and outmanoeuvred and outgunned them in the battle that followed. The colourful tale had become legend. Huntas inhaled and blew long streams of smoke from his nostrils. Kimo waited patiently. It was expected, part of the format for old men telling young men tales. "We won, thanks to Mr. Yale."

And his guns, thought Kimo. Still, it was a victory against huge odds, and commendable. Mr. Yale had again played his cards well.

"Size, you see, is no measure of a man." Huntas puffed so heavily on his clay pipe that his face disappeared behind the screen of white smoke.

In old Hawaii, men would have challenged such a statement. Hawaiians used to revere large leaders, men and women weighing three, four, six hundred pounds and more, whose royal stomachs needed to be massaged, *lomi-lomied* by servants, to aid digestion after consuming gigantic meals. Yet Mr. Yale's littleness certainly discounted any relationship between size and ability, for he had proved himself over and over a man of spirit, a worthy *moi*.

Huntas closed his eyes and withdrew into the seductive comfort of selective memory. Kimo felt a rush of pity for the old man, for a life lived in bondage, exposed to every whim and danger, graced only by the haphazard goodwill of his current owner. Yet the water carrier seemed content enough with his lot in life, living day to day as he did, with no outward show of discontent or want for more, so maybe Kimo's pity was misplaced. But slavery was a large and cruel part of Indian culture in the Pacific Northwest and he wondered if and when it would end. Some Indian wives of the fort men even kept slaves. He hadn't quite grasped how it all worked, for some seemed treated well enough — almost as family — while others were utterly brutalized. When he thought about it, there were days he felt much like a slave himself. All fort employees were, in a sense, slaves to the Company. The only difference was that your bondage ended after three years, and you got paid for it. If you were smart. But if you owed the store too much, your contract would be renewed, extending that bondage for another three years. Or five, in some cases.

"Do you ever visit the village, Huntas? Do you know the Fanons?"

Huntas cocked his head. "There is only one. Rose."

"Can you tell me about her?"

"Her father, Jacques, came to Fort Vancouver and married the Nooksack woman, Lawi'qum, and brought her with him to Langley when we first built the fort. When he left and didn't come back, Lawi'qum married the Kwantlen man, Neetlum."

"Why did Rose's father leave?"

"Voyageurs, they come and go, never staying in one place. Jacques, he stayed a long time. More than most. So why ask about the girl?"

"I met her, that's all, and was curious about her background."

"Her backside, more likely!" Huntas laughed. Kimo, offended, ignored the crudity.

"Can she see whoever she pleases or must the man speak with the father?"

"Kwantlen women do as they please."

Good. He didn't want to break any tribal rules.

"By custom, though, the father arranges marriage when the time comes. But since Fanon is likely dead, maybe Neetlum will. But maybe not, for the girl is only half-Kwantlen and has a mind of her own." Kimo palmed Huntas the last two wads of tobacco from his battered tin, thanked him and walked away. The old man's maybe-maybe not blather hadn't been much help, but now at least he knew he would not transgress tribal custom by walking with the girl.

"But don't waste your time, Kanaka. I tell you, she will choose Kwantlen."

Huntas' words reached Kimo's ears across the compound, carried on the wind and irritation suddenly pricked him. What could a slave possibly know about Rose Fanon's intentions? Or anyone's, for that matter? It had been a mistake to ask him in the first place. He should've asked the clerk Annance, instead. He spoke many languages. Half-Abiniki and educated as a schoolmaster, François knew more about the Indians and their customs than anyone. Yes, he'd ask him.

He suddenly felt homesick. It came like that sometimes, inexplicably, arriving out of thin air, hitting him like a blow in the solar plexus. He longed for the sun, for the comfort of home and family but he breathed deeply and forced himself to face the present. As much as he missed Hawaii, he would put it firmly out of his mind. He was here, this was now. Each day that passed brought him closer to his goal. He was as content now as he had any right to be, with the fort, its occupants, and his surroundings.

He'd just like to get to know the girl, that's all. Then he had to ask himself in all honesty if his interest wasn't charged by his sexual drive more than he cared to admit. In Hawaii, sex was no more than a casual, happy sharing between two people. The missionaries hadn't yet been able to change the easy-going Hawaiian attitude to physical satisfaction, and women obliged happily, no strings attached. Moku said the Kwantlen were like that too. Still, the haoles felt differently and Rose Fanon was half haole. He decided he'd better re-think this situation.

He longed now for a change. One more week and they'd be done with cutting pickets. The wood had to be four to five inches thick, and exactly fifteen feet high, so it was hard work. He'd been lucky. The carpentry at the fort didn't involve particularly fine skills, and he had coped well. He, Moku and Pali continued to raft the pickets down river from points upstream, while at the fort, the Canadiens squared logs for the bastions.

The following Sunday, on his afternoon off, Kimo obeyed Company rules and scrubbed his bunk, then washed his laundry outside in one of the communal tubs. His mother had done his laundry in Hawaii and he'd never given it a thought till he'd had to do it for himself, first on the ship, then here. He should've thanked her more often. Washing tested the men's patience, so that now they talked of hiring Indian women to do it for them. It wasn't that they felt demeaned by it; it was the precious time it stole from their few hours off. When he finished his wash, he hung his clothes to dry and headed for the riverbank.

The fort was much like the ship. It was hard to find privacy anywhere when you wanted to be alone to think. His thoughts roved home to Hawaii. He hadn't written yet. He'd do it when he got back. He'd write for Moku as well, since he had never learned. Maybe it was his imagination that the day had an Island feel to it, for the sun shone unusually bright and the cloudless blue sky trailed long ribbons of pink. The fresh smell of wood smoke borne on the breeze tickled his nose. No matter where you walked in Langley, you couldn't escape the pungent smell of newly felled timbers.

ROSE, PADDLING ACROSS the river, thought it was a glorious day. Even the river seemed to be having a fine time, running with a surge and a gurgle. She beached her canoe west of the dock, climbed out with her basket in hand, then spotted Kimo in the distance.

"Hello, Kanaka," she called. "How are you?" She walked towards him smiling, and he was taken aback. What to call her? Rose? Miss Fanon?

"I'm well, thank you, Miss." He stopped short, hobbled by uncertainty. She looked different. She wore a blue and white cotton European-style dress. The dress was long, with sleeves that stopped half-way between her elbow and her wrist, fitted neatly at her waist and scooped low, but not too low, at the neckline. He wondered if she'd sewn the dress herself. He found himself staring at her, comparing her with the picture in his mind's eye that he still held of her at Semiahmoo, when the Cowichan called her *Aleela,* the Salmonberry Woman.

"Call me Rose. What should I call you, Kimo or Kanaka?"

"Whatever you like. Kanaka is what Hawaiians call each other. It means 'human being.'"

"I prefer Kimo, then."

"I was going for a walk," he said. Then on impulse, "Would you like to come?"

She hesitated briefly, then smiled. "Yes."

They walked along the riverbank away from the fort, chastely, he with his big brown hands at his sides, and Rose with her hands clasped around the handle of her basket, nervously in front of her body.

"Tell me about your family," she urged when the silence between them grew overlong. He talked of his mother and father, of Pikoi and old Keaka and Hopoo. He described life in Hawaii and she listened intently, intrigued to learn that the white Captain Cook had reached that distant land, that he had died there in a battle with the Hawaiians.

"They returned in my great grandfather's time and claimed our islands for Britain. We had our own names for them then, Nihau, Kauai, Oahu, Molokai, Lanai, Kahoolawe, Maui, Hawaii, and others, but the English renamed them the Sandwich Islands.'

"I like the old names better."

He hadn't thought about it much. The whites had widened their island world, brought them new ways of thinking as well as a new name. What choice had they? Native spears were no match for haole guns. Still, many changes had been necessary and good, so the whites were deemed more clever, more knowing. But now, with the girl's simple "I like the old names better," his Hawaiian soul stirred.

"After that, ships came more often and whalers too, and men started to leave on them, mostly out of curiosity, to see the world beyond our own. Our Islands have become the stopover for ships trading in the South China Seas. They pay high prices for furs in Canton, up to $100 a pelt."

"I thought all our furs went to England."

"They do, but after that, they're sent to China on the East Indian trading ships." He knew Russian-American furs went there too, directly. Competition was keen between the Russians, Americans and English for the Chinese market. That pelts from Langley could end up on the head of someone in far-off China astonished Rose. These were people she'd only vaguely heard of, who lived at the other edge of the world, another race, yellow-skinned, with strange dress and stranger customs.

"How long have you lived in the village, Rose?"

"Since I was three. My mother, my naha, is Indian. My father was a voyageur, one of the first men here. When he left, my mother married Neetlum. I have a half-brother Sandich and two half-sisters, Snana'y, and Wawas'u. You met them the day of the fire."

"I thought you might be half-French, with a name like Fanon. Do you speak the language?"

"Yes. Not as well as I'd like though. I was a child when my father left. I listen to the voyageurs, but their language is well . . . salty at times." She laughed, eyes sparkling with mischief. "I can curse and swear like the best of them."

"That must come in handy at times."

"I save it for special occasions."

He liked her laugh, the quick response. It struck him the hardest part of a man's contract with the Hudson's Bay Company might not be in enduring the killing work pace, but in staying celibate. Tough, hard, no-nonsense contract men, here for a while then gone. Some would take Indian wives, but others would never think of it. Men of iron, he judged. For himself, all he wanted was honest friendship. Anything else would complicate his plans.

Rose liked him. He was different from the men in the village, open and gentle. He'd tried hard not to frighten her at Semiahmoo, and he'd led her away from the carnage of the Lekwiltok raid. But he was from far-off Owhyhee, which meant he'd return there when his contract expired, and she would never allow herself to become involved with a man who would leave as her father had done.

He told her about farming in Hawaii, about life on board the *Thomasina*, about Billings and the chained man Collins, and she talked of her mother and her family. He'd heard talk of natives copying the white man's ways, clearing land to cultivate the earth and grow potatoes, but when he spoke of it, she laughed at the idea.

"We've always grown our own kind of potatoes, *wappatoes*. Their roots grow in low wet land all along the river. They taste much like the fort's potatoes, only firmer."

He wondered then at the view the girl must hold of the two races whose blood she shared, and about assumptions the whites made of the Kwantlen people. This was the one thing at the fort that irritated him. Everyone was pigeon-holed, categorized from high to low. Put in their box, labelled and destined to remain there forever. The Indians were no better, of course, for they had their own caste system from high chiefs to slaves, just as the Hawaiians had before the haoles arrived.

When Rose talked about the potato-like wappatoes, Kimo told her about making *poi* by baking, pounding, moistening and fermenting the root of the taro plant. Whenever he thought of farming, he pictured in his mind's eye rows of potatoes, a small fenced area for a few cows, a pig maybe. No chickens. Though in reality, he would put up with them, their eggs and meat being too precious to dismiss. A farmer here could make a fair living, he reckoned. Of course the land would need to be cleared. A tough job around Langley, where trees were so enormous that one stump he passed every day was big enough to contain his childhood home. Once the trees were down though, the land held possibilities. Not for him, of course, for his future lay in Honolulu, where the taro fields awaited him, and sunshine and warm seas.

"It's almost dusk and I should go," Rose told him regretfully.

"I'll walk you to your canoe. Will you come again?"

"When?" she asked. Her directness surprised him. No wavering. No coy batting of the eyelids.

"Next Sunday?"

She hesitated, wondering if her stepfather would approve of her seeing this Kanaka, or if he'd allow her use of the canoe to do so.

"Same time. Here, where your canoe is tied up now?" he prodded. For a moment, he thought she would refuse.

"Yes." He felt awkward, like a twelve-year-old, with no understanding of proper social behaviour. It was this place. He didn't know if he should even shake her hand. She was already in the boat reaching for her paddle when he decided he'd done enough fretting over conventions, which seemed to be of little consequence in this wilderness place anyway. He was a man and he liked this girl, so he leaned over and kissed her quickly, on the cheek, as he would have any woman at home.

She felt like she'd been scalded. Her hand stopped reaching for the paddle, as his eyes met hers. Her pulse leapt like a frog. He'd kissed her on their first outing! Not the compulsory kiss on each cheek that to the French meant nothing at all except a casual greeting. But one single kiss, which did certainly mean something, on her cheek. What did it mean in Hawaii? What did it mean here to him?

He pushed the canoe from the riverbank, unsmiling, and neither the Kwantlen nor the French-Canadian in her knew what to make of him. She raised her arm briefly, then waved. He watched her paddle away, and cursed the way he suddenly felt diminished in this place. What was a man supposed to do? He knew the answer well enough in Hawaii, but here? Damn this uncertainty. It would be much easier not to get involved. He'd be better leaving her alone. After Sunday, he'd stop seeing her.

He worked hard next day to keep his mind occupied. The long summer days provided more daylight hours and he had come to enjoy the fort most in the evenings, when the bustle of the day receded. Then it had a character different from daytime, and the evening smells intrigued him — of wood shavings, foods cooking, of smoke and worn leather, of fur bales and the sooty smell of coals in the blacksmith shop.

Sunday arrived. He met Rose and went walking, and forgot about not seeing her again. He pecked her cheek chastely as before when she left and made arrangements to meet again. And again.

Work continued unabated at the fort. More workers arrived on the *Cadboro,* voyageurs from Fort Vancouver with their Columbia wives, and this made life more pleasant for the fort people. The store bustled dawn to dusk with the Indians bringing in not just pelts but food supplies, deer, elk, cranes, ducks and geese for barter. Men hoed and harvested the potato fields, packing the red potatoes in kegs for cold storage, and continued to clear ground for planting wheat and peas the following spring. The smith sharpened axes and made and mended tools, men worked the pit, made barrels, cleared stumps from the pasture, tended the animals. There was no end to their chores. Sentries kept a close eye on the never ceasing Indian traffic along the river. The Indians moved villages frequently, visiting and trading with neighbours and with distant tribes. Their large wooden rafts balanced upon two or more canoes passed the fort daily, piled high with trade goods and household items.

Fall came and went and Christmas approached. Moku woke him early one morning in December with a shake.

"Come and look outside!"

He yanked his pants and boots on, drew a warm sweater over his head and stepped outdoors. A blanket of white covered the landscape. A light wind blew, enough to make the bare trees wave in a world of white silence. He'd never felt snow before and laughed out loud, stretching his arms to catch the flakes in his cupped hands. He sat on the ground and let the snow have its way, turning his face skyward and licking the cold flakes off his face before they melted. The snowflakes drifting through the trees sounded like the hushed voice of the sea ebbing through the sand on the beach at Oahu, whispering as it pulled away, "Ssh! Ssh!" He gloried in the beauty of it. The fort trappers quickly devised snowshoes, in case it lingered. But before the week was out, the white ground turned a crusted gray. By then Kimo's warm Hawaiian bones felt brittle with the stabbing cold and he had few regrets when the thaw began, and turned the fort ground into a slurry of mud.

Christmas, when it came, transformed the place. Every man attended the "smoker" at the mess hall in the Big House. It wasn't what Kimo expected, for alcohol flowed freely even though it was morning and a Christian holiday, but Mr. Yale gave each a gift of meat or poultry of their choice. Kimo chose turkey, and gave it to Rose for her family.

He attended the fort's Christmas party that night, and this, too, shocked him. It was a riotous affair of singing, dancing and drinking, concluding with a brawl between jealous men over a wife dispensing her favours too widely. The two drunken men staggered down the steps of the Big House, throwing their jackets to the ground, rolling up their sleeves, while the silly wife sailed like some coquettish ship alongside. The husband's egg-shaped belly hung over his breeches while his opponent reeled tipsily in circles around him. Kimo left. He felt homesick and he'd had a steady soaking of drink. He needed to distance himself, to separate himself from the taste of this first, not-so-merry Christmas at the fort.

New Year's Eve was equally wild, but in the morning, Peopeo and Como brought their Kwantlen wives to visit. One look at the bronze women, wearing colourful native jewellery and haole women's long dresses, and Kimo's heart caught. He was suddenly transported home, where flesh was golden, where women with flowers round their necks and flowers in their hair, reclined languorously on the sand, with Diamond Head silhouetted against the skyline, its crater rim sharply defined, as warm surf flung dying ripples across the sand.

Then he was back in Langley, smiling at the native women who reminded him so much of the barefoot women at home. And of Rose. When he thought of her, his heart expanded. It was tempting to think about entering a marriage contract, but that wouldn't fit his plans. Or hers, either. For now he understood the Company's marriage contract, and it didn't favour the local women. A man could take a "country wife" and when he chose to leave, his only obligation to the abandoned wife and children was financial. As long as he found a replacement husband as a source of income, he could cancel the contract.

He couldn't do that to Rose. She was beginning to occupy a great deal of his thoughts. He really should see less of her. But truthfully, she'd become a bright light in his life at the fort. He'd finally written his first letter home. It would be months before he'd receive a reply. He hoped it would be from Hopoo, for he would write far more than Oolea.

JANUARY AND FEBRUARY were dreary months, as rain bombarded the coast. March blew in and men woke again to the wonder of falling snow. It didn't stay, but melted quickly and by evening, all traces were gone. Next morning, Peopeo sent him to the Big House. One of the voyageurs had fallen sick and needed blistering. Kimo would take his place in the Express to the Cowlitz. They did this now and then, blistered a man on the legs to draw out the bad humours. Blistering, for Kimo, was as repulsive as leeching. Yet it was true that some men improved afterwards. He'd seen similar oddities before, when Keaka had healed people by casting dry chicken bones. Even if the missionaries hadn't taught otherwise, a thinking man would have to question how dry bones, or entrails, or stone pebbles, could possibly cure a sickness. Yet they did, at times. The power of belief, he supposed. Still, as long as the poor voyageur was being blistered and could be ill for weeks, he'd gladly take his place in the Express.

His health was always good in spite of the wet and cold coastal winters that felled, often severely, so many of his countrymen. Frequently these days he would be the first to be called as a replacement for a sick man. Already he had made half a dozen trips while other Hawaiians who had served more contract years never made it out of the sawpit.

In clear weather, there was nothing finer than paddling to the Cowlitz. The Company had chosen a beautiful location, halfway between the Columbia River and Puget Sound for its farm, which now comprised thousands of acres. Kimo enjoyed canoeing the riverways, absorbing himself in the silence of the countryside on these trips to the farm to exchange goods and mail. It was a welcome break from routine. The dark mountains that had felt menacing before now seemed friendly, soaring skyward, wrapping the river and valley in their secure embrace. They wore a spring covering of snow from the peaks down to the tree line, and Kimo felt a sudden urge to explore them. He knew nothing about mountain climbing, but promised himself it was something he'd do before he left these shores.

"Aloha, Kimo Kanui!"

They had just reached the Cowlitz, and the Langley Express was easing its way to tie up at the wharf when he heard the shout. The tone was deep and hearty, as if from a long lost friend, but Kimo turned to find it was the wretch, Ahuhu, waving at him. The hearty welcome was utterly false, of course, but there was no avoiding the man. He paced back and forth impatiently while the Langley men unloaded their cargo, but failed to offer any help, though every other man on the dock did.

"So, what are things like up north, Kanui?" He didn't wait for an answer. "No better than here, I wager. Life is hell. They work you like a dog then punish you for nothing. I was in Nisqually four months and that was hell, too. We should never have come."

Kimo had been to Nisqually with the Express. It was the new fort near Tacoma where they raised sheep and longhorn cattle to feed the forts, and it was as fine a place as the Cowlitz.

"I've no complaints," he said and turned away, but Ahuhu caught him by the arm.

"Look!" He rolled up the stained left leg of his gray cotton trousers and displayed a reddened ankle, bruised and scabbing, encrusted with dirt. "Look what they did! Curse them! A whole month I was in irons!"

"I'm sorry, Ahuhu." He meant it. No man should wear chains.

Ahuhu oozed resentment. You could feel it coming off him in waves. He looked angry enough to explode.

"What happened?"

"Nothing worth chaining a man for. I drank a little rum . . ."

"On the job?"

He looked away. "No. I got sick, Kanui, and missed work, that's all."

"You'll get sicker if you don't clean that leg." You could see it was infected. The man was a mess. Open sores festered along his stubbled chin. His dark eyes had sunk into deep holes in his head. His lip was cut. Cloaked now in grievance, he appeared older than Kimo remembered. Likely he'd drunk himself into a stupor, and not turned up for work. Strict as they were, the Company wouldn't chain a man for one infraction, so there had to be some other offence. Before Kimo could question him further, and without so much as a farewell aloha, Ahuhu turned away and left the dock, heading back towards the farm. Men parted wordlessly to let him pass and Kimo felt pity for him. Fort men bonded easily one with another, from loneliness and from facing common dangers, but it was clear from their pointed silence that few called Ahuhu friend. There had been others like him at Fort Vancouver when Kimo was there, low types who gambled and drank to excess, men who fought at the drop of a hat and ended up in leg irons. Thank goodness no man had been chained in Langley, not since he'd arrived and he didn't think they would be. One had been sent back to Vancouver for being drunk and trying to bring women into the fort at night, but that was before Kimo's time. The men there now were all trustworthy and reliable. They bore discipline well, pulled their weight and seldom complained. He fingered Keaka's dolphin. The gods had been good to him after all, when they'd sent him north.

He always stayed alert on those trips to the Cowlitz, for he remembered the early Lekwiltok attack on the Express that Huntas had talked of. But nothing untoward ever happened. Except once, and men spoke of it for weeks. They'd set up camp by the riverbank when an odd little short-legged dog appeared, a round, white, woolly ball of a thing that looked more like a baby lamb than a dog. It skittered excitedly between the bales with a bark so faint, you couldn't hear it unless you stood beside it.

"Must be Indians around. The dog's one of theirs," the Iroquois said. "They shear it and mix its fleece with goat hair and goose down to make blankets."

The animal made a nuisance of himself around the camp but no one minded, for it was a little thing, quiet and friendly, till two small black bear cubs appeared at the edge of the water and the startled dog went into a frenzy.

"Keep your eye on them," McKay warned.

"They're just babies," Kimo said, amused at the tiny dog circling the lumbering cubs.

"Dangerous all the same. The mother will be close by, so watch out. They move fast. They're powerful strong and their claws'll rip the flesh off you in a second. They'll be scavenging for salmon along the river."

The cubs hung around and proceeded to sniff about the camp. The men clanged pots and threw things at them but the cubs refused to leave. After a while, the biggest one stretched its neck, brown muzzle up, sniffed the breeze and shuffled forward, grunting towards them. It "whoofed" the air out its nostrils in a muffled bark then slashed open a precious bale of pelts with a swipe of its sharp claws.

"That's it!" McKay rose to his feet, lifted his musket reluctantly and shot it, so close you could see the cub's little eyes blink. It toppled with a cry at the water's edge, making a small splash. The other cub fled wailing strangely like a human baby, bounding off into the trees.

"Now we'll have peace," McKay said, "and roast bear for supper."
The men were happy. Bear was fine meat, a welcome change from
fish, as long as it wasn't a grizzly. The superstitious Indians would
never eat grizzly, for they believed the animal held special powers. A
grizzly carcass must always be burned. But this was a black bear cub,
young and tender, so received their approval. The head, tail and feet
would be cut off and the cub skinned, leaving a small bloody carcass
no bigger than a half sack of meal, to be parboiled and then slow
roasted.

By sundown, the aroma of the roasting meat tantalized the men.
They complimented the cook, sliced the succulent roast and ate.
Conversation died and every man scraped his plate clean, swiping
the last of the juices up with chunky bannock.

"The bear's delicious," McKay said to the grinning cook. "How
long did ye boil it before ye roasted it?"

"Bear?" The cook struggled with English. Puzzled, he pointed to
the shallows. The cub carcass had drifted with the tide and remained
intact, tangled in the reeds.

"In the name of God, what did ye cook, man?"

He barked. McKay gagged. Forks dropped and clattered as men
choked over their plates, disgorging half-masticated food. The Indians shrugged and continued to eat placidly without batting an eye.
Kimo had eaten dog as a child on Oahu, but had forgotten the taste.
Now he felt curiously isolated, neither as disgusted as the whites nor
as calm as the Indians, but he set his plate aside and ate no more.
When he told Rose later, she laughed over the incident. The cook
winked at Kimo as men told the tale in the mess hall on their return,
but he was never sure if the dog had been cooked by accident or by
design, or if indeed it was dog at all.

March went out on a gentle wind, bringing with it an astonishing
event, the run of oolichan along the Fraser. Kimo watched, fascinated, from the riverbank, in the shadow of towering Tlagunna —

Golden Ears, the fort men called the mountain, after the sunshine that lit up its twin peaks. The natives raked in tons of the tiny silver, smelt-like fish with giant wooden rakes, combing them off the surface of the water into their heaped-up canoes. He'd never imagined such abundance.

"Every spring the oolichan arrive first," Rose told him. "We call them 'saviour fish' because, after a hard winter, they can save the tribes from starving."

The Indians smoked and dried the nutritious fish and made oil from it. The entire process required a frenzied amount of work in a short time frame, and everyone pitched in. Nothing was wasted. A ton, twenty-five thousand or more fish rendered only twenty-five gallons of oil, which they used for fuel and cooking and for trading with other tribes along the "Grease Trails," named for this oolichan butter. So much, Kimo thought, for the idea that the natives were indolent. As far as he could see, they knew exactly what they were doing, worked industriously and managed the oolichan fishery in time and tune with nature.

In Hawaii, they had no great river like the Fraser. They caught their fish in the sea, and in two kinds of *loko i'a,* fishponds, inshore and sea ponds. Inshore ponds formed when groundwater flowed seaward through porous lava, filling depressions in the rock. In these, *'ama 'ama,* mullet, and *'awa,* milkfish, would breed well. And they had open-sea ponds, controlled with rock walls and vine sluice gates that connected the pond to the sea, and utilized changes in the tide. Small fish could get in, fat grown fish could not swim out. Overall, he thought the Hawaiians and the Kwantlen understood fishing better than the haoles.

Work continued as before and the move to the new fort took place rapidly, once the basic structure was erected. Men moved items over from the old fort piece by piece, and left the timbers for the Indians to salvage. After settling into the new quarters the Kanakas shared, Kimo tossed restlessly in his bunk, too tired to sleep. In the months he'd been here, he'd seen things he never could have imagined. In Hawaii, life had been predictable. He had worked hard in the taro fields, but there was time to sing and dance, to swim and surf, to sit idly in the shade for shelter from the simmering heat. Each day you knew clearly what the morrow would bring. Here, you never knew what to expect and he liked that edgy feeling of excitement, the dangerous thrill of insecurity and unpredictability. And he was learning things from the strong men he worked with. They took pride in their fort. Good men. Blunt as rocks they were, but that was how they lived — without fuss, with simplicity of language and everything else. He'd come to judge, and be judged by, the men he worked with. If you pulled your weight — no excuses, no sloughing off — that was their measure of a man. They depended on each other for survival, and quickly decided in your favour or not. No waffling. The Company might make a great deal of the colour of a man's skin, but the men didn't. In enemy territory, you don't care what colour a man's skin is, brown, red, yellow or white, or if he's the son of a lord or a lowly water carrier. You just want to depend on him, and his worth as a man.

Apart from the Lekwiltok raid, which still distressed him, Kimo wasn't sorry he'd come. The land was wild and beautiful like its native people, strange and full of legends and superstition. Like old Hawaii in many ways, only colder! At first, nothing had fit his tropical sense of beauty, but now he could appreciate the grandeur of the place, and the amazing river, the Fraser, that brought life to the people who lived here. The land was strong. You could feel its power. And from this small fort on the edge of the wilderness, he sensed he was gaining power himself, through coming to know the larger world of men.

He remembered the mating eagles dancing, circling the sky, and the feather that had fallen at his feet. McKay said it was just a feather, no more, no less. But the Hawaiian in him knew better. It was a message. The gods had spoken. And the message was for him.

chapter nine

SPRING REMAINED COLD and wet, and men lingered over dinners with appetites keener than knives — and not just for food. Their appetite for conversation was equally keen. Kimo had been surprised at the men's propensity to gossip, but there was little else to do after work. They eagerly consumed news and were all desperately interested in each other and in the daily commerce of their neighbours, and in the other forts. The forts were interconnected and dependent upon each other, and a threat to one could be a threat to all, so every man paid heed when the voyageur Antoine burst his way noisily through the door at dinner.

"Dose Yankee traders have bin up da Nootka Sound again." Antoine was tall and thin, brown as the Kwantlen, with long, untied hair hanging loosely past his shoulders. His thin, hawk-like nose hooked aristocratically, like that of the Iroquois. Dark eyes flashed with irritation. "Just las' week. Day gave 'em guns and axes an' everything, an' all cheaper dan us. Dere's no stoppin' dose Boston guys."

"We're in trouble if we don't do something soon. The Indians will stop trading with us altogether," the clerk beside Kimo frowned. He was short, barely twenty, thin and gaunt, with blue eyes and poorly barbered brown hair that fanned out across his narrow shoulders.

"An' who can blame dem?" Antoine swigged tea in gulps and complained with a mouth full of bannock, "Day best do something quick or we all be out of work here at the fort."

Kimo was only now piecing together the politics of the land. Britain and America had signed a treaty in 1818 setting the border from Lake Superior along the 49th parallel to the east face of the Rocky Mountains. But there they stopped. Everything west of the mountains (from the Spanish holdings that ended 42 degrees North, to Russian Alaska, which began at about 55 degrees) was open to anybody. A great westward movement of pioneers was beginning in America, and their numbers and hunger for land made the British nervous. Boston traders plying the West Coast waters were also making the British nervous.

"Any word from Governor Simpson, Monsieur?" Antoine asked the senior clerk at the end of the table. He was a gray man, with gray eyes and gray hair. He wore gray trousers, and his gray shirt might have been white, had it seen regular washing. Even his skin was a pallid gray and he wore a permanent air of injury. Kimo guessed he was sick, if not in body, then of life. The clerk hesitated, swirling tea flecks around the bowl of his cup, which he obliterated with a sudden shake of his wrist before placing the cup down on its saucer again. Everybody knew Sir George was in Hamburg negotiating a deal with the Russians in a deliberate move to drive out the Americans. He cleared his throat and a gravelly voice emerged.

"Yes. A deal's been signed. Plans are being drawn up now for Langley, Cowlitz and Nisqually too. We've to increase production all round, build up the dairy herd, add a creamery. They want tons of butter by year's end, and more vegetables too."

"So that's why we got all those cows," Moku said. Last trip, the *Beaver* had chugged in with another load of California dairy cows and they'd spent a weary day unloading the beasts off the ship. They'd herded the bewildered beasts, with their steamy breath crystallizing in the wintry air, into newly built sheds, for shelter from the cold.

Weeks later, the hoped-for news arrived that Governor George Simpson had indeed arranged to lease part of Southeastern Alaska from the Russians, who had been trading with the Americans. Now that trade was cut off, the Russians would be buying Company goods instead, supplied by the forts. Antoine was happy.

"Dose Boston guys, day will be mad!" he crowed, and toasted Governor Simpson with rum.

The men continued to expand the fort, to accommodate the Company's new plans, and the influx of workers who would be arriving to implement them. They arrived on the *Beaver* — a dairyman and his wife to take care of the herd, the fort's newly appointed butter maker, a blacksmith, more Hawaiian labourers, and Ovid Allard, a big bearded man with an aura of quiet integrity about him that Kimo liked on sight.

Peopeo greeted the Hawaiian labourers with aloha, took them under his wing and explained the operations of the fort. Kimo judged them all decent men, tall and strong, thankfully not an Ahuhu among them. He showed the men to their sleeping quarters, where the single Kanakas lived, separate of course from the white employees. Those with native wives moved across the river, near the stream men called Kanaka Creek, where all the men with Kwantlen wives lived with their families. On impulse, and as a gesture of friendship, he offered to write letters home for them. A few Kanakas at Fort Vancouver were literate, but none in Langley, except himself. He had Keaka to thank for that.

"Mon Dieu, you can read and write? Why didn't you say so?" François Annance beamed at him. Kimo had been slow to make friends with the half-white, half-Abiniki former schoolmaster. He had a wild look about him, an air that commanded respect. If not respect, caution. You didn't mess with François Annance. *A teller of tales,* some haoles said of him, disparaging the tradition of ancient peoples to embellish, in order to increase understanding. Kimo pegged him for a man in harmony with his environment. He'd helped build the original fort and knew the land and people. If food supplies ran low, it was Annance who left the fort to hunt. He'd come striding through the fort's big doors two or three days later with a deer, or an elk, or a row of geese strung on a pole over his shoulder. He had almond-shaped, cat eyes, black flecked with gold, above a long, aquiline nose. He wore a fringed buckskin jacket, blanket trousers and leather boots. You would never take him for an educated man, though he spoke English and French fluently, and a dozen Indian dialects. A more competent man at the fort would be hard to find.

" I have books I can give you, if you want them, Kanaka."

If he wanted them! So many times he'd longed for reading material. He'd never thought to ask François, or anyone else.

"Merci. I'd like that, François. I haven't read a page since I came."

"English or French?"

"English."

"Pick them up after dinner."

Kimo did, and carried four dog-eared books carefully back to his room. *Robinson Crusoe* by Daniel Defoe looked interesting. *A New Complete English Dictionary, Peculiarly Adapted to the Instruction and Improvement of Those who have not had the Benefit of a Learned or Liberal Education: To which is prefixed a Compendious Grammar* by D. Bellamy, he placed at the bottom of the pile. *Gulliver's Travels* by Jonathan Swift looked good, too. The last was *Selected Poems,* a book by Alexander Pope. He hadn't read much poetry, just childish rhymes. It wasn't something they'd studied at the Mission. He flipped the pages.

> A little learning is a dangerous thing;
> Drink deep, or taste not the Pierian spring:
> There shallow drafts intoxicate the brain,
> And drinking largely sobers us again.

He didn't know what a Pierian spring was, but he liked the image. He placed this with the other three. He'd need extra candles to read by, but he could trade his rum ration for them. He couldn't wait to get started.

The fort fairly bustled after the arrival of the new people. Everyone worked hard as before, but the influx of manpower made projects go faster. The fort farm on the Langley Prairie had expanded constantly till it covered many hundreds of acres, though flooding sometimes washed away great stretches of it. As soon as men cleared another patch of ground, more potatoes were planted, and barley, wheat and peas. The dairy herd, initially begun with 29 cows numbered almost 500, and the piggery had grown to house 200 pigs.

When the dairyman's helper came down with a fever, Kimo was assigned to work with the herd. He didn't like the idea. Apart from unloading cattle off the ship, he'd never worked with stock before and had no wish to deal with them.

"Lay your head into her side and take a firm hold," Mr. Finlay advised him the first time he had to milk a cow, "so she knows who's boss." Finlay was a wiry man, mid-sized, with an open face and eyes that wrinkled in the corner. His skin was deeply tanned from working outdoors, and he'd taken charge of the herd immediately, arranging the animals in their stalls and organizing the sheds to his liking. The cow Kimo was milking defiantly lashed out her tail, slapping the skin of his neck sharply enough to raise a long welt. After a week or so, once the temperamental beasts grew familiar with him, they stopped bunting him and grew more docile at milking time. He came to like their large soulful eyes and sweeping-brush eyelashes. Of their fast whipping tails, he remained forever suspicious.

Mr. Finlay milked three cows to every one of his, but Kimo improved as time went by and he slowly gained the hang of it. He learned to differentiate between them. He learned you should never milk while fretting over troubles, for the animals sensed it and would tighten up and hold onto their milk. But if you worked calmly, the cows would slacken their muscles, and with each gentle tug, the white milk would spurt from their teats evenly into the pail.

Mrs. Finlay made butter from the cream. She was a bright little woman, with a ruddy complexion and a ready smile. She'd pour the milk into shallow pans to set overnight, so the cream would rise to the surface. In the morning, she'd skim the cream off with a wooden spoon and leave it to sit till its surface shone and tasted slightly sour. She knew just by looking at it when it was ready for the churn. Then she'd pound it with a large wooden dasher, a stick with paddles on the bottom till the cream separated into buttermilk and tiny pellets of butter. The buttermilk went to the piglets and the young heifers out in the pasture.

Kimo found he enjoyed working with the animals and tending the farm and fields. Company servants had to work where commanded though, so he was recalled for carpentry work frequently, but he didn't mind as long as he was outdoors. He was under contract after all, and must do as he was bid, so he took each day in stride. At night, he was so exhausted, he barely read a page before his eyelids closed, and sleep claimed him. But he did try to read every night.

He'd begun with Defoe's *Robinson Crusoe*. The little brown book was smaller than his big hand, the print so tiny he had to hold it at the end of his nose to read it. The cover was worn and frayed at the edges so that you could see the strands of loose thread. He didn't know why that surprised him. In Oahu, they used cloth, tapa, to write on, too. It was a true story, according to the inside cover, and he'd read it keenly but ended up disappointed. He couldn't comprehend the extent of the man's fear at being stranded on a tropical island, as if that in itself were dreadful, for it was warm and he soon found food and water. He felt sure he himself would feel worse if they dropped him in England, where, so Billings said, cold and fog and lack of money could kill a man. Crusoe's loneliness, though, he did understand. Still, after some time the man managed to find himself a dark-skinned friend to keep him company and make life easier for him, and in a wink he turned him into his servant.

A haole story, he'd decided, and blew out the candle.

"Fire! Fire! Get up, Kimo! The fort's on fire!"

He forced his eyes open. It was still early evening but he'd been so exhausted he'd dozed off on his bunk right after dinner. His nose twitched violently as his nostrils picked up the strong smell of smoke. He reached for his boots, yanking them up swiftly. His first thought was that someone had torched the place.

"Indians?" he barked at Moku.

"No. It started in the smithy. The fire's eating it up!"

In the dusk, families scrambled from their quarters out to the compound in a daze. He could see flames leaping skyward in jagged pointed fingers above the blacksmith shop. Men ran wildly in different directions as he raced with Moku towards the smithy. His mind reeled. What if they lost the fort? It would be disastrous to be without shelter in this wilderness.

A shifting pancake of smoke layered itself overhead, forming strange gray shapes, swirling in wide arcing circles directly across the stockade. The wind suddenly gusted, swelling the hungry flames like blasts from the smith's own great bellows, urging tentacles of red fire across the compound.

A battery of conflicting commands crisscrossed the stockade, shouted through the smoke by anxious men, while Kimo's brain scrambled to prioritize their needs.

"Water! More water!"

"Move the gunpowder!"

"Here! Over here!"

"Shift those boxes! Move the bales!"

"Quick, the powder!" He raced with Moku to help the men struggling to roll the heavy barrels of black gunpowder away from the bastions and the magazine to a place of safety.

Rose had gone to the trade store late, and just had time to pick up Neetlum's nails before the Clerk closed. She was about to head for the river when she sensed a change in the air. Uneasy, she paused, instinctively scanning her surroundings, already half prepared to flee. Then her nose twitched. Smoke! Smoke meant fire. And fire brought terror to the forest. She panicked momentarily. A tumultuous commotion reached her ears as shouts and screams erupted across the normally quiet fort. A spray of sparks and an arrow of flame suddenly shot skyward above the palisade walls, and she caught her breath. The fire was in the fort!

"Fire! Fire!" A horn sounded, again and again throughout the compound. The fort's big gates that had just closed, swung open and Ovid Allard ran through, carrying a stack of ledgers outside. Rose watched as people darted every which way, stumbling and colliding through thickening clouds of smoke.

One of the fort's clerks appeared suddenly in front of her, bounding over a heap of baled goods like some frightened frog. She recognised the thin, white-faced young man from the trade store but didn't know his name. He grabbed her wrist and rammed an armful of folded woollen blankets against her chest. Startled, she stumbled backwards, then found her feet unsteadily.

"We cannae lose our trade goods!" the freckle-faced man exhorted her anxiously, wide-eyed above his skeleton-like cheekbones. "We'll no' survive here without them!" She ran with him, half blinded by the pile of blankets that reached above her head, to lay them in a heap outside and away from the walls.

"Fetch help!" he pleaded. "Quickly!" She ran back into the confusion of the compound. Through choking gasps, she relayed the clerk's message to the first man she encountered, who turned immediately to conscript another, and the two set off running. The next time Rose saw them, they were exiting the burning store, stooped over coughing, carrying great bundles of blankets, furs and supplies to safety. She did what she could to help, lifting and shifting packages. With every trip she peered through the smoke searching for Kimo. A knot of men furiously fought the fire in and around the burning smithy. She could decipher only vague, ghost-like shapes through the screen of gray smoke, but knew he'd be there. She hoped he'd stay safe, for the flames had come to life, leaping monstrously now, higher and higher towards the sky, causing waves of heat to roll across the compound, smarting her dry, itching eyes and prickling her burning skin.

Through the smoke belching from the smithy, Kimo could see no more than his arm's length in any direction. He tried to remember what was in the adjacent shed. Stacks of boxes and feed for the animals. Then he heard a loud whinny and realized there were horses in the lean-to behind the smithy, waiting to be shod. They should've been in the outside barns, but the two must have been tethered there in the afternoon, waiting for the farrier to re-shoe them for work in the fields next day.

"Bring blankets!" he bellowed at Moku, and tore along the dirt path faster than he thought possible. The terrified animals, snorting loudly with fear, stamped their hooves in panic. A fierce roar like thunder filled his ears as wooden storage boxes and crates ignited across the shed. He could no longer see through the acrid smoke. Fire spurted across the roof beams overhead, illuminating the night sky like some brilliant comet. His skin burned, his eyes were scratchy and dry.

"Come on, Moku!" he urged impatiently, peering through the smoke at the distorted shadow that was Moku returning, flying towards him like a spectre through the smoke. Another burst of sound erupted as a hay bale on the far side of the shed suddenly ignited with a crackle and whoosh, then the far side of the shed caught fire. A columnar spiral of flames rose into the night sky. Men passed each other in haste, fleeing gray shadows amid the suffocating smoke. Hot tears stung Kimo's eyes, streaming down his cheeks, dried by the heat long before they reached his chin. Choking from the smoke-filled air, he ran to meet Moku, and seized an armful of blankets.

"Soak them in the water trough. That'll give us some protection."

The choking stench of burning things, of wood, of charred hay and scorched leather enveloped them. The hot stink of manure dropped by the terrified horses reached Kimo's nostrils as they led the animals, whuffling, heads and shoulders covered with wet blankets and snorting with fright and panic, away from the burning shed. Fear suddenly overwhelmed the big stallion and the heavy horse bucked without warning, lashing out with a vicious kick to the lean-to wall.

"Whoa, boy! Whoa!" He nearly lost his balance as the stallion bucked hard again, fighting against his reins, rearing up in fierce protest against his rescuer. Then the animal's leg broke audibly with a loud snap as he flailed out against the heavy metal stanchion near the door.

"Damn! What a waste!" Kimo swore in frustration. They'd need to shoot the animal now, or slit its throat and save the powder. Damn it anyway.

The two men dragged the animals towards the split-rail pens outside the stockade, and tethered them securely. The stock, chickens and pigs would be safe enough from the fire, he reckoned, but the horses' fearful scufflings added to the din, as they snickered and whuffled with fright, cantering here and there, bunting each other. Maddened chickens squawked in circles between and under and through the animals' moving legs.

Kimo spotted Rose on the way back. He hadn't known she was at the fort. She stooped to lay a pile of blankets on the ground and straightened up, pushing her hair from her eyes with a weary gesture, and he saw the side of her face smudged dark with soot. His feet propelled him towards her of their own accord. The thought she might have come to harm hit him deep in the solar plexus, and his walk quickened unconsciously to a run.

"Are you all right?" He gripped her arms, riveting his eyes on the dark smudges on her face. Her hair was a fly-a-way mess, and she looked drained, but thank God, the marks were only smoke and dirt, not bruises.

"I'm fine. What about you? Your hair's scorched."

"It's nothing." He shook his head, anxious to get back to the blaze, now he knew she was safe. "Will you be all right?"

"Yes. Go! Do what you have to do."

Mrs. Finlay ran by, wailing dolefully about her cream pans. Back at the store, men and women continued their desperate struggle to save the fort's supplies, but the suffocating flames gradually encircled them. Forced to retreat, they watched the fire swallow up the store's precious goods. Moku managed to grab some clothing from the Kanaka's shack, as well as Kimo's books. Their possessions were so few, it had taken only moments, but he barely made it outside before fire raced up the walls. The women wept in frustration. The men seethed in silence. Every eye reflected desperation and despair.

As she paddled wearily homeward, Rose pitied the people of the fort. All their hard work, gone up in smoke. Reduced to ashes. Including her own dream of finding work there. When she returned next day, men and women drifted gloomily in twos and threes through the smoldering ruins and blackened stumps, trying to assess the damage in the morning light. Their tired faces reflected dejection and there was an odour of anxiety about the place, as thick as the fire's smoke had been. The only thing that lifted people's dark mood and provided a measure of relief, was the daring rescue of the Finlays' baby from the fire. A brave dash by Ovid Allard through the leaping flames of their burning house had saved the child's life. A grateful Mrs. Finlay walked about with the baby clutched to her breast, looking for all the world as if she would never lay the child down again, while gallant Ovid Allard for his bravery sported burned tufts of hair and badly singed eyebrows. The baby's deliverance and the fact no one had died cast the only positive light on an otherwise black day. They had feared for Brulé, the new blacksmith, for a time, for he'd been sleeping in the smithy till his accommodation was ready, but he too escaped unscathed.

"That's all we could salvage," Kimo said, indicating a small pile of trade goods, a few pelts, some powder, and salmon. He'd listed them on a sheet of paper for François, along with half a dozen muskets and some kegs, and a handful of tools. "Everything else has gone — furniture and food, most of the pelts. Up in smoke."

"What will happen now?"

"We begin again," he said matter-of-factly. His kupuna always said the way to take trouble was to leave it. He reckoned that was true, for the sooner they rebuilt, the safer they'd be. Mr. Yale had already begun to reorganize. The men were glad. They knew word would spread fast through the tribes that they were vulnerable. There was always the possibility of another Indian attack.

And as the fort people began to rebuild their stockade, fortune smiled on Rose, for she was hired to work there after all. She kept her interview neutral, acted appropriately humble, and signed on as "Laundress." That was her official title, but like every employee, she was expected to do whatever was required, which sometimes included work in the new creamery, helping the ever-cheerful Mrs. Finlay.

As time passed, she formed friendships with the women newly arrived with their husbands, and tended some of their babies. Mr. Yale's wife gave birth to a baby girl, Aurelia, who remained temporarily with the mother in her little house in the Indian village.

Rose didn't like laundry that much, for it was heavy work and some days her back ached sorely from the effort. She occasionally saw Kimo during the day, not to talk or spend time with of course, but to wave a quick hello in passing. Her language skills improved quickly. She spoke French with the Canadien boatmen, English with the Finlays, adding their Scots vernacular to her repertoire of tongues.

Rose's presence around the fort provided fleeting flashes of warmth in Kimo's labour-intensive days. He began to look for her more keenly, and the day she passed carrying someone's baby on her hip, his insides turned queer. He turned away and worked harder than ever, deliberately focusing on the task at hand.

The men forged ahead expanding the fort. With the extra man-power on hand, buildings were erected in a surprisingly short time, propelled by necessity and a little fear. People took more care with fire around the fort afterwards, the cooks and blacksmiths. Even the labourers took extra care with their candles.

Kimo thought about the fire often. In Oahu, the old ones believed the goddess Pelé brought fire, lava and lightning bolts, upon the people. Keaka would claim that Pelé was angry, and he'd be casting spells to find out why, and with whom.

But Keaka would be wrong. This was Langley. Pelé belonged to Hawaii. To *old* Hawaii. The fort's fire had sprung, not from Pelé's darts or lightning bolts, but from sparks from the blacksmith's furnace. Purely and simply. Mr. Yale confirmed this. Kimo believed it to be true. Still, he rubbed the dolphin at his neck, wishing somehow he could feel its *mana,* sad that its power eluded him, for he felt in need of reassurance.

All the men did. They'd grown weary trying to establish this fort. So many things had gone wrong. Flooding had forced them to relocate to safer ground. They'd had to battle for their lives when the Lekwiltock attacked. Then fire had burned it to the ground. The superstitious among them wondered if the gods had decreed the fort's demise, and wondered what disaster would strike next.

Kimo thought differently. He'd talked with the clerks. It was earthly power, not heavenly that directed their lives, and it came from those men in black frock-coats and shiny beaver hats in the Hudson's Bay office in London. They read their ledgers in warm comfort, focussing on bottom lines. How could such men comprehend the harsh reality of life in their distant outposts, the passions, the fears, the brutality men dealt with day by day in order to survive? They wanted furs, and if obstacles arose to block their acquisition, solutions would be determined by the stroke of a pen. Floods? *Simply move.* War? *Fight, and if necessary, kill.* Ruined by fire? *Then rebuild.* Kimo felt it would make no difference if another disaster happened. That, as far as the Company was concerned, Fort Langley would stand fast. If it had to be moved, or rebuilt or defended from time to time, so be it. The supply of furs must continue. The ledger men would scratch a line on a page to end their discussions. Then, wearied by the effort of directing other men's lives on paper, they'd lift their haole pinkies and drink tea from fine china cups. From Canton, purchased by local beaver pelts.

He believed this. The gods had no part in what happened here. Their voices had grown dim, to the point of nothingness in this place. He rubbed the dolphin at his throat but felt nothing. He let himself go quiet, so quiet he could almost hear the sound of his blood surging through his veins, but still he felt nothing. Heard nothing. Pope had written *"Know God and Nature only are the same,"* and it had set him thinking. If God and Nature were one and the same, then there was no supernatural power ordering the universe. So what did you rely on? He didn't think he liked the answer.

He returned to his quarters early, for he wanted to read more of Annance's books. It had become his nightly ritual. *Gulliver's Travels* was more complex than *Robinson Crusoe,* though he didn't see that at the beginning. He'd read several chapters before he realized what Swift was doing, and he'd had to go back to the beginning and start all over again. Then it felt like uphill ploughing, backtracking occasionally and tackling it anew to fully understand it, which he suspected he never did. But in the end, he liked it more than Defoe's, with all it had to say about how badly human beings treat other, different human beings.

The thin book of Pope's poetry challenged him, stretched his mind and he liked that most of all. He didn't understand the references, but he found himself returning to the poems frequently. The images appealed to him. He liked the language, thought it musical. Pope he read, and read again, each time trying to catch the references, feeling he'd achieved something when he did. Images would float from the page, and he learned to snare them like a butterfly in a net, before they escaped him altogether. Then he'd feel them, play with them till some window of his mind finally opened and comprehension flooded in and he would walk around smiling all day as if he'd conquered the biggest wave to hit Makaha beach.

chapter ten

THE MORNING MIST THAT hovered between rain and fog lifted with the May afternoon sun, making the roof of Rose's cedar house steam for a while before finally drying out enough to sit upon. She had invited Kimo to the village to celebrate the arrival of the salmon along the Fraser. He'd expected a potlatch ceremony, for the Indians found any excuse to hold one — a wedding, the birth of a baby, building a long house, taking a new name, harvesting wappatoes, anything at all was reason for a potlatch.

He'd attended one with Rose and her family, held by the Musqueam downriver, for the raising of a pole. The chief had called out the names of the heads of families, and gave them blankets, pelts, tools and carvings in an extraordinary show of extravagance. The display of wealth raised the donor's standing in the community, but Rose explained this had to be reciprocated later on a grander scale.

The fort people thought potlatches did more harm than good, impoverishing many in the struggle to keep up. Which was true, he supposed. Still, he had to wonder what was worse, giving away your possessions in a show of pride, or accumulating them as the haoles did, often for the same reason.

The salmon celebration was not the potlatch he expected though, but more of a religious ceremony and the roof's slight slope provided a good view of the activities taking place below.

"The first is the scout for the entire population," Rose said, pointing to the salmon, "and if we don't treat him with respect, his people might be offended and not come back. Whoever catches the first spring lays him down, head facing upstream, so the salmon will run in that direction."

"You don't believe that."

"Certainly. Why not?"

She'd told him her father was Catholic. He thought she would be too, but now he wasn't sure. Below, an elder cleaned the fish reverently with fern leaves and cut down the backbone with a special, old stone knife. He placed short sticks across the body of the salmon to stretch it flat, and roasted it on a split stick above the fire.

"We have to eat it before the sun goes down," Rose said. When the elder finished, she climbed down from the roof and returned with flakes of fish cupped in her palm for them to share. He chewed slowly, pondering the long journey of the fish who made it back to the place of their birth, the ones with the will and the heart, and also the ones who failed, who couldn't finish the task that nature forced upon them to swim thousands of miles to complete.

When the fish was eaten, the villagers danced. Once in a while he'd heard their drums from the fort, but this was the first time he'd seen them celebrate close up. They danced in circles, pounding drums and chanting, shifting from foot to foot, and swirled in great wide arcs with outstretched arms. The men wore conical hats, made partly from human hair, with feathers at the crown. Their robes were made from otter and bear, lynx and marten. Some wore white wool blankets; others beautiful capes of loon and duck feathers that gleamed in the thin sunlight.

Kimo admired their magnificent robes, but truthfully, he was not moved by their dances. He preferred his own. Hawaiian movements with hip, knee, foot and hand were fast and joyous, or else slow and sensuous to a degree that had shocked the haoles. He recalled the last luau he attended in Oahu, where men and women walked barefoot on the warm sand with gifts in their hands of flowers and fruit and fish, and hearts full of aloha. He had tried to explain aloha to Rose — both a greeting and farewell, and how it signified affection, sympathy, kindness, love. Aloha encompassed all that was warm about Hawaiian culture, hospitality, friendship, giving and sharing. It was the essence of Hawaiian life. Then his thoughts returned to the Kwantlen village, and he felt suddenly bereft, under a sky less blue than Hawaii, with a sun less warm, and he was glad of Rose's presence beside him.

The roof gave him a wide view of the villagers' homes. The carved door posts impressed him. He recognized the raven, eagle, salmon, frog, wolf and bear, and Rose patiently explained their meaning for him. The raven created all things, and was the most important being, the trickster who could become alive and make anything happen. The eagle meant power and prestige, and was the symbol of friendship and welcome. The salmon represented good luck, and was the giver of life, offering his body to feed all his earthly brothers. The frog was the voice of the people, symbolizing innocence, stability and communication. The wolf meant family and togetherness. He held special spirit power that men needed to acquire to become great hunters. The bear had strength, power and human-like qualities and people welcomed him as a high-ranking guest. There were others, the owl, the moon, the sun, the orca, the hummingbird, the thunderbird that drew his eye. He didn't see any single standing totems the voyageurs talked of finding in other villages, though, but they could be away from his view. The door posts below were simply designed, sparingly painted, yet they possessed a stark kind of beauty that appealed to him.

When the dancing ceased, Kimo walked with Rose through the village. He didn't fear the Kwantlen as he had before, for they had proven themselves friends of the fort, but many tribes nearby remained a threat. Danger lurked in the forest and round each bend of the river, so he lived by McKay's advice. Never let your guard down, and expect the unexpected, if you want to stay alive till your contract expires. Yet, in spite of the danger the Indians posed, his heart went out to them. The tribes must eventually bow to the more advanced culture taking root in their midst. Much good would come from this, but not without pain and loss. The Hawaiian in him knew that.

He told Rose about the books Annance had given him, and when he saw how this excited her, he thought he'd ask François for some in French for her. He recited a verse or two of Pope, and she liked the musicality of the rhyme, liked that a long story could be told this almost Indian way. She nodded when Kimo quoted Pope's "God and Nature only are the same."

"The Kwantlen have always believed that. Indian gods *are* in nature — in trees and stones and mountains and rivers." Her Catholic father had taught otherwise, of course. "I'm surprised the Pope would say such a thing, though."

Kimo laughed. "Not *the* Pope, Rose. Just a man, Alexander Pope."

"Oh. Then it's just the opinion of an ordinary man?"

"Yes, a thought he wants to share with his readers. That's all. You can take it or leave it."

"I'll leave it, thank you," she said, a little edgy, embarrassed for confusing the two. The sum and total of everything she knew about the head of the Catholic church was that he was white, and lived in Europe. So was the man Pope. How was she to know?

Kimo let the conversation drop and left the village to canoe the Fraser leisurely to Whonnock and back. The natives clustered like bees here and there along both banks. There was an air of expectation, of excitement among them, as they busied themselves preparing for the great spring run.

Next day, the run began in earnest and the entire village took part in harvesting the salmon. Smoke from the village fires drifted clear across the fort. They would repeat this in July and August, with the sockeye run. The fort became as frenzied as the village then and everyone was called to pitch in. Men ran from the wharf carrying fish to other men and women, with Indian helpers, who cut it up. They then ran with the cut fish to the shed, where others waited to salt it. The new cooper, Cromarty, stirred cauldrons of brine all day long. Kimo helped him make barrels to contain the fish, and some days he too, helped make the brine. The sheer quantities of fish astounded him. He was used to plentiful fish in Hawaii, but nothing there could compare with this bounty. Except their colour. In Hawaii, fish were gloriously beautiful.

"Blue and red, pink and yellow, black and green and purple, every colour of the rainbow," he told Rose. "And we even have a fish, the *humuhumu-nukunuku-a-puaa* that grunts like a pig." She had laughed outright at the improbability, not knowing it was true, and he allowed her to laugh without dispute, amused by the sound of her voice.

He visited the village the following two Sundays while the run continued before it tapered off. There appeared to be a division of labour that worked well. Women dried the fish on frames, while the men fished and gathered wood. They used a variety of traps, spears and nets. They built weirs and scooped up the fish with long handled dip nets while the fish piled up against the obstructions. Later, after smoking and drying, they stored it all away in specially woven baskets.

"You could slice this smell and package it!" he said to Moku, when they fell exhausted into their bunks late into the run. The stink of fish and brine permeated everything. Their clothes reeked of it, even after laundering. No matter how hard you scrubbed, the smell persisted. He was glad the run was tapering off. Another day or two, they'd have enough for all their needs, and for export to Hawaii. Moku cut into his thoughts from the other side of their shack.

"Those Indian women sure know how to gut fish. There was a girl helping Mrs. Finlay. Her name's Khatie. She's deft with a knife. I'm meeting her at the gate Sunday afternoon. Thought we'd go walking."

Moku had kept company with several local women this past year. Now he clearly had his eye on another. "Walking," he'd said. He'd done a goodly share of "walking" this past year. Kimo rubbed the koa dolphin at his neck unconsciously. He felt irritable and tired. He didn't approve of Moku jumping from one relationship to another, the way he did. Truth to tell, he pitied the Kanakas who were stuck here, forever renewing contracts with the Company in order to stay with their Indian wives and children. Never to feel the sun of Hawaii again. Never to wade in the surf, feel hot sand under your feet. It was unthinkable. Forming ties here was a trap too many lonely men fell into. He hoped his good friend wouldn't make that mistake. For a mistake it surely was.

The run had no sooner ended than a fur brigade arrived from the interior. You could hear them from Whonnock, miles upriver, firing off their muskets and as they canoed into view, their voices rose above the water loudly singing their boat songs. It was an event to be celebrated, for the Company was experimenting with different routes to the Interior, since they feared being cut off from the Columbia. The journey from Fort Kamloops to Langley was dangerous through the canyon, with its narrow precipitous walls and miles of churning rapids. Yearly brigades could comprise fifty men and four hundred horses, and both men and beasts died on the canyon route. The Company had tried a route through Seton and Anderson Lakes to the Lillooet River, down Harrison Lake into Langley but that didn't work, so now they planned to erect another fort, Yale, further upriver, with a portage at Spuzzum. They were also considering a possible route from Fort Kamloops, through the Coquihalla Mountain Pass to a planned new fort, called Hope.

"Hope," Moku said with a snort, "because you hope what's ahead of you is better than what you left behind!"

Kimo counted twenty canoes in the approaching brigade. Eight men sat in each canoe, two by two, on wooden seats suspended from the thwarts. Every canoe was piled high with furs — otter, beaver and mink pelts. The fort cannon boomed out a welcome for the fleet, and everyone ran to the wharf to meet them.

"Trouble coming fast, *wiki-wiki*." Peopeo said, as the brigaders quickly unloaded their cargo. They were a colourful lot, shouting and strutting about the wharf in moccasins, wearing bright red stocking caps and shirts with shoulder-length yokes, soft collars, long sleeves and soft cuffs. Baggy pants were tied below the knee with coloured woollen garters, in the same pattern as the fringed sashes round their waists. Knives, tobacco pouches, pipes, and fancy carved drinking cups hung from their sashes.

They were small men, well-muscled and without exception bulging with powerful, overdeveloped shoulders. Most were half-French, half-Huron Indians, with a wild look about them. When they finished unloading, they made their way to the steps of the Big House where the Chief Clerk waited to greet them. They were in great good humour, and eagerly drank the rum provided, two ounces for each man.

Peopeo was right, though. The brigade brought trouble, and it came fast. The day after they arrived, two voyageurs brawled over a bottle of rum, and this triggered a rash of fights that continued throughout the men's month-long stay. They couldn't settle a dispute without a knife in their hands. Friction grew daily, within the brigade itself, and between the brigade and the fort workers.

"How do they get away with this?" Kimo asked Peopeo. They wrecked tables and chairs on a whim, usually over someone's head. Property damage escalated dramatically, and you had to mind your feet when you went to work in the morning, dodging around heaps of broken bottles.

"We need them," Peopeo said. "It's that simple."

Kimo wondered why anyone would choose a life so cruel. Men died on the fur trails. Horses, by the dozen, toppled to their deaths down steep mountainsides. Men toiled from dawn to dusk paddling rivers and wild rapids, toting heavy goods over long portages and dangerous precipices. Some even threw themselves off cliffs, out of despair and desperation. They endured dreadful hardship and brutality, and you had to admire their strength and courage. If any man had the right to boast, it was a brigade man. Those who survived were free spirits who relished the unfettered life and the challenge of battling the wilderness. But it was hard to swallow the havoc they created at the fort. The men's propensity to strut like peacocks didn't help, and the women grew indignant having to dodge their amorous advances.

"No man worth his salt would tart himself up wi' all these feathers and fancy gee-gaws," McKay declared with disapproval. It crossed Kimo's mind the Scots also produced their share of fancy trappings on occasion, such as kilts and bagpipes, but he wisely refrained from saying so. He decided to go about his business and turn a blind eye to offensive situations when they arose. Till one night, when he could not.

Rose was to meet him at the riverbank. When he arrived, he found her under assault, screaming, pummeling the chest of a drunken voyageur. He was nuzzling Rose's neck, forcing her backward with his powerful arms, when Kimo hauled him to his feet with one yank of his big fist. He hoisted the man into the air by his red waist sash.

"Get off her, *cochon!*"

The man was moon-faced, dark and swarthy, with small pinhole eyes and he reeked of rum. He wriggled free, dropped to bent knees and drew a knife. Kimo ducked the moment he saw it flash in the sunlight, but the blade sliced him on his chin, just below the jawline on the left side of his face. It was swift, sudden and unexpected. He felt the blood trickle from his lower lip then he reacted with a furious one-two punch to the man's stomach that left the stunned voyageur doubled up, gasping for breath in the shallows. He threw the man's knife far into the river.

Rose had stumbled backwards when Kimo grabbed the voyageur, and landed by the water's edge. Shaken, she regained her feet. Kimo reached for her hand.

"Are you all right?"

"Yes." She touched his cheek. "You're bleeding! Come home with me, and I'll clean that cut, Kimo." He pushed her canoe into the fast flowing water, jumped in and paddled across to the village. Rose and her mother patiently cleaned his wound. It was a shallow cut, long but not deep, so would heal quickly. Watching them side by side, he saw how much they resembled each other, though Lawi'qum was small and plump where Rose was slender. Her parents treated him with cool respect, but Kimo knew they did not approve. Neetlum in particular. He had discussed her future with several braves but Rose had resisted his attempts to arrange her life. He had not pushed too far. She was not his child, but for his wife's sake, he wished to see her settled. But not, if he could help it, with a Kanaka, who was of such low status at the fort. This much Kimo had figured out.

The rest, he learned from Huntas. In the early days of white contact, intermarriage seemed a good thing. Now, it was no longer so, for the white men could go away, leaving their women, passing them along to other men. Some women could thus be prostituted, passed from one man to the next, till they grew old and unwanted. Keeping company with the big Kanaka, in Neetlum's view, was folly. He'd made that clear to Rose. Kimo knew this. So, visits to her house had been avoided. Till now, when he vowed to see her safely home to the village as long as the brigade stayed at the fort.

He remained alert around the brigaders, but even so, days later he landed in the river while seeing Rose off in her canoe. He had just stepped back after untying her rope when someone struck him from behind with a heavy plank board. He had been moving at the time, but it caught and smacked the side of his head enough to drop him to his knees. By the time he rose, stumbling in the shallows, Rose had jumped from her canoe and whacked the assailant right and left with her yew paddle.

"Coward!"

As the man took off, Rose and Kimo collapsed laughing with relief, onto the beach. He rubbed his head, found a swelling already the size of an egg. Rose had delivered at least as good a bump to the voyageur.

"You swing a good paddle, Rose Fanon."

"And don't you forget it, Kanaka!"

He laughed then. She could be sassy as a goose at times.

With the arrival of the brigade's furs, the store had become the busiest corner of the fort, packing the furs for shipping, and selling goods to the men going back up river, though they didn't buy much. They couldn't exceed a ninety pound bale; otherwise the packhorses left behind upriver while the voyageurs paddled downriver would be overloaded. Rose laughed at this.

"They limit the size to accommodate the *horses*? What about the poor men?"

The regulation load for men was two pieces, or 180 pounds, for a regular portage, but on occasion if a man fell sick or a horse died, some carried three 90 pound bales. Kimo and Moku helped at the store during this busy period, baling and packaging trade goods. The furs had been cleaned and dried, then pressed and flattened for packing when they received them. The two men then baled them, tied them tight and made sure they weighed exactly ninety pounds, before sprinkling them with tobacco juice for insect repellent. Lastly, they wrapped large low quality bearskins around them. They'd be shipped south to Fort Vancouver, then sent to London, England.

Rose, and the women at the fort, sighed with relief when the brigade men left.

"Never mind," Kimo said. He'd been talking with Peopeo. "One of these days, they'll stop coming altogether." She could not foresee such a turn of events.

"Food will soon be more important than fur. We need it to supply the other forts, and for export. We're shipping out tons of salmon now. Look at the cattle we're raising. Butter production is up. We have acres of new fields under cultivation. It's just a matter of time."

Was the fort really moving that way? In the past months, she'd seen the herds and crops expand on the large prairie seven miles south. The fort *was* thriving, and looked rather splendid in its new location, commanding a view up and down the river. Mr. Yale appeared happy with his new wife and baby Aurelia, and a second child was expected soon. There had been no further disasters at the fort since the fire months ago. People ate better. Apart from salmon, they ate salt pork from their piggery and beef from their cattle. So when Kimo announced an addition to the fort to supplement the fort's larder, Rose was incredulous. "A house for *what?*"

"Pigeons. We're going to breed them. Like chickens. They're a treat when baked into pies, so we're building something to house them at each side of the bastions."

"And when will you finish the accommodation for the people? Before or after your pigeon palace?"

"Oh, that's done. Finished. *Pau.* Come, I'll show you." The new family quarters were comfortable but small (fifteen by twenty feet), each with its own fireplace, and separate from the others. Indeed, with the new personnel, the fort fairly bustled. The store at the wharf was busier than ever, trading in wire, blankets, tools, guns, tobacco and other goods. The natives used collar wire from the store for making snares and women traded for vermilion, their favourite cosmetic. The bright red pigment of mercuric sulphide was in high demand as a paint also. Kimo thought the Company lucky to have the genial Mr. Allard managing their trade. Rose said the Indians thought so too, for they'd had traders who treated them with contempt before, but Allard never did. He was scrupulously fair, an excellent interpreter who spoke several languages. He hired a few Indians to work at the fort, carrying wood and running errands, and paid them with potatoes, a little vermilion and beads from the store.

The commercial relationship between the two races brought increasing prosperity to the Indians, but Rose laughed at any hint the Indians were servile to the traders in any way, for the Sto:lo still maintained their traditional culture and economy.

"From the beginning, you needed us more than we needed you," she reminded him. "And if it weren't for Mr. Allard, you wouldn't trade half so well as you do!" He had to agree. She surprised him sometimes, with her perceptions.

Life at the fort remained structured. Survival demanded it. Work was hard, from six o'clock in the morning to six in the evening for all employees. Kimo had discovered the Company's wage scale, and supposed it was determined by skin colour. Hawaiians earned from seventeen to twenty pounds a year, whites thirty to fifty pounds. He had no idea what Indian employees were paid, for he'd never asked Rose, but he assumed much less than the Hawaiians. Saturday afternoons, Company rules decreed they must scrub and tidy their living quarters. They had rules for everything. At noon on Saturdays, each received four ounces of rum, and was allowed to buy a pint apiece for Saturday night's party. Kimo didn't always drink, and bartered his rations on occasion for something else. Last month he'd acquired a fine muslin shirt.

He and Moku were scrubbing their quarters as usual on Saturdays, when Moku sat down, fidgeting with the scrub brush in his fist, passing it from one hand to the other, clearly agitated. His big open face grew serious then he drew a long breath.

"I'm going to get married, Kimo. I want to settle down with Khatie."

Dismay swamped Kimo. It wasn't that he didn't like Khatie. He did, and he understood Moku's loneliness but it was folly to plunge into marriage here in this place. Moku was twenty-four, two years older than he was. Old enough to make up his own mind. He had no right to say anything, but couldn't contain himself.

"Aw, Moku! Have you gone *lolo?* We're more than halfway through our contract! You've only been seeing her a few months. Is there a reason?"

"Reason enough. I love her."

"I mean, is she in *pilikia?*" Hawaiian women used herbs to pre-

169

vent pregnancy. He didn't know if Indian women did the same.

"No, she's not in trouble, as far as I know."

"As far as you know? What kind of an answer is that? What will you do come renewal time? You better think about that!"

"I have thought about it, Kimo. Look, all the reasons we left Hawaii — they're still there. We go back, life will still be for the alii. For the rest of us, it's a poor existence, eking out a living working the fields or the docks. Think about it. In time a man could set himself up here and make a living from the land. With hard work and a good wife, he could have a decent life. Could you do as well in Honolulu? How far will your wages go when you go back?"

Kimo remained silent.

"You don't approve," Moku accused.

"You didn't ask for my approval."

"And you're not offering it, are you? What kind of aikane are you?" Moku rose and left the room. His anger seemed to linger and vibrate in space, disturbing Kimo. It was the first real disagreement they'd had, and he felt uneasy. Moku was salt of the earth but he ran at the world full throttle, ignoring obstacles. He paid no heed to caution, particularly when it was needed. But truth to tell, it was one of the things he liked best about Moku, his wholeheartedness, that made him sometimes incapable of being prudent.

He reached for the koa dolphin at his neck, and rubbed it thoughtfully. He'd been right to speak up. He had to look out for his aikane, if his best friend couldn't look out for himself. This would pass. Moku would return to Hawaii, he felt sure. He'd just need time to change his mind, that's all.

He rose and went outside but Moku had already disappeared. He sat on the hut's wooden steps and let his mind drift. Instead of the shack's cold cedar step, he was transported to the warm ground of Oahu, squatting in the shade of the ancient hau tree, big as a house, on the beach, where women with golden flesh wearing leis danced the hula. Beyond the beach, through the fringe of coconut palms, the ocean shushed up the sand, spewing white foam, and beyond the reef with its colours of jade and emerald and turquoise, the blue sea grew bluer as it reached the horizon. He heard the sounds of music, soft voices singing, dissolving into a love song, and from beneath the palms, laughter. In his imaginings, there was no vexing wind, just the gentlest breeze, long sighs. He walked through the monkey pods, through the bananas and mangoes growing wild, and when he reached the wide-spreading, flame-red poinciana, he felt heat from the sun warming his skin.

Then he shivered, and returned to the present. What did Rose call the sun here? *Snookum.* There was little snookum in this place today, only enough that when he opened the door, thin shafts of light sliced through and landed on the dusty, uneven wood floor. He entered the shack, looking for a warm shirt to throw over his shoulders to ward off the chill. When he drew the garment from his drawer, the eagle feather he'd picked up last year fell and drifted to the floor. The floor needed sweeping, scrunching as it did with blown dirt, as if someone had spilled a bag of salt. He picked the feather up and dusted it off, intending to put it back in the drawer, but instead he held it, turning it round and around in his hand slowly. Once again he sensed it meant *something.* He just didn't know what. As he returned it to the drawer, the door opened. He turned, expecting Moku, but it was Pali in the doorway.

"I was at the Big House when the Express came in, Kimo. There's a letter for you. The clerk's holding it."

"Finally," he said, starting for the door. He flew to the Big House, where the clerk was maddeningly slow to retrieve his letter. As the man pushed it across his desk, Kimo stepped back, feeling a hammer blow to the chest. Fear, intuition, the gods, he had no idea where the knowing came from, that something dark had come to greet him. His fingertips touched the paper and felt as if they'd touched hot coals. He stared down at the envelope, passing it gingerly from hand to hand before letting it sit on his open palm. Finally he closed his shaking fingers around it. He moved outside, down the steps before he opened it in the trapezoid of sunshine that lit up the near corner of the compound.

Dear Kimo,

Aloha! I write for your mother, Kalama. She and Pikoi are well, but she sends you sad news.

Auwé! Your kupuna, Keaka, has died. It came not from sickness, but from old age. He grew tired and slept often through the days till one day he fell asleep altogether. They talked of mutilation in his honour, but he forbade this months ago, saying it was no longer proper. Also, losing his teeth gave him much trouble in the end, sucking his food.

I hoped for a Christian burial, but that would have displeased him so he was buried by his sons and grandsons singing melés in the old way, beneath the kamani tree by the falls.

Oolea sends good wishes. He has a son. His name is Kapahei, a lusty boy with feet the size of a banana leaf. Your mother is happy, Kimo, believe this. Pikoi has planted a garden behind their shack and tends it every day and they have food enough to share.

We miss you. God keep you in his care, and Aloha.

Hopoo.

Moku stood in the compound, but Kimo passed him by, eyes glazed and wide like a mutant owl. He stared at the horizon then broke into a slow trot. He changed pace, picked up speed suddenly and ran, black hair flying, straight through the fort's heavy wooden gates down the path to the river. Moku caught up with him, squatting near the water's edge in the shadow of an old willow, chanting to himself. Moku eased himself down and sat cross-legged in the dust beside him.

"Bad news, Kimo?"

"My kupuna, who raised me, has died."

"Auwé! What happened?"

"Old age. Months ago." He renewed his chant. Moku sat beside him and folded himself into a hunched, silent ball. Kimo remembered the chants the old man had taught him, and these carried him now away from the green Pacific Northwest back to golden Owhyhee, to rejoin his ancestors. He called up his father and his grandfather, reliving their lives together. He recalled his birth, his childhood, his youth, his manhood. He smelled again the glorious white jasmine and fragrant plumeria in his mother's sweet garden. He felt himself climb the coconut palm beside Keaka's hut, whacking the ripe nuts off with his machete, hearing them fall with a thunk on the lanai. He heard the roar of surf in his ears, the sound of voices singing, but when he opened his eyes, it was the Fraser he saw, not the Pacific; a willow he sat beneath, not a palm; and it was cold and gray, not warm and sunny. None of that mattered, except for the regret he felt for not being there when the old man died.

When at last he rose, he reached his long powerful arms to the sky and with the tips of his brown fingers, threw Keaka's name lightly on the wind. "Aloha, Kupuna."

"Time to go home, aikane." Moku put his arm around his shoulder.

When they returned to their shack, the Kanakas poured him a cup of rum and he drank it gratefully. And another. And drinking the rum, he understood what he'd never understood before about the death custom of cutting off a finger, poking out an eye, or breaking teeth. It was like losing a piece of yourself when you lost someone you loved.

When sleep did at last come, he dreamed he floated across the world's seas in the grandest of ships, clouds and waves transporting him from one continent to another till he arrived home on Oahu. From the far Koolau Mountains, the trade wind drifted down in wisps to Honolulu, gently swaying the banana leaves and ruffling the palms. Air, balmy with the scent of ginger lily, fluttered through the lacy algaroba trees as men and women reclined on the beach beside the outrigger canoes.

They were all from his ohana, all faces he knew, even the old uncle who made a living diving for octopus, and Keaka, alive again, regaling them with tales of Maui's brave deeds — Maui, great demigod of Polynesia, who fished up the land from the depths of the sea with hooks tied to heaven, who raised the sky under which men had previously crawled because there was no room to stand, who made the sun stand still by snaring its legs and making it promise to cross the sky more slowly.

Kimo called out to them, but they paid no heed, not even Lili, garlanded and bedecked with flowers, working on a half-made hala lei, or fat Oolea, sitting cross-legged in the shade polishing a calabash made of sandalwood. Alarmed, Kimo stayed aside, on the edge of their life looking on as the sun blazed down, not knowing he was asleep, yet knowing. The perfumed air grew heavier. The monkey pods drooped, folding their leaves in the late afternoon heat, as surfers, black specks on the horizon, crossed the lagoon. The fragrant scents of Hawaii, of breadfruit and hibiscus, and plumeria in bloom, wafted on the warm breeze then merged in his dream with the smells of Fort Langley, of salmon curing, smoke curling up in spirals above the salmon sheds, of wet cedar boughs, reeking of the scents of the forest, of cut pine, and the sweet smell of newly sawn wood. Wood for building coffins. The Indians buried their dead in boxes and tied them high in the trees for protection from animals, but his family had wrapped Keaka in tapa, dug a hole beneath the kamani tree, and laid him where he could hear the rushing waters of the falls. In his half-sleep, he smiled, for his kupuna had taken a step into the future after all, by ensuring no one would break their teeth for him.

His kupuna had died, and something died with him. Old Hawaii had been kept alive in the memories of old ones like Keaka. Soon, they would all be gone, and no one living would remember life before the haoles. He had been the family's link to the old days, the old ways. Now, that link was broken. The ohana would never be the same. Life would never be the same. He felt a searing sense of loss. A door had closed forever. *Pau.*

chapter eleven

Kimo woke at dawn. He rose, reaching for his clothes. His shirt threw a healthy reek from the sweat of his week's work, but it was two days to washday, so he had no choice but to shrug it over his shoulders, nose twitching. Six of them shared the room now — five it would be, after Moku moved his gear across the river. It was small, enough to contain a table, chairs, a tiny cupboard and their rope beds. He would have to cut some hemlock branches soon to re-stuff his pallet, for it was so flat and uncomfortably thin from leaking contents, that the rope strands had begun to rub at night.

His thoughts returned again to Oahu and his grandfather. Keaka always said men died from the same thing in the end, lack of breath, and Kimo reckoned that was true. His thoughts shifted to his mother and Pikoi, and his ohana. He prayed to Amakua, his family god and to Kane, the giver of life, and to the Christian God as well, to keep them safe. One day he'd sing a proper auwé for Keaka. It would pain him to do it here though, for the gods might not hear it in this place, so far from home. He had not heard their voices in a long time. That didn't distress him, but left him sad and puzzled, as if he'd misplaced something that he shouldn't have, and he was left wondering if he'd ever find it again.

The Kanakas in his hut all gave him death gifts, little tokens from their meagre possessions — a *tiki,* a wad of tobacco, a piece of jerky, some shells. They accompanied him to the river, faced west, and threw their gifts into the water, chanting a low melé, and he was grateful for their support. Then he went to work at the cooperage, making kegs, but all day spoke to no one. He'd see Rose later, and he'd be ready to talk by then. Truthfully, she had become the bright light in his life.

Rose paddled to the fort every morning to begin work at six o'clock. Whatever she'd been seeking at the fort remained elusive. The women at the fort were like women anywhere, some kind, others less so. She discovered there was a hierarchy among the wives. White wives ranked first then native wives of white men. These wives lived in the fort. Native wives of voyageurs, and women married to Kanakas lived outside the fort. Alas, there was no escaping rank. Rose never lost her sense of being outcast. In the village, she remained half-white. At the fort, she was half-Indian. But she waited patiently for the unknown to occur, sensing somehow she was meant to.

Saturdays were washdays. Her back ached with the heavy laundering but she stifled her discomfort and did what needed to be done with as much compliance as she could muster. The entire day was taken up scrubbing men's soiled work clothes. She prayed for good weather to hang them out to dry; otherwise the wet things stretched themselves out on wooden frames indoors, making her nostrils pinch with the smell of damp woollens. The soap stank. The large yellow slabs contained so much lye, you could just about scrape hides with them.

Tuesdays she pressed clothes all day, using the heavy triangular sad irons Mrs. Finlay brought from Scotland. She'd heat them on the stove in relays, always having one ready, piping hot, gingerly lifting it with a wad of cloth wrapped around its handle to prevent her fingers from burning. It never quite worked though and she always had one finger or another wearing a blister. Other days she helped in the creamery and on occasion, was called on to tend the women's babies.

Mrs. Cameron, a recent arrival with her husband, took Rose under her wing. The woman was small and round, with fair hair and blue eyes, a back straight as a ramrod and she spoke with a musical lilt. Rose wondered why the Scots spoke English and never conversed in their own tongue, as did the other non-English people at the fort. She learned they were a conquered people, whose Highland customs, dress and language had been banned by the English.

Kimo, mending a stool at the time, overheard their conversation and thought Hawaii fortunate to be so distant from England. What luck the English had no troops with them to enforce such a cruel law in the Islands. Now he understood those proud Scots in the pay of the Company. Loss made them hard as steel. But gave them deep compassion.

"Do you ever wish you hadn't come?" he asked the woman, and Rose eyed him sideways.

"I'd lie if I said I didn't. But I've a good man, a bonny bairn, a roof over my head. I've no regrets. But if I did, what could I do about it? No good looking back if you're building a future."

He liked the little woman, with her down-to-earth, Scots tweed sensibility. He left them churning butter and his thoughts shifted to Moku. He'd packed his gear and paddled across the river to live with Peopeo, Como and the other Hawaiians in the village. A week later, he'd signed his marriage contract with Khatie. Como had stood witness for him. Kimo was disappointed that Moku hadn't asked him, but knew it was his own fault.

"I didn't think he'd go through with it!"

"Why wouldn't he?" Rose said, when he told her. "It's not Moku who's taking the risk here. It's Khatie. He can go home when he wants and leave her here with their children. The Company keeps promising to bring in an ordained minister to solemnize vows, to make marriage proper in the sight of God. They say he'll arrive soon, but even so, how does that guarantee a man will stay? Besides, Moku and Khatie don't know the Christian God, so why should a Kwantlen and a Kanaka need a priest to proclaim them legally married anyway?"

Rose had a point, but he said nothing. The die was cast. Another Hawaiian would not return at the end of his contract. Of this contract, anyway.

A celebration was held at the village after the ceremony, and in the evening everyone attended the party across the river at Kanaka Creek. Kimo made the crossing as dusk was falling. Sounds of merrymaking drifted across the river on the breeze, and the lights from the torches set into the beach flickered like stars, reflecting in the rippling water. He smelled and heard the celebration long before he beached the canoe on the pebbled shore, with smoke rising from the long deep *imu*, the fire pit dug into the shale, pork sizzling, potatoes baking in the ashes, and the smoky scent of burning sweetgrass.

Long planks lay on the ground covered with mats and a variety of food bowls. It was neither hot nor sunny, yet a luau of sorts had materialized on the banks of the Fraser, reminding Kimo sharply of

home. The fort's clerks all paid courtesy calls, and most of the voyageurs attended along with the Kanakas, except for Kimo. But he too
had come, finally.

He made his way up the sloping bank and Moku rose to his feet.
Kimo reached inside the sack slung across his shoulder, and drew
out a long open-ended lei made with wild aromatic green ferns. Had
this been Hawaii, it would have been of maile leaves. It was beauti-
fully wrought, intricately pleated, and had taken hours of work. He
placed it around Moku's neck, draped it so the open ends fell in
graceful lines from each shoulder, then hugged him. The two men
stood, arms about each other, speaking in Hawaiian for many minutes.

Kimo turned to Khatie and drew from his sack a circle of flowers
of wild roses, hawthorn and light ferns. He placed the lei around her
neck, kissed her, and blessed her in Hawaiian. Khatie was smaller
than Rose. When she smiled, her cheeks plumped out and two dim-
ples appeared so unexpectedly, it was hard not to smile. No wonder
Moku was charmed. Khatie returned his embrace and as he turned
to move away, he caught sight of Rose beside the fire pit with the
cook who'd roasted the dog at the Cowlitz.

"I sure hope that's pig," he said, nodding at the animal cooking on
the spit, and the cook laughed.

"I set a place for you," Rose said.

"I wasn't going to come."

"I knew you would. Pali told Peopeo you were working on their leis
and a fine cedar box . . ." Nothing could be kept secret at the fort.

The feasting began and the night air reverberated with music and
dancing. The Kanakas chanted a wedding melé for the couple and
rose to dance the hula. On bent knees, they gyrated to the pounding
drums and sang lustily and surprisingly well in unison, and in tune.
Kimo danced also, the Hawaiian way, openly suggestive in front of

Rose, who lowered her eyes at times, making him laugh. Later, as rum was passed around, they found a willow near the beach to sit against and talk.

He'd drunk too much, something he'd avoided since the night he'd overindulged with Billings' stolen keg. The rum loosened his lips and he talked about returning to Hawaii to plant taro, to sit on the beach and listen to the waves rolling in on air sweet as perfume, and watch the Hawaiian sun roost on the brim of the horizon in a brilliant display of orange and violet, peach and purple.

He'd been emphasizing his intention to return to Oahu at the end of his contract so many times lately. Hawaii sounded so beautiful. She couldn't blame him.

"How could you have left all that in the first place?"

"It isn't always beautiful, Rose, not for ordinary people. Ugly things are happening in Hawaii, just like here, with men fighting for power and for territory."

She'd never been far from home, but knew how difficult she would find living alone in a new land a world away, with strange people and customs. She understood his longing to return. She didn't like it, but she understood it.

"It seemed such a great adventure at the beginning. Mind you, a month at sea soon changed my thinking." She knew about his sea voyage, about life on board ship and of the man Collins, clanking his wretched chains across the *Thomasina's* deck. She didn't know he'd nearly died. The rum propelled him to tell her now.

"If it hadn't been for Moku, I might not have made it," he said, shocking her. He'd never mentioned sickness before. Even now he hesitated, as if it were something to be ashamed of. He'd collapsed while mending sails with Billings, falling suddenly with a loud thump, spread-eagled across the deck. His chest felt as if it were being squeezed under a great boulder. He'd sweated and shivered as the deck spun giddily around his head and a dreadful nausea overwhelmed him. Moku had carried him below, where the ship's surgeon, a tall no-nonsense Cornishman, ordered him isolated, moved to a bunk away from the crew's hammocks.

"Billings said I got sick on purpose," he laughed now, "because only officers rated bunks." A rash of angry red spots had appeared across his neck, armpits and groin and flared over the back of his body. His glands swelled and his left ear throbbed painfully. He slipped out of consciousness and from some place where his mind detached itself from his body, he decided the red spots that killed his father had come to claim him too. Whispers reached him from a long way off.

"Not measles. Maybe scarlet fever." Then after a paroxysm of coughing tore at his lungs making him whoop, "maybe even whooping cough." Fearing convulsions, they decided to leech him. Moku had never heard of such a thing.

"They can help," Billings assured him. "They drain off the excess blood with their sharp little teeth and jaws, their saliva numbs the wound, dilates the blood vessels and stops the blood from clotting. It may be the only chance he's got."

Kimo opened his eyes and saw the surgeon reappearing with a glass jar with some brackish water inside, and a few wilted green leaves. Black slug-like leeches clung to the inside walls. The surgeon picked two fat ones about four inches long from the jar and placed them on the skin at Kimo's temples. He tore at them frantically, peeling them off and throwing the offensive things on the floor.

"Aolé!" The foul-looking slugs disgusted him. He retched violently in the metal basin that Moku deftly managed to scoop beneath his chin in time.

"You won't feel a thing," the surgeon coaxed, as a thin trickle of red blood oozed slowly from the tiny puncture wounds the leeches had made on Kimo's broad temple before he ripped them off.

"No!" His throat felt choked with sausage, closed up, so that he could barely find breath to raise a whisper. He clutched at Moku's shirt, and the big man's fist closed reassuringly over his fingers. Moku conferred with the surgeon. His size alone intimidated most men, whatever their rank, but the doctor had treated men from the South Seas before, and knew not to discount the power of their beliefs. The leeches were returned to their jar. Kimo, reassured, sank into an exhausted stupor. He wanted to speak but his tongue felt nailed to the roof of his mouth. Billings leaned his pock-marked, potato-white face over Kimo's bunk.

"Kanaka, if you won't have the leeching, you must drink all you can, even if it makes you sick. You need to keep up your strength, or you'll end up food for the fishes, understand?" Kimo heard, miles away, from an uncaring distance.

He tried to stay awake, but couldn't, and swam in and out of consciousness, dreaming dreams within dreams, where time stretched then shrank, fusing and confusing future with past. All the people he loved encircled him, tossing over his shoulders the wide fishing net used for their family *hukilaus*, hauling him in like a fish off the reef, tugging at him in his dream, his mother, Pikoi, Keaka, Lili, Hopoo and others, till finally he fell exhausted onto the safe, sandy shore and slept deeply at last, thanks to the laudanum the ship's surgeon had mixed in his boiled drinking water.

He woke to Billings hovering over him like some expectant father, and to Moku who had forced boiled water down his dry throat every few hours for two whole days. The cook killed a bird from the clucking hens penned on deck, to cheers from the entire crew, and Moku teaspooned drops of precious warm chicken broth down Kimo's parched throat. He was able to swallow the mushy brew without the urge to send it scudding back across his blankets, and his eyes no longer burned like firepits drilled into his skull. When he realized where he was and why he was there, he smiled to himself. No one need break any teeth on his account just yet. He'd recovered quickly, walking the decks, breathing great lungfuls of clean, sweet air.

"And Moku, when you were sick, spoon-fed you?" Rose spoke softly in his ear, drawing him back to the present. Her dark eyes chastised him. "How could you not support him in this?"

"He's making a big mistake."

"You're sure that's what he's doing?"

"Yes."

She looked at him pensively. "Does his family in Hawaii know?"

"He doesn't write."

"You do. Did you offer to write for him?"

He hadn't. It dawned on him only then that Moku would probably have asked him if he hadn't been so opposed to the marriage. He'd finally written home himself, thanking Hopoo for his letter with the sad news of Keaka's death. His reply had gone by the Express to Fort Vancouver to await the next ship to Hawaii.

He wondered if Hopoo would continue to write on his mother's behalf. He'd hoped Oolea would write, but he was grateful to hear from Hopoo. He was shrewd for a man of the Christian faith, and a better judge of character than others he knew. If Hopoo said his mother was happy with Pikoi, it would be so. And Kimo was glad of it. He kept the letter under his mattress and read and re-read it.

He suddenly realized that neither he nor Rose had spoken for several minutes, that she had fallen silent. It occurred to him that it didn't matter, for there was now a language between them that was theirs alone, one that would take a lifetime to develop between other couples, if it ever did. It was a subtle thing, indirect and wordless. It was in a look, in the closing of eyes, and even in silence. It was a language belonging to them, different from others, of signs and silences shared. Now, that silence spoke clearly across the space between them, unsettling him strangely.

"Is something wrong, Rose?"

She turned to look at him, with an expression he couldn't read, and hesitated. He admired that in a woman. No hasty rhetoric. Words seldom fell from her lips before she thought them through.

"We have to talk, Kimo. I meant to before, only I didn't want to deal with it. But now it's time." She drew her breath, and released it slowly. "I think we should stop seeing each other." She spoke flatly, suppressing emotion, eyes cast down, shuttered, to avoid his, even while enunciating each word clearly, crisply so there was no chance he'd misunderstand. Still, he thought he'd heard wrong.

"Stop seeing each other?"

"You heard me." She looked him straight in the eye, challenging him.

"Why?"

"Because if you are going away, it would be better to make the break now."

It was a quiet still evening. The silt of the evening sun drifted through the draping willow boughs that overhung the edge of the river. She spoke without recrimination. No edgy judgement entered her tone. Just acceptance. She just sat looking at him, waiting patiently for him to speak. When he did, words poured out of him, heavy with disbelief, and slightly slurred from the rum.

"And lose the next few months together? That doesn't make sense. Has this got something to do with Moku and Khatie?"

She shook her head, but he didn't believe her. Of course it did. She was playing poker but he wouldn't let her win. He was going back to Hawaii. His mind was made up.

"We've been seeing each other for a long time, but if you go back, we are going nowhere." Her voice trailed away.

He stared at her set face. If he'd met her in Hawaii, things would be different. They wouldn't be living this unnatural missionary existence.

"You said all along you'd never be a country wife."

That was true. She'd never take the gamble that Khatie took today. She didn't want a man who would pack his bags and wave goodbye, like so many did, uttering the "Here's your new husband — he'll take care of you" speech. He'd never asked her, though, never tried to persuade her, which pained her too. In spite of her defences, he had become a large part of her life. There had been times when she'd weakened, when he might have talked her into a living arrangement, but any hope she had of him staying was always too slender. And today, he'd made his intentions plain all over again, with every word he'd spoken so lovingly about Hawaii. He was going home.

"You knew I was leaving when my three years were up. I made that clear from the beginning. What do you want from me, Rose?"

"Rien! Nothing!" She lapsed into French when she was angry. If he wouldn't voluntarily stay, she wouldn't ask him. "I won't go on like this, waiting for the axe to fall. It would be easier and cleaner to do it now, swiftly." She made a rapid slashing gesture across her throat with her small wrist, suddenly appearing more Indian than white. She looked so unhappy, his rising anger evaporated.

"Look, let's go for a paddle. Away from here, where we can think straight."

"No. We should have faced this sooner, Kimo."

He'd ingested a good deal of rum, enough to fog his brain, but still he knew she was right. Logically a swift clean break would be easier than a slow leave-taking that would drag out painfully. He should have thought of it first. Hell, he had. Many times, but he'd dismissed the thought. Now he felt angry, tied in a knot of guilt and confusion.

He was at a loss for words. Things he should have said lay silent on his tongue. Thoughts scattered unspoken, like tiny fragments of shattered glass. Didn't she appreciate how difficult their situation had been for him? Working to exhaustion point had been his salvation. He did care, enough not to leave her in a sorry state when he went back to Oahu. There had been many nights when he'd wished otherwise, when he'd thrown himself into the cold Fraser to bathe, or found an axe to chop wood. But he'd assiduously avoided trapping himself, for that's how he thought of it. He planned to leave this place with no regrets, no guilty conscience. One of the upright iron men of the fort.

Rose had ruined things now. He felt a sense of dislocation, as if he were losing his bearings. He didn't want her to corral him, halter him. Then it would only be a matter of time before he was reined in and broken to harness, like Moku, tamed and saddled with a wife. But he would not be trapped in this place, in this Langley, in a web, no matter how fine the weave, or the weaver.

"What do you want, Rose? That we should just walk away and not see each other again?"

"You will be the one walking away, Kimo. Now or later, it amounts to the same thing." She'd waited so long for him to say he'd stay. Moku had promised Khatie months ago that he wouldn't leave and Rose had hoped that Kimo would rethink his plans too. But he hadn't. And wouldn't. He couldn't have made that more plain. She would have no part in his future.

Today's wedding festivities had driven the spike home, and set a fearful discontent vibrating within. A sense of injury enveloped her and she felt dislocated. She didn't like the rush of resentment sluicing through her, but there was no silencing the cry of her discontent.

"You do what you have to do, Kimo, but I must too. Tonight, we say goodbye." She didn't recognize her own voice, it sounded so compressed. Still, she must do this. It could not be prevented.

"Rose, wait!" He believed he could coax her, make her change her mind. He couldn't comprehend her being so stubborn. It was so unlike her. She sat there proud as royalty, a cold queen, distant and aloof — so damned *Indian,* he thought angrily! Deep in his bones, a slow burn took hold. He wanted to shake the life out of her. "Why throw away these last months together?"

"Precisely because there will be nothing afterwards." She spoke quietly to him, as if he were a child who didn't comprehend the situation. The odd thought came to him that Mrs. Cameron had done her job well. Rose rolled the "r" the Scottish way, precisely the way the little Scottish woman would have said it.

She thought the tension in her would cut off her air supply. He would never know what it cost her to speak this way. Words stuck in her throat, but she pulled them out, and threw them down, shards at his feet.

"It will be easier if we make the cut swift and clean."

"Like you would for some wild animal?" he asked cruelly, the rum giving him voice. He couldn't prevent anger igniting in his chest. That it should end like this! He rose, unsteadily, hands at his sides balling into fists. She rose and faced him and he moved towards her. She could smell the rum on his breath, but didn't pull away and remained rigid within his bear-like hug till he could no longer stay silent.

"Don't do this, Rose!" His words vibrated along her nerve endings. She wanted to take back all she'd said, but it needed saying, and he'd given her his answer. Now she gave him hers.

"Walk away, Kimo."

"We could have so much longer together." He tried to coax her and rubbed her collarbone.

"No. Go now, Kimo. Please. Just go." She shrugged her shoulders, and he dropped his calloused hands. Both stepped away, shrinking from each other like solitary cedars in the forest exposed to the drying wind.

He watched tears gather beneath her dark eyelashes. Her eyes were enormous, luminous now. He was suddenly shattered. Feelings he never knew existed swamped him. He needed to fight her now. She had taken him outside his experience. He wanted to dry her tears but he knew if he did, he would lose command of himself. For someone so positively certain of his destiny since he arrived here, this was a devastating realization.

He didn't move, so she did, turning and walking away from him quickly, without looking back, picking her way one small moccasined foot in front of the other. He stood for several minutes staring at her straight back, then he too, turned away. He found his canoe and jumped in, then smacked the cold water angrily with each dip of the paddle as he stroked fiercely across the river back to the fort.

A week passed and Kimo did not see Rose at the fort. His decision to leave remained firm. This was what he had always wanted. Yet he felt miserable. He'd come to know many of the Indian women around the fort. Several had caught his attention, and from time to time their eyes had met. He wasn't blind to such interest when it presented itself before him, and he knew he could find satisfaction quickly if he chose to pursue it, and to hell with Rose Fanon. But she filled his mind more than he had intended and her absence became like a rusty blade picking at his heart.

Another week passed and still he had not seen her. Four days later, as dusk descended, he was trekking from the fields to his quarters when he was stopped abruptly by the fort's water carrier.

"Owhyhee! There's trouble on the Semiahmoo Trail."

"I heard." There had been a skirmish early in the week, when the Langley Express returned from the Cowlitz. Indians had raided their campsite during the night, yet the sentry had heard nothing. The

Company was sending a party south to locate them and retrieve their stolen property.

Huntas stuck his clay pipe between his teeth, and without another word turned on his bowed legs and headed for the well. Dust feathered up from the earth of the compound as he shuffled along in his moccasins, leaving a trail in his wake like a dying comet. Kimo stared after him, sensing he'd been challenged in some way he couldn't define, then he found himself walking the path to the creamery. He hesitated briefly, then knocked on the door sharply.

"Hello, Kimo." Mrs. Finlay greeted him warmly, wiping her hands on the long cotton bib apron that reached almost to her toes. He'd expected Rose, and swallowed his disappointment.

"I've come to pick up the stool that needs mending." They were forever breaking milking stools, so his lie wasn't too far fetched.

"I haven't seen it, but we have a bench with a leg that needs fixing. Can you look at that? It's awkward for setting the pans on when it's so lopsided. Rose propped it up before she left, but the pans are heavy and it won't stand their weight for long."

"She left?"

"Last week. Didn't she mention it? She took time off for the family's trip to Semiahmoo."

"No." For one heart-stopping moment he thought she'd quit the fort. "Did she say when she'd be back?"

"No." That didn't surprise him. Indians had no concept of time, so heaven only knows when she'd be back. Then an alarm bell sounded within, and it struck him, like a hammer to his chest. He took his leave, completely forgetting the broken bench, and by the time he reached his quarters, worry gnawed around his innards like a hungry worm. He sat the bones of his buttocks upon the cold step outside. He no longer felt hungry and he didn't want to enter the confines of his quarters and breathe in the less-than-fresh air.

It was growing late yet the evening remained clear, for he could see the dark mountains across the river poking their jagged fingers at the mauve-layered sky. The fort's labourers were drifting across the fort in twos and threes, the evening shadows throwing out long lines in front of them, making them walk on their own stringy likenesses.

When he did finally take to his thin pallet, he tossed all night on the bed ropes like the *Thomasina* in a squall. His mind replayed what he knew about the disturbances south of the fort. Eight days ago a trapper came in with news of braves raiding tribes in the Puget Sound area. Then five days ago they had been spotted near the Cowlitz, where they'd stolen goods from the Langley Express. Now they'd been sighted along the Semiahmoo Trail. Rose and her family were in that vicinity right now.

He rose and dressed early, needing to begin the day, though it was too soon for breakfast or work. As soon as the cockerel crowed over in the chicken coop, he headed for the Big House. He was finding it hard to breathe. Rose was somewhere between the Fraser and the Columbia with a pack of angry braves running around. If they found her, anything was possible. She could be captured and made a slave. Or raped or killed. His mind exploded at the thought, and the impotence of his situation frustrated him. If this was Hawaii, he'd have left instantly to find her, but it was Langley, and he was a servant of the Hudson's Bay Company, and bound to do what they told him to do, and when. He'd have to go in their time, not his. If they let him.

He waylaid François Annance the moment he opened the door of his hut just after dawn. He almost didn't recognize the voyageur. In the dim morning light, Annance's Abiniki half appeared to dominate. Nothing about the angles of his face or the deep set eyes hinted of the white blood running in his veins.

"François, I want to be in the Express when it leaves."

"Could be trouble. The list's not out yet. Are you volunteering?"

He'd remembered Billings' advice and had never volunteered for anything before. Now he nodded. Annance eyed him curiously.

"Rose Fanon's out there somewhere, with her family," Kimo said tightly.

"Then I suppose someone could take sick, and you'd have to take his place."

"Appreciate it." His voice reflected false calm, but his stomach pained him, as if he'd swallowed a hive of angry bees. He couldn't eat, so skipped breakfast and sought relief in the mindless salve of habit, spending the time rubbing bear grease over his boots. The oily polish stank, but it did a fine job of waterproofing the leather, and he'd put off cleaning them for days. The morning air felt cold, so he pulled on a pair of mutilated woollen gloves. He'd cut the fingers and thumbs off at the knuckles, freeing his fingertips to handle tools while keeping his hands warm. He reported for work at the cooperage, but couldn't keep his mind on the task at hand. Every minute seemed an hour. Finally the clerk's messenger told him to report to the wharf in two hours to join the party leaving on the Express for Fort Vancouver. François had done it. He was in the canoe.

Specifically they were to scout for the hostile Indians encountered on the previous journey north, and do what was necessary to ensure there would be no repeat of the theft of Company goods. *Do what was necessary* left considerable room for discretion. He located Khatie.

"When did Rose and her family leave? And when are they likely to be back?"

"Seven days ago. I don't know when they'll be back. A few moons, maybe, or more. They come home when they're ready."

He thought he'd pop a vein. The Indian attitude to timekeeping didn't baffle a Kanaka as much as it did the whites, but even Kimo couldn't comprehend the extent of their easygoing notions about the passage of time.

He returned to his quarters, fighting to control the dog organ that had surfaced in his brain, calling for her return, screaming for vengeance if she were harmed. He had less than half an hour to sharpen his knives, oil his musket and pack his gear before joining the men of the Express down on the wharf.

chapter twelve

THEY WERE A MOTLEY CREW at the dock, Scots, English, Canadien, Indian and Owhyhee, even the water carrier, Huntas. Kimo recognized the Hawaiians from the distance, three brown, muscular, straight-limbed men, nearly a head taller than everyone else, except for the Iroquois.

"I thought Billings told you never to volunteer," he said to Moku.

"I didn't," Moku said, but he winked and raised his palm and the two clasped hands.

"Fit yourselves in best as you can," McKay said, for there was less leg room in a canoe with husky Hawaiians than with wiry voyageurs.

"Quickly, mes amis. Vite, vite!" urged Charles, the Canadien.

"Aw, hit him with a paddle!" muttered Moku under his breath, as the men took their seats. Within minutes they pushed off, paddling along the Fraser towards the mouth of the Salmon. Canoeing was second nature to Kimo, one of the things he liked best, on a clear, fine Sunday afternoon, paddling the river with Rose. It lifted the spirits, and when the sun glanced off the water in sparks of light, you felt you were in the centre of the universe. But today the Fraser presented its dark side, and the wind held them in its teeth as it raced along the river, feeding spinning currents and turning the air white with spray. And as the men put their shoulders to their paddles and pulled harder, Kimo withdrew into himself. His companions focussed on reclaiming the Company goods and punishing the thieves. His focus was on Rose.

As the canoe entered the Salmon River and headed south, the wind eased. No man in the craft seemed disposed to talk, and Kimo felt the silence as an ache within his skull.

"Indians!" McKay suddenly croaked. A few quick strokes pulled them to the bank. "Two of you, come!" Pali rose with Moku, but Kimo caught his sleeve. The big man nodded and sat back in the canoe, and Kimo took his place. He and Moku followed McKay and the Iroquois at a steady half-run through the underbrush, bent over low, dodging adroitly around cedars and cottonwoods that stood like sentries.

"CLICK! CLICK!" The grating sound of hammers locking into full cock met Kimo's ears and he came to a sudden halt, rearing back abruptly behind the Iroquois, nearly slapping into the Indian's back. Four braves stood side by side, muskets at shoulder height, pointing directly at the chests of the Bay men. The Indians were barefoot. Long black bearskins covered their shoulders and torsos. Where Kimo stood, wet moss hung like laundry from the cottonwood branch above, and it was difficult to see where their oiled black locks stopped and the fur began. No one spoke.

Kimo's sharpened senses brought everything into focus: the wind littering leaves across the forest floor, rustling them in tumbles at his feet, breaking the silence. Birds soaring overhead, carried on the wind like torn bits of paper. Trees rising like spears into the sky. An arrowhead of geese flying across the horizon, plaintive honks lingering on the air, haunting the treetops.

The Iroquois stood still, holding his musket loosely in his fingers at the end of his arm, mid-thigh level. He said something in Chinook in a conciliatory tone to the armed men. They didn't reply. He spoke again, gesturing with his big hand. His palm looked hard as saddle leather. So did the man. Kimo admired his courage. Not a glimmer of fear showed as he faced the Indians' guns. Cat-eyed in the shade, his face took on the appearance of a strange monolith as light slicing through the trees played over his high cheekbones.

One of the Indians spoke, but none moved to lower their guns. The Iroquois spoke again and finally the muskets were lowered. McKay and the Iroquois stepped forward and shook hands with the Indians. Tension had wrapped itself like a cable round Kimo's chest. His lips when he licked them felt broken and cracked. The Indians talked, signalled their leave-taking and backed slowly away. They retreated a few yards then melted into the trees.

"What news?" Kimo asked anxiously.

"Not much," McKay replied. "Things are quiet around here, but not good south in Klallam territory. They were nervous and wanted to be on their way."

Kimo felt as if his chest had been squeezed. There was a history of killing between the Company and the Klallams. Some years before, Company trader Alexander McKenzie and four men had been captured and robbed by Musqueam natives near the confluence of the Fraser and Pitt Rivers. Annance had gone to their rescue. But on their return trip, McKenzie and his men were killed by Klallams on the Hood Canal. The Company retaliated by raiding a Klallam village, killing twenty-one people. If the braves who stole from the

Express *were* Klallams, they would not look kindly on Kwantlen people, known friends of the fort.

The men returned to the canoe and paddled till the Iroquois gave a signal to portage. They left the Salmon River and trekked to the Nicomekl in silence. They quickly entered the narrow river and paddled to Mud Bay. They dragged the canoe onto the shingle and scouted the area but found no sign of recent campers. They proceeded to Semiahmoo and made camp for the night. There was no sign of the family anywhere along the bay. That clearly meant trouble. Kimo's thoughts came and went and he could no longer control them. Had they reached their destination safely, then left? Had they encountered trouble? Did they run, or fight?

He lay listening to the crackle of the fire, rubbing the koa dolphin at his neck. Don't let me down, Kupuna, he prayed. If your charm still has its power, don't let it fail me now. But because he hadn't felt its mana for so long, he asked the Christian God to look after Rose and her family too. If he'd known the names of the Indians' gods, he might have asked them too. But that thought passed quickly. He didn't believe in them. Doubt permeated all his religious thought now. He had turned into Hopoo's "Doubting Thomas." If Pope was right, and God was Nature, there would be no help forthcoming except from what nature could provide. If that meant the power nature gave to men, right now it didn't seem enough. He doubted Pope as well.

The night was clear, though the chill air of spring threatened and there was a smell nearby sharp enough to make your eyes water. He moved his blanket farther away from Moku, who stank from the reek of tobacco juice. They all did, having anointed themselves liberally to keep away the wood fleas and ticks. Pierre Charles took his place as sentry while the men grouped around the fire in their blankets. Some chose to sleep near the canoe. Within minutes, a rumble of snores exploded, popping like gunfire across the campsite, cutting into Kimo's nerves like broken glass.

"We might as well hang up a sign saying "Here we are, come and get us!"

"Relax, Kimo. The sentry's posted. Go to sleep," Moku said.

And though he thought sleep would never come, it did at long last. He woke at daybreak as the sun was rising, lighting the sky to a pearly gray and creeping down the dark mountainsides to provide just enough light to see. Annance and the Iroquois came through the trees, returning from a pre-dawn scouting of the bay. They had found a campsite whose fire pit ashes were cold, but recent. From it, they'd retrieved fragments of burned papers.

"It's our mail, that's for certain. They likely kept the pouch. Looks like they've moved on, but not that long ago. We've a good chance of catching up with them if we press on. Which way, Sakarata?"

The Iroquois hesitated. He was seldom uncertain, but he'd found two sets of tracks that crossed, heading both north and south. "If they went north, they'd have to return this way."

"Your best guess?" McKay stood up, and shouldered his gun.

"South."

"Let's move south, then. You two," McKay signalled Kimo and Charles, "stay here, in case we're following the wrong trail. If they went north, they'll come back this way."

When the canoe moved on, the two decided for safety to leave the large campsite the men had occupied during the night and scout the area for a more secluded site. Charles was in charge. That was understood. He was small but strong, with a pointed fox-like face, green, deep-set eyes, and a shock of whitish hair that stood on end. He wore a ready smile and was known to carry his weight without complaint, which is how men measured one another here. They circled the area and chose a spot where previous hunters had left a small fire ring. Kimo offered to set the fire, which turned out to be dismal, producing more smoke than light or heat. He went to fetch more wood, and it was then he spotted something high in the trees. He called for Charles then clambered up and found a rough cedar plank platform suspended between branches, loaded with tied bundles.

"Pelts. They're ours," he called down. He'd baled enough to know. "That means they'll be back to pick them up."

Kimo clambered down. "Now what?"

"We'll have to look for them. They must still be nearby. But one of us has to guard those pelts. You choose, Kanaka." The voyageur ranked above him. He didn't have to defer to Kimo's wishes in any way. Yet this happened often now with the Kanakas, and even among the voyageurs, for many couldn't read and called on him to write for them also. He recognized the Canadien's gesture of respect.

"Merci, Charles. I'll scout. If you need me, fire off a shot." He could not bear the idea of sitting still.

"Be back by sundown."

The Express had continued south, so Kimo decided to backtrack and run parallel to the shoreline from Semiahmoo towards Mud Bay, then circle back. He felt disoriented, like a kite in a gale, blown hither and yon by the winds of his emotion. He stopped for a moment, sensing the air, and let the atmosphere enfold him. Semiahmoo Bay had turned dove gray, with ribbons of mist wafting above the waves, stretching toward the shore to catch at the trees. The pale sun, searching for a gap in the clouds, found one and lit a path across the surface of the bay to where he stood on the shingle. He filled his lungs, then set off again, taking his bearings from the natives' great white rock, the boulder cast there long ago by some sea god from far across the ocean to prove his strength. He had his musket, powder and shot, and his knife. He left the beach area and moved at a fast trot through the moss-covered trees, dodging here and there, taking detours through every mud pond and standing pool of water, in case he was tracked. He was wading through a pool of brackish water when he heard an owl call and he stopped in his tracks.

It was still daylight. This was no owl. He waited several minutes and wondered if his imagination had run amok. Then he heard it again, one long hoot, two short, then two long. He swung himself onto a low branch of a large cottonwood. Methodically he climbed the trunk till he reached a wide fork that would sustain his weight, and hunkered as low as his big body would go. He drew the musket up silently, but didn't cock it for fear the noise would draw attention in the stillness of the forest.

Then he heard a vague rustling beneath him, sounds of branches being lifted and separated carefully. The leaves of a bush eight feet away quivered and settled and quivered and settled and moments later, the hoot of an owl reached his ears again, louder this time, almost below his feet. A man's head appeared beneath him through the tree branches. He dropped, landing on the balls of his feet, bending his knees into a half-squat, ready to strike. Fractions of a second before he smashed the black skull with the butt of his rifle, he pulled back.

"Sandich! I might have killed you, *keiki!*"

"Kimo!" The boy sank down on the forest floor with a thump, his bony ribs pumping in and out as he fought to breathe. Kimo extended his big hand to pull the trembling boy to his feet.

"My parents have been captured!" he blurted, "and my two sisters. I was cutting wood, and when I returned, they were tied up. I think they're Klallams. Rose was away picking reeds. I hid till she came back, and we've been following them since."

"Where is she now?"

"Not far. We separated for a time. We thought it safer." The two set out at a lope. Sandich was nimble on his feet and moved quickly through the trees. "My uncles met a Lummi east of the Cowlitz whose traps had been stolen. He said the thieves went north, so they decided it was too dangerous for the women and babies, so they took them home."

They reached a boulder beside some heavy bushes. Sandich stopped, cupped his hand and three times made a clicking in his throat that sounded like the "chick-chick" of a woodpecker. Seconds later Rose appeared through the canopy of trees wearing her brushed cedar skirt and moccasins. A reed cape covered her upper body and shoulders. Kimo thought her about as fine a sight a man could see, and drank in the sight of her, like water in the desert.

"Sandich! I was frantic! You took so long!" Her head spun from one to the other. "Kimo! What brought you here?" *She* had, but he didn't say that. Instead he battened down his internal hatches and delivered the official Company line.

"Thieves robbed the Express, and we were sent to retrieve the stolen goods. We found their campsite at Semiahmoo. The Express has chased them to the Cowlitz but two of us stayed here on watch and found our pelts stashed in the trees. So, the raiders are still around. I was looking for them, and circling my way back when I heard the owl call. That was a dead give-away, by the way, Sandich." The boy looked sheepish.

"We figured on the woodpecker if it was safe; the owl if there was danger. We thought if they heard the owl, they'd go away. It's bad luck, the death call," he said defensively.

At night perhaps. In broad daylight, not likely. They'd have come to investigate. But Kimo said nothing of their courageous imbecility.

"So what do we do now?" Rose whispered. On top of her fear there settled a thin icing of wonder that he had come, that he had found her.

"You are doing nothing," Kimo said. "I'm going after them."

"We're coming with you."

"No. It's too dangerous. You stay."

"We know this place. You don't. We're coming, right, Brother? "

Sandich picked up her cue. "Right! We'd just follow you anyway."
Kimo swallowed the urge to swat him.

"Then you must do exactly as I tell you. Exactly. Agreed?"

"Agreed," they said in unison.

"Let's go."

One man, one woman and a nine-year old boy. Not good odds,
Kimo figured, but at least he had his musket. It was nearly an hour
before they caught up to the raiders. Kimo spotted their sentry and
signalled to Rose and Sandich to keep still. The two crouched like
snails inside a large hawthorn while he sprinted several yards ahead
to climb a tall, wide cedar. He went up swiftly, hands then feet, the
way he climbed palms in Honolulu, but now with a musket slung
over his shoulder. Rose, in her hiding-place, felt her heart skip a beat
as she watched his ascent.

They heard the brave before they saw him coming towards them,
arms uplifted, swiping at branches barring his path. He didn't know
what hit him as Kimo dropped from the tree straight as an arrow. He
timed the fall perfectly, lifting and bending his knees half-way to the
ground to boot the man in the chest, seconds before he gripped the
brave's windpipe. Rose saw the brave sprawled on the forest floor
with Kimo standing over him and felt a rush of vertigo. He wasn't
dead, just unconscious. When she went to Kimo's side, he seemed to
look through her as if he were somewhere else and she didn't touch
him. The three of them dragged the man out of sight, gagged him
then tied him securely to an alder with his own deerskin belt, and
covered him with leaves.

"Stay here. I'll circle around then come back," Kimo said. "Don't move." He handed Rose his knife. "Just in case," he said, and left.

She stared at the blade in the palm of her hand. Would she find the power, or courage to use it?

"I can take it," Sandich offered.

"No." She tucked the blade in the back of her waistband where she could feel the steel press against her skin through the layers of pleated cedar. The two crouched low to the ground. Rose's heart beat loud as a drum, and she willed it to stop palpitating. It was worse now than before, when there were just the two of them to worry about. Now she was terrified for Kimo's safety too. The tension was affecting Sandich. Beads of sweat gathered along his thin arms and throat. She reached out and touched him reassuringly.

Kimo had been gone so long that Sandich grew fidgety, picking at some bulbous black slugs that draped themselves across the leaves of the thicket. Rose signalled for him to stay still, while she herself fought to ignore the cramp that seized her upper right thigh. She half-rose, biting her lip, and rubbed the tight knot of pain cramping her leg. It was the worst thing she could have done. A painted brave stood ten feet from their hiding place, musket pointed straight at her. His face lit up like a candle as he triumphantly called out his find. She froze momentarily, her mind in a fearful whirl, then she did what she had to do, for she could think of nothing else. She walked towards him, away from Sandich, on legs that threatened to liquify beneath her, her heart fluttering like a trapped bird frantic to escape its cage.

The brave grabbed her arm and shouted excitedly to his companions, dragging her with him back to the campsite. She staggered behind, intentionally slow and noisy, shrieking so Kimo would know that she'd been caught. The brave slapped her across the mouth and ordered her to stop wailing. Her cheek stung and her lower lip swelled up from the sudden pain of her own teeth biting it where he'd struck her. She tasted blood on the tip of her tongue and unintentionally swallowed it as she stumbled forward.

Lawi'qum lay huddled with her daughters, tied together with their backs propped against a cedar log that had been washed up on the beach. Neetlum lay on his back beside them, blood from the cut on his temple blackening in the morning sun. Rose was dragged over and dumped like a sack of flour beside him.

The group's leader was about forty, short of stature but stocky, and through the black and red and white streaks of paint, she could see pockmarks from the white man's disease across the left side of his face. His black hair was oiled, parted down the crown and tucked behind his ears. She kept her eyes down, hoping fervently he would see only Indian when he looked at her. Inside, she screamed silently for Kimo, praying he would come, wondering if he had heard her cries.

Neetlum had been watching the Indians closely, and realized they were not of one tribe, but from several, likely cast out for some transgression or another. Outcasts lived by their own rules, banding together, raiding villages, looting, killing. He feared the inevitable for his wife and daughters: slavery or death. He strained against the ropes binding his wrists till his hands swelled from clashing against each other, skin broken and scraped with chafing. A large blue fly crawled busily over the dried blood on his temple, tickling him and he shook his head violently, vainly trying to rid himself of the insect.

Rose stopped crying. She pressed her purpling lips together and tried to take stock. She gauged the noise level carefully before whispering to Neetlum.

"Father, Kimo's with Brother." She thought he hadn't heard, for he showed no emotion, not even the blink of an eye. But moments later, he rolled slowly onto his side and whispered back.

"Has he a gun?"

"Yes, and I have his knife."

"Pass it here, Daughter."

She waited till the guard looked away, then deftly retrieved Kimo's blade from the band of her skirt and slid it along the ground into Neetlum's waiting fingers.

With Kimo accounting for the one in the forest, there were six Indians left. Four she could see — three around the fire and one guard. They wore coverings of thin pelts over blanket trousers, and all walked barefoot, but one. They spoke different dialects, interspersed with Chinook, so she could only pick up words here and there. The brave barking orders, she took to be their leader. He was Klallam, but the man seated with him was of another tribe, for he was tall and rangy as Huntas. That left two others somewhere in the trees.

She stared hard at her knuckles. Neetlum would need time to cut his ropes. A distraction of some kind. She breathed in, filled her lungs then slowly exhaled her fear. She pushed up unsteadily from the ground and balanced herself.

"No, Daughter," Neetlum rasped, his voice breaking. She ignored him. She wiped the drying blood crusting her lip, willed herself to focus, and like some butterfly winging its first flight, propelled herself forward.

The guard spoke sharply to her, drawing the attention of the men at the fire. He ordered her to sit but she ignored him. When he moved to strike her with the butt of his rifle, her stomach curled in a spasm of fear. She pushed it down hard, through to her feet, and kept going.

"Let her come," the leader shouted, amused, from where he squatted low beside the fire. She took her time. Her cedar skirt shushed softly as she sashayed slowly around the far rim of fire, deliberately drawing their eyes away from Neetlum. She heard

Wawas'u weeping and her throat felt choked, as if her heart had jammed upwards and she could feel it pounding in her ears.

The leader finished chewing the pemmican in his hand. He stuffed his mouth with bannock and spoke with his mouth full, pointing at Rose. He made a crude comment and laughed suggestively, which drew a round of laughter and snickers from the other men.

"Sit," he ordered, slapping the ground beside him, bidding her like some mongrel dog. She stepped around him deftly, lowered herself between the leader and the tall brave beside him. She could expect no quarter from them, but maybe she could use them.

She folded to the ground on her knees and touched the tall brave's leg deliberately, looking across at him provocatively through her eyelashes. He gave off an unpleasant odour, and she had to swallow her fright, for his eyes were large, almost round, and he wore the scars of many battles on his face. Not Salish, she realized, and shook. He didn't move a muscle and she thought she'd guessed wrong. Then suddenly his hand shot out and he made a grab for her leg. The leader immediately reprimanded him sharply, and the man leapt to his feet, rifle in hand. Everyone fell silent.

The Klallam, stone-faced, wiped his lips with the back of his hand then rose slowly, inch by inch unravelling himself. Though shorter, he challenged the tall brave. With hunched over shoulders, he stared at the man through half-shut eyes and suddenly barked an order. The short burst of Chinook words erupted staccato-like, harshly from his throat, like bullets. The tall brave hesitated, fighting a duel with himself, his face a study of resentment. He was bigger, more powerful, and Rose thought he would surely meet the challenge, but he suddenly conceded. He lowered his head and folded to the ground, resuming his cross-legged squat.

"Now what?" she thought frantically, and held on to the panic in her stomach. She didn't know how much longer she could keep their attention. "My mother is Nooksack," she pleaded. "Klallams have no quarrel with the Nooksack."

"The man is Kwantlen," the Indian said abruptly. He suddenly grabbed her hair, and pulled her head back roughly towards the light. Her eyes smarted from the pain.

"And you? Half-breed!" he said, sharp and hard as a hammer blow. Rose suddenly shuddered with fright as he shoved his hand roughly beneath her cape and groped her breast. When his cold fingers touched her flesh, she spat contemptuously in his face, with all the power she could muster.

Everything stopped dead. The silence screamed at her. No bird flew. No insect buzzed. No leaf fluttered. The air seemed to coagulate. None of the Indians moved, caught in silent, lustful anticipation of their leader's response.

The astonished brave stared at her, frozen in provocation and abject disbelief. She stared back at him, frightened and mesmerized by the sight of her own white saliva beading and dripping slowly down his painted face. She felt certain of one thing. Now she would surely die. He rose and slapped her face twice sharply, stunning her, spinning her head from one side to the other, and she thought her neck would break with the sudden jolt. Tears spurted from her eyes uncontrollably, but she stifled a cry.

Kimo didn't. He howled a screaming-loud, other-worldly yell, that echoed frightfully across the clearing as he broke through the trees. He dragged two shuffling braves with him, wrists bound together with cedar roots and dumped them on the ground in front of their leader. Relief flooded in Rose's breast. He'd come! But then fear immobilized her. What could one man do against many?

The Indians leapt to their feet to aim their weapons at Lawi'qum and the girls, but they froze, for Neetlum was already leaning over their leader, pressing the cold steel of Kimo's blade against the Klallam's throat. Kimo strode forward.

"Tell him I want to talk, Neetlum!"

Neetlum conversed in Chinook all the time, and understood English well enough, but he ignored Kimo now and pressed the knife against the Klallam's throat till the tip disappeared into the folds of his skin.

"They are s'texem, worthless! They would have killed us, Kanaka."

"I know. But I must speak with them."

Rose thought her step-father's warrior power had come again, for his eyes gleamed with anger as he continued to hold the knife steady at the man's throat. He hesitated briefly then nodded.

"Pick up his musket, Daughter, and keep him covered."

She crawled forward and grabbed the man's weapon. The exchange was a blur, so quickly done that even Kimo, who expected it, was surprised. Neetlum suddenly acquired the musket, while Rose held the knife at the Indian's throat. She held it steady, and when he looked at her with disdain and spat, she met his gaze with defiance, refusing to drop her eyes. Neetlum primed the musket and moments later exchanged it again for the knife. Rose received the weapon gingerly. Truthfully, she was terrified, for she'd never held a musket before. They were notorious for going off by mistake and wounding their owners, but she dared not think about that now, for the Indians still had their guns pointed at Lawi'qum and the girls.

"Tell him I want to talk," Kimo said. Neetlum spoke sharply to the Indian leader. When the man nodded, Kimo dropped to the ground and sat cross-legged facing him. He laid his musket on the ground between them.

"Tell him we know they stole from the Langley Express, that our men are searching for them now, and that we found their cache at Semiahmoo Bay."

Neetlum and the Klallam exchanged words. "He says he knows nothing of any cache at Semiahmoo."

"Tell him we can make a trade. He can have his braves back, and the one in the woods, if he lets everyone go."

"He says, the Company killed his people. Innocent villagers."

"Tell him that was a long time ago, that Klallams killed Company traders, innocent men, too. We know nothing of that quarrel. Ask him to let this family go."

Neetlum translated. The leader said nothing.

"Tell him this. If he kills this family, he will be hunted down. The Indians are few. The whites are many. They have more guns, and more people will come, as many as leaves on the trees."

"He says, this family is Indian. The Turned Up Noses will not avenge them."

"Tell him there are many warriors at the Langley Fort, not just Englishmen. The Kwantlen are their allies, their chiefs related by blood. They *will* seek vengeance. A Klallam should know that."

The Indian paused. "You spoke of trade. What is your offer?"

"Your braves back, and the one in the woods, if you let everyone go."

"We keep our prisoners," the Indian repeated.

"Then you will die." Kimo nodded to Neetlum, who pressed the cold blade against the Klallam's neck. A tiny trickle of blood beaded around the point of the knife. The braves with their guns trained on the family took two steps towards them. Wawas'u wailed, but Lawi'qum hushed her, and she bit her lip in silence.

"You too will die, Kanaka, or one of the prisoners. At least one will, before you can reload."

"No trade, Kanaka!" another voice cut in, and recognition drove through Kimo's head like a sharp spike. He felt slightly sick. Ahuhu stepped away from the two armed Indians and stood before him, a small twisted smile on his face. "We're keeping the women."

"So, you've become a runaway, Ahuhu."

"Yes. And glad of it!" he spat, and squatted on the ground beside Kimo. He was dressed like the Indians, but unclean, and wore across his torso tired-looking pelts that dangled to his knees over blanket trousers.

Through the shock, Kimo wondered what he'd done with his European clothing, his trousers and boots. Traded them? Gambled them away? He could certainly pass for Indian at a distance, though he was the only one wearing moccasins. The forest floor was likely too cold for a barefoot Kanaka.

"I'm free now," Ahuhu said. "Glad to be rid of that damn fort."

"How free is a man if he can never go home?"

"At least I won't be in leg irons any more."

"Blame yourself, Ahuhu. You broke the rules. They paid you to do a job and you didn't do it. But this? You know runaways are always caught and punished. You'll find yourself in chains again before you know it."

"Only if they catch me, and I don't plan to get caught."

"Then you'll never leave this place. Don't be a fool."

"I'll find a way."

"If you stay with these men, you'll have to move around constantly, never staying in one place. Let this family go. They've done nothing to you. What use are they to you?"

"We can sell them to one of the tribes as slaves, for food or clothing. The women we'll keep, at least the young one. A man gets lonely on the move."

"No!" Kimo placed his hand on his rifle butt. He wanted to smash Ahuhu's face. "The woman is mine! The trade is all, or nothing." At that instant he caught Rose's eye and thought how slight she looked, yet how strong and determined. Her beauty almost hurt him — a rose strong enough to push its way through stony ground.

Ahuhu stepped forward to dispute Kimo's claim, but the leader spoke sharply to him, and he instantly dropped back, cursing Kimo in Hawaiian. His subservience shocked Kimo; then it came to him. Ahuhu would have to align himself with some tribe or another, to survive. The fool had simply exchanged one form of bondage for another. It was clear who truly led this pack. Though right now, Neetlum had a knife at the Klallam's throat and Rose a musket levelled at his chest. But the Klallam's braves still held Lawi'qum and the girls in their sights. They were at a standstill. Kimo addressed the Klallam again. He fought hard for control. They had beaten Rose, and would do worse. He reined in his anger, needing to stay calm. There were six lives at stake.

"I have the pelts you stole." His mind raced. He'd watched natives trade a fathom of dentalia, an armspan of shells, for a slave. Sometimes four pelts could buy one, though often it was as much as ten.

"Ten pelts to let the family go free," he said finally, gambling the Klallam would save face and leave with something rather than risk losing this fight, which would draw further Company wrath upon his head. Kimo knew he had no right to make such an offer. The pelts were Company property, worth a great deal of money, and he was obligated to return them. He could end up in chains for this.

The Indian hesitated, eyes cold as little dark pebbles in the shingle, beneath straight black slashes of eyebrows. Neetlum pressed the knife deeper into the folds of his neck. The trickle of blood thickened. The two other braves still stood, stone-faced, their weapons aimed at Lawi'qum and the girls. The heavy silence pressed down upon them and Kimo felt his chest tighten, as if drawn up by a ratchet.

"Ten pelts won't even buy a rifle," the Klallam spat. That was true. The store traded twelve for one.

"Twenty-four. Twenty-four pelts," the Klallam said.

Kimo hesitated. About half the cache. Enough for two rifles. Not much for six human beings. Who could argue with that? Even as he asked himself the question, he knew the Company might, for in Canton one pelt alone could fetch $100 — a huge loss from that perspective. Where fur was concerned, native lives didn't account for much in Company eyes. They saw tribal warfare, slavery and brutality, and concluded life was cheap among the savages, forgetting history and their own slow march to civilization. But these people were human beings, with as much right to life as any other. He'd signed a contract, promising to defend the property of the Company, but he could not bring himself to counter the Klallam's offer. To do so would demean Rose's family, demean humanity, if he haggled over the value of their lives.

"Twenty-four pelts. Agreed."

"Where? When?" said the Indian.

"Any time. Now, if you like. They're under guard, at Semiahmoo."

The Indian hesitated, then grunted assent. Kimo nodded to Neetlum, who slowly withdrew the knife from the man's throat. The Indian rose to his feet and signalled his braves to gather their gear. Rose stepped back, lowered the musket and passed it to Neetlum. A long relieved breath escaped her that the thing hadn't exploded of its own accord in her shaking hands.

At the tree line, Sandich raised his fist in triumph. Kimo had instructed him where to find Charles and the pelts if things went wrong. Now Kimo urgently signalled Neetlum to take his family and leave. You couldn't be sure the Indians wouldn't change their minds.

"*Quickly,*" he mouthed. Lawi'qum and the girls scrambled to their feet. They backed silently through the trees, except for Rose. She waited for him.

"Go! Go!" he waved frantically at her, and after a second's hesitation, she too vanished.

chapter thirteen

THE RAIDERS AND KIMO set out for Semiahmoo Bay at a fast trot. When he reminded them of the injured brave he'd left in the forest, the Klallam shrugged and indicated they might pick him up on their way back.

"They won't," said Ahuhu, his voice heavy with certainty. He fell into line beside Kimo. The last thing Kimo wanted was this man's company. He disgraced the name Kanaka.

"Look at yourself, Ahuhu, running with a pack, like an animal. What are you doing with these men? Their own people don't want them."

"They treat me better than the Company ever did."

"For as long as it suits them, then what? Turn yourself in. You'll maybe spend time in chains, but you've survived that before. If you keep your nose clean, you could be back on a ship to Oahu soon enough."

"I've got plans. I'm heading south. They're looking for men to work the docks in Sacramento. Good pay."

The fool didn't have the brains to figure how to get there without sailing on a Company ship, nor would he have the backbone for the hard work involved in any kind of long trek south. He'd never make it to Sacramento.

"Anyhow, it's too late to go back now," he said gruffly.

To the fort, or to Hawaii, Kimo wondered? Had the man gone down so many wrong roads, that he didn't know how to get back? It came to him suddenly that Ahuhu must be "spirit sick." He was thinner now. Slack skin hung from his face, as if looking for somewhere to go. Unwashed, he threw off a reek like old socks. Open sores covered his face and his once wide eyes pinched down. He bore little resemblance to the powerful bully who'd boarded the *Thomasina* three years ago. Kimo almost felt pity for him.

"What else got you into trouble, Ahuhu?" There had to be something more, apart from the drinking. Ahuhu shrugged carelessly.

"We'd sneak a pelt off a bale once in a while, pass it along to one of the Indians. He'd bring it to the store with other skins and trade it all over again. We got away with it for a while, but somebody talked. The others will be in chains for months, but I ran before the smith got to me." His bravado returned. He brandished his musket. "Mine," he said. "And shirts, tools and blankets, we used for gambling. Vermilion and cloth would buy us *klootches* whenever we wanted."

Kimo smashed the side of Ahuhu's face with all the force he could muster. The Hawaiian staggered with surprise, and slumped down on one knee, then fell sideways like a drunk in a doorway. Kimo rained blow after frenzied blow on Ahuhu's head, hate lodging in his throat like a fishbone. Ahuhu had argued for Rose, yet he'd been buying native women in Fort Vancouver where venereal disease, the "Chinook Love Fever," was rampant. Kimo's insides burned like *aa,* the lava of Hawaii. The thought of what might have happened to her enraged him. The Indians halted to watch, but on a signal from their leader, none interfered. Kimo finally stopped when his stomach heaved and he needed to wretch.

"You bastard!" Kimo wiped his mouth then rubbed his bruised knuckles, but ignored the pain. Ahuhu rose, stumbling to his feet, his battered face blood-covered from cuts to his right eye, now half shut and swollen. A wide gash had split his mouth across the upper lip. He spat blood, and a tooth, from his bleeding mouth.

"I curse you, Kanui!" he raged. In the old days, a curse could reduce a man to fear and trembling, but Kimo barely lifted an eyebrow. He rejected superstition now. Partly from the missionaries' teaching. Mostly by his own inclination.

"I turn my back on you, and your curse," he replied evenly, and slowly turned his back. Even the raiders understood the symbolism. The Indian stepped between them, uttered a guttural order and gestured to Ahuhu to move to the rear. Kimo picked up his musket and they loped in silence towards Semiahmoo Bay.

As he moved through the trees, his rage subsided. Ahuhu had drifted too far, like others caught in the void in Hawaiian society. The kahunas used to seek out and punish those who broke *kapu* laws, and fear of their wrath could make people ill, and some would even die. But once the old kapu system was abolished, people no longer feared the kahunas or the breaking of kapu. The missionaries had come to fill the void, but they hadn't done so, not yet, and men like Ahuhu had no moral compass. He had to know the risk involved in consorting with klootches at the fort. Driven to seek favours from the fort's men, either by necessity or inclination, they contracted and gave back more than they or their partners ever bargained for. He'd seen men salivating from mercury overdose, before their treatment was changed to ointment. Some claimed they were cured this way.

Others said there was no cure, only respite from time to time. But to risk the health and life of an innocent human being against her will, was more than thoughtlessness or ignorance. It fell into the realm of evil. When Ahuhu died in this place, he would die alone. No man would sing an auwé for him, and his soul would not return home.

When they arrived at Semiahmoo, Charles was nowhere in sight. Kimo knew he'd be hiding, watching, so he spoke to empty space, imparting information to the trees around the campsite, feeling slightly foolish, before the wily voyageur chose to show himself. He came through the underbrush slowly, alert, musket cocked.

"The Company, dey won't be happy you gave away der pelts, mon ami. Zut! You be in big trouble, Kanaka."

Kimo knew that. So much money was tied up in that baled fur. He'd end up in leg irons for sure. He'd been thinking about it for hours, wondering how long his punishment would last. He'd rather have a bad flogging than be chained like a dog, but it was more than likely he'd get both anyway. And if they went by his contract, and the unthinkable happened and he had to make up the loss, he'd be working here for more years than he'd planned. The thought choked him.

He climbed the cedar, slashed the ropes tying the bale to the platform, rolled it over on its side and slit the ties. He counted out twenty-four beaver pelts and let them thud to the ground. Two braves quickly rolled up twelve skins apiece and roped them into small packs. The Klallam gestured south with his arm, and the group trotted away. Ahuhu was last to leave. He called no aloha as he followed the others, the Hawaiian in him dead already.

They returned to the large campsite on the beach, to await the return of the Express. Kimo collected the wood for their fire. He wondered if Rose's family had retraced their steps and found their canoe. Otherwise the trip back to Langley would be arduous for them on foot. How far south had the Express gone, he wondered, and when would they be back? And how was he going to tell them about those pelts? Every time he thought of it, a sick worm wound through his stomach.

When he returned with the wood, Charles had set the tripod up over cold ashes in the used fire pit on the beach. The Canadien drew flint and steel from his fire pouch. It was a pretty thing, of blue cloth worked through with beads, with coloured tails that dangled, that he'd made himself, so different from the plain tin box that held Kimo's tinder. Sparks flew and the fire took readily. Moments later, a voice reached them from the beach.

"Klahowya!" Kimo turned, to find Neetlum picking his way carefully along the shingle with the family trailing behind him in weary single file.

"I come to thank you, Kanaka." They'd found their transport, canoed to the bay, and hidden themselves till the raiders left. They looked exhausted. Rose's shoulders drooped. Her face was swollen and bruised. He moved to help her spread reed mats on the ground. The women and girls sat huddled together for warmth, along with a subdued and solemn Sandich.

"My son will speak of this for many moons," Neetlum said. Kimo didn't doubt Sandich would wear everyone's ears out later, recounting the day's events. As Charles busied himself at the fire, Lawi'qum offered some dried salmon and peas for their meal, and asked Rose to pick berries for tea.

"We 'ave enough for all," Charles said, but clearly there was not, so Rose set off and Kimo offered to go with her. She looked fragile, as if she would keel over now the danger was past. She stumbled when she lifted her basket, so he took it from her hand. They hardly spoke as they picked their way through the trees, distancing themselves from the others. The moment they were out of sight and sound, he dropped the basket and she walked straight into his arms. Neither spoke. They just clung to each other wordlessly.

He felt her shiver from the pain that still clung to her in small burrs, tiny patches. He had tried hard to stop caring for her but she had ruined his plans, confounding him. Like a sailor waiting for a squall to pass and die away, he'd expected his feelings to blow over. It was odd that in other facets of life, he felt in control but where Rose was concerned, now, all of a sudden, he had none. He'd watched her today, shamed and frightened by the braves. She'd surprised him by fighting back, distracting them, attempting to play the coquette, though from his own wider experience, not too well. The notion was so ridiculous, it made him smile faintly now. He'd nearly gone *pupule* at the thought of them hurting her. Insane at the idea of anyone touching her, except himself.

The day had also wrought a change in Rose. It struck her forcefully that life could change in an instant, that living fully involved risks. She would stop thinking about what lay ahead, for she'd done that too long. Now suddenly her insides churned against the dam of restraint her fear of his leaving had erected. Today that dam broke, and she drooped against him now, fighting for air.

The day's events had started a fuse in Kimo. He'd wanted Rose from the moment he realized he might lose her. Maybe it was some innate human need to create life in the face of death. He'd been celibate so long, he didn't know if he'd find control. He felt as if he were through the whitewater, beyond the breaking Oahu waves, waiting in the calm outback for the giant smoker, the one you hope to control, the one that roars over you like thunder before it drags you below.

Rose knew that against all odds, she was alive now and the moment was too precious not to live fully. She loved him. On the far shore of her mind, only half conscious of reason, she decided to place her future squarely in the hands of the gods. She wore her reed cape but now she fumbled with its ties, hesitating when she remembered white prudery.

"Maybe . . . you ought to close your eyes," she whispered.

"Not," he said, "for every pelt in the Bay's storehouse," and he watched her untie the reed sash around her waist so that her cedar skirt fell away, like dry leaves off an autumn tree.

She had fought so hard to be cautious, to be prudent. But now she threw prudence to the wind. She made the first move, or maybe he did, hauling her against his chest. Passion rose in him like fire in dried hay, and he drew her with him. Yet even as they came together, an alarm rang in some far corner of his brain. Honolulu still beckoned. He ought to back off. There was still time. Yet he knew it was too late, that nothing in the world could stop him now.

A bird sang somewhere, its echo fluttering over the treetops. For Rose, the calming sound of his Hawaiian voice, a strong deep bass ebbed and flowed through her and she knew she would hold this time in her heart always, even if he left. This was love, snared by the present, wild, desperate, compulsive, and utterly blind to the morrow.

WHEN THEY RETURNED to the camp, Rose joined Charles and her family at the fire, but Neetlum drew Kimo aside.

"I would speak with you, Kanaka. Alone." He indicated a driftwood log nearby. Kimo sat down and waited for the Indian to settle beside him. Neetlum's lips tightened around the stem of his stained pipe. His blunt fingers, the colour of ochre, gripped the chipped clay bowl. He sucked softly, flexing and twitching his wide nostrils and Kimo waited for the tobacco to enter Neetlum's lungs. When it did, he exhaled with satisfaction then readjusted his bones where he sat, straight-backed and cross-legged on the ground. Kimo honed his knife, scrutinizing the Indian from beneath his black eyelashes. He licked his forefinger and ran it along the edge of the blade, testing it for sharpness, and waited.

A heavy woollen shirt, made from a Hudson's Bay blanket, fit well across Neetlum's shoulders and broad chest. His hide breeches were old and sagged loosely on his haunches. Oiled hair cascaded over his shoulders and Kimo wondered vaguely if Indians had problems with lice, as the men at the fort sometimes did. The Indian's face remained expressionless. He had intelligent dark eyes, but Kimo wasn't sure if they were calculating or just self-righteously wary. He had something to say, though. It was written in code on his mouth, arcing down in a crescent.

"We are in your debt, Kanaka."

"There is no debt, Neetlum."

"Yes. We're free, thanks to you. But I wish now to talk of my daughter. Four men from the village have spoken for her. Kwantlen women marry early. She has been late deciding."

He was opening the door for an offer. Not very wide, but it was open. Kimo knew Indian women married young, some as early as twelve if they'd begun menstruating. For men, eighteen was the norm. If he were Indian, he too would be old for marriage.

"It is merely a matter of choosing between families now. Her mother is anxious to have things settled."

Kimo said nothing. He was watching Rose tend the fire, surrounded by the colours of the day, though here they were nothing like those of Hawaii, where colours bloomed arrogantly, commanding your eyes. Here, you *felt* the day, with all its changes and your eyes slowly came upon the colours. And when you found them, they didn't demand attention, but gently called for it. As Rose stirred the contents of the kettle, evening colours surrounded her. Red flames flickering in the fire's core, fingers of orange reaching upwards hugging the black cook-pot, gray wisps of smoke rising in puffs into the azure sky. The forest shades blended together to form a cover of greens — of pale white hue, of yellow and blue, of black and even purple, exuding life, living things, and the scent of it reached out and touched him. He inhaled deeply.

"So, Kanaka, when does your contract end?"

"Next month."

"Then you return to your own land?"

"That was my plan." He knew he should say more, but a sudden surge of irritation made him feel perverse, so he added nothing. He didn't believe Rose had feelings for any of the suitors Neetlum spoke of. Would Neetlum force a decision on her? Would she let him?

Impatiently he flicked off a beetle that emerged from the rotten bark, shiny and black, the size of his fingernail. Inexplicably angry, he jerked to his feet and hurled the knife he was honing far into the bay. He was no longer thinking of the plans he'd made, but of possibilities, hanging like apples on a tree that you could just pluck off at will. The knife formed an arc against the sky and fell towards the bay, gleaming in flashes of light before it cut into the rippling water. The waste suddenly shocked him. To discard a useful tool verged on sin in the wilderness. If not sin, then folly. Where had such anger sprung from?

Night fell and the family made their beds separate from the two men. Kimo found several pieces of dry cedar, almost two feet in diameter and four feet long, which he hauled from the brush to stack on the fire to keep it burning through the night. He took his time stoking the flames, glad the logs were long and heavy, since he felt a pressing need to kick something. He couldn't sleep now, thanks to Neetlum. He didn't blame the man. He was only trying to secure Rose's future. There were men, Indian and white, who regarded women as possessions, to be bartered away for some tool or article of clothing or position they wanted. Neetlum didn't, and Kimo respected him for that. He lay awake in his blanket, and thought of Rose sharing it. He watched the night sky, waiting for sunrise, while the waves of Semiahmoo Bay whispered insistently with each ebb and flow, speaking to him in a fusion of sound too low for him to discern their message.

Rose lay awake too. She sensed his withdrawal since his talk with Neetlum. The thought of being without him tore at her like eagle claws. She wished she could share his blanket. The moon, round and ripe and the colour of mustard, glistened above the crest of the trees. The pain of the day slowly ebbed away with the tide, and she slept at last, as the blue night threw a shawl of star-spangled dark across Semiahmoo Bay.

She woke early and bathed. She coaxed last night's dying embers into life and dried her hair, running her fingers through it by the fire. She had a large measure of oatmeal bubbling in the iron cook pot and a kettle full of tea ready before the others joined her. They were still eating when the Express appeared across the bay. Kimo caught Rose's eye for a moment across the fire.

The knowledge of what could happen because of the lost furs had been hovering over him like a wall of water about to curl in upon his head. He dreaded the thought of being chained like an animal, but he'd been prepared to face that to free Rose's family. Now he'd have to pay the price. He laid his plate down and turned to Charles.

"Well. This is it. I have to tell them about the pelts."

"What pelts are dose, mon ami?" the voyageur said gruffly, pouring cold water over their fire, spreading the wet ashes, sniffing and inspecting them to make sure no spark lingered. "I seen no pelts other than dose dat's left, none at all." He rose and extended his arm to shake Kimo's hand, and winked. The words soaked into Kimo's brain and he threw his arms around Charles, hugged him soundly then thumped his back.

"Ah, Charles, thank you. Merci, mon ami. Merci. I can never repay you." He pumped the voyageur's hand up and down.

"Next week's rum ration, maybe?" Charles retorted, with a lop-sided grin.

The Express men had searched in vain, of course. When Kimo reported his encounter with the raiders and their capture of Rose's family, McKay pressed for details. Charles jumped in.

"He tole dem we'd punish the hell out of dem if day didn't let the Kwantlen people go — just like we did when the Klallams killed the McKenzie men, and day sure didn't want dat. So here day are, all in one piece," he waved his arm with a flourish to where Neetlum and the family stood silently aside.

"No sign of the goods?"

"Only these," Kimo replied, indicating the small pile of pelts. He could hardly look McKay in the eye.

"We found dem stashed high in the trees," Charles continued to elaborate, more at ease with the conspiracy than Kimo, who remained nervous. "Someting more might have been stored der, but," the Canadien shrugged his shoulders, "no sign of anyting else now."

There was nothing more to be done, but return to Langley. As they packed their gear, Kimo noticed Huntas leave the men grouped on the beach and walk towards Neetlum. They drew aside and the two squatted on the ground, talking head to head for several moments, till Neetlum turned and signalled Lawiq'um to join them. Huntas then left husband and wife to speak together in private.

Kimo caught up with him by the canoe. "What was all that about?"

"The Departed," Huntas replied in a low, hushed voice. Indians would not speak the name of the dead. Or any name, for that matter, except at a feast or a potlatch. If they talked about one living person

to another, they'd use "So-and-so." Indians at the forts learned to discard the custom, but death, apparently, had brought Huntas' old instincts to the fore.

"Who died?"

"The girl's father," he said quietly. "When we were in Fort Vancouver, an old Iroquois who now works at Fort Garry, he told me *The Departed* drowned, years ago, in the rapids on the Assinaboine."

"How can that be, when the Company had no record of his death?"

"He left them. He and some other Canadiens, they went to go work for the free traders on the Red River."

Men at the fort gossiped about free traders. They'd been opposing the Bay's right to all land use in the country. Around the Red River in particular, they created problems for the Hudson's Bay, who threatened legal action to stop them. Kimo understood. It had been the same in Hawaii when, till recently, only the alii owned the land. The Hudson's Bay were the alii here, but their hold would be broken sooner or later. Sooner, he guessed, with the free traders growing bolder.

"When did he die?"

"The Iroquois didn't know, but it was many moons ago. Those free traders, they began working the Red about a year or two after he left." He nodded towards Neetlum. "I told the family it was just months after, though."

"Why?"

"We say he died sooner, it looks like he would have come back, except for the accident. The girl, and her mother, they will feel better."

Kimo wanted to speak with Rose, but she had her back to him, huddled with Neetlum and Lawi'qum. His kupuna had told him years ago to learn something from every man he met. He'd thought that meant gleaning knowledge from the haoles, but today he realized you could learn something even from an old slave.

He rejoined Charles and the Bay men for the trip back to Langley. Rose's family quickly clambered into their own craft, and the two canoes started out in loose convoy together. The Bay craft sped along faster, widening the distance between them. It had more difficulty along the winding Nikomekl though, and left the river to portage sooner than Neetlum's craft. They stopped before entering the Salmon River, waiting for the family to catch up, then set off on the final leg home.

Rose wept no tears for her father, for she had done her grieving years before. But she felt a deep sadness within. So many questions would remain unanswered. He was an expert boatman, so how could he have drowned? Did they find his body and bury him properly, or was he left at the bottom of the Assinaboine? Regret surfaced for the years she had wasted blaming him. But through the sadness, there was an easing, and sense of relief. Had he not drowned, her father might have come back. It was possible. Other voyageurs had done so. She clung to the possibility, knowing it was faint but needed to believe that she *had* been loved — had been worth loving, after all. Would Kimo think so — enough to stay? She had lost one man. Would she lose another?

Every stroke of the paddle reminded her that May was around the corner, that she could be facing a future without him. She loved him. He was not like other men, either in her village or at the fort. Though a lowly servant of the Company, a labourer by the contract he signed, he was his own man, unfettered by convention and more intelligent than his "betters" at the fort realized. This same class-consciousness provoked the conflict between herself and her step-father. He couldn't understand why a half-white would settle for a lowly Kanaka instead of one of the unattached whites at the fort. Both races, Rose decided, imprisoned people into caste systems from high to low. As an outsider from birth, she judged this cruel and a waste of human potential.

When the canoes reached Langley, the Bay canoe pulled in to the dock while the family headed to the village. Kimo waved briefly at Rose as they passed. On the path to the fort, he caught up with the water carrier.

"Thank you, Huntas. That was kind of you. It'll help old wounds heal."

"*The Departed* was my friend and a good man. Maybe he *would* have come back some time, after a few years. Anyhow, it's good the girl can think so. She'll make a good wife for any man, Kanaka," he said pointedly, "but that's up to Neetlum, of course. And the girl, I suspect," he laughed, "since she has a mind and tongue of her own that she puts to good use."

chapter fourteen

IN THE DAYS THAT followed, Kimo thought about Rose's father and the Red River traders. He respected the Company and would be true to his contract, yet he understood the traders' wish to walk free in this land, to act independently, to be more than a mere pawn in the service of some other. The land was too great to be controlled by one entity. And though he didn't condone the pain inflicted on Rose and her mother, he could understand Jacques Fanon's bid for independence. He had understood that fool Ahuhu's bid for freedom from the Company too, only the wretch had chosen the wrong way and would never find the right one now. While the Ahuhus of the world would end badly, he reckoned the free traders would succeed, eventually. It was a thought that pulled at him. And stayed with him.

While he was working in the fields pulling stumps, Khatie arrived with a message from Rose that her mother was ill and she would not be coming to the fort. With no meetings with Rose the days seemed long and tedious. Then Pali fell sick and Kimo had to work in the sawpit, ending up miserable with aching muscles, every orifice filled with sawdust. At his first opportunity, he paddled to the village but found only Sandich who told him Lawiq'um was better and she had gone with Rose to take rosehips and other herbs to treat a neighbour with scurvy.

Sandich scampered around Kimo's canoe. "Nicamous was just here, too. He can shoot straighter than anyone in the village. Guess how many rifles he's offered for Rose?" Kimo hesitated, hating to ask.

"Four! And blankets, too!" Sandich crowed.

Kimo took his leave. The boy clearly had a new hero to worship. His mind raced. You'd need four dozen pelts to trade for four rifles. And blankets too. This Nicamous must be a wealthy man in the village. Kimo did some quick calculations to figure out how long he'd have to work to pay for even one rifle and winced. Unreasonably he suddenly wanted to cleave the man in two.

A few days later the Langley Express arrived bringing two new Kanakas. As he walked to the landing, he saw them helping to unload the trade goods. They were powerful, broad-shouldered men, who laughed easily with one another. "Aloha," they called as he approached, faces wide with smiles, as if he were kin. Both came to hug him, exchanging names, making near incoherent inquiries about this and that, faces filled with emotion. They'd lose some of that spontaneity over time at the fort. They all did, he realized, though the Hawaiians were still like that among themselves, in the haven they'd created at Kanaka Creek, living according to their own customs, their own ways. If he stayed, he'd find that a comfort.

Over dinner, the fort people bombarded the newcomers with questions about Fort Vancouver. The young Kanaka was a new recruit, in his first year. The other had signed his second contract with the Company, after six years spent in Fort Vancouver. The place buzzed with talk, they said, about Oregon expanding, and the huge numbers of American settlers arriving, so many they now outnumbered the British. They talked of the outright probability, not just the possibility, of America taking over the Territory, and Kimo wondered what this would mean for the people of the Columbia. Some men already had decided for America, while others supported Britain.

The Kanakas said Mr. Polk wanted the voters in Oregon to put him into office. That if he became President, he would annex Oregon from northern California at 40 degrees latitude to Alaska, at 54 degrees. The Doctrine of Manifest Destiny, he called it, to expand America from coast to coast.

Kimo didn't know what to make of it all. He fell into bed late and slept fitfully till daybreak. Waking came slowly, as thoughts wove and interwove through the confusion burrowing in his soul. When was the last time the gods had spoken to him? He couldn't remember, but gods of heat and fire did not live long in this cold land. Indian gods lived here, in the trees and stones, in the rivers and mountains, but he had never heard their voices either. The only voice that he heard, faintly, was the echo of the white man's God, from his days with Hopoo at the Mission. His thoughts roved there now. So much still called him back, for instinct and custom required a man be buried where he was born. And yet . . . and yet . . .

In the morning, Kimo found one of the new men smoking outside the shack, beside a decayed moss-covered stump that wore a crown of salal and feathery stalks of sword fern shooting skyward. A thatch of dust-coloured hair, curly and thick, covered his head. His nose was broad, beneath dark sepulchre eyes that sat deep in his skull and the skin pulled tight across his cheekbones had the texture of dried parchment. If you pinched them, Kimo thought, they'd crumble to dust. Kimo greeted him with aloha and squatted beside him. He took the customary roundabout approach, enquiring after his sleep, commenting on the weather, and sat in silence for several minutes before asking him what he thought was likely to happen between the Americans and British.

The Kanaka hit his broad chest with his closed fist and cleared his throat. He opened his mouth wide to cough, and surprised Kimo with a long, pink tongue covered to the tip with blue patterned tattoos. One of Kimo's old uncles in Waimea had a tongue like that. He'd always wondered about the pain involved in tongue tattoos. Bad enough in the usual places, on body or face, but there, where the tiniest ulcer felt like a mountain?

After more coughing to clear his throat, the Kanaka found his voice. "I have seen many changes since I came to Fort Vancouver six years ago. I think the Americans will eat up the continent, the way they're going. They already occupy Mexico's northern territories, Texas and California."

"Will they have the means to accomplish this, Pokua?"

"Who knows? But it looks fairly certain they'll take Texas and California from Mexico, and go to war over it, if need be."

"And will they go north to the 54th parallel as well, and fight for that too?"

"Borders get fixed one way or another. No one can predict what will happen, but the Americans outnumber the British now. Five, six times as many. They're coming in covered wagons across the Oregon Trail, hundreds, thousands of them to work the land. The Willamette Valley is fertile, good land to farm. They're already building across the entire Territory."

"Can't the British stop them?"

"How? They can't turn all those people back now. It's too late. No one knows what will happen next."

"*Mahalo nui*, Pokua," Kimo said, thanking him. A fine mess, he thought, and rose and walked away, wondering what this would mean for the British forts if the Americans took over. *When* the Americans took over, for that's how things seemed to be shaping up. He talked to Pali about it later. "Maybe we've been caught napping."

"We? You're siding with the British, then?"

"They pay our wages. They were here first. I can't see myself changing sides now."

"Britain's so far away, maybe they don't know what's going on here in the Northwest. Or else they just don't care."

"But land is land, and men always fight over land. Because they've done nothing till now to stop the American settlers, doesn't mean they won't."

"True. And if the Americans are prepared to fight Mexico for Texas and California, they won't hesitate to fight Britain for the Territory. Half the Columbia men support them anyway, and their 'Manifest Destiny' to take over the continent."

But as many didn't. And those who didn't were angry. So war, it seemed to Kimo, was more likely than not. It was hard for him to sleep that night for thinking how this struggle between America and Britain might affect the Hudson's Bay Company and their great base at Fort Vancouver. And the smaller forts, including Langley. His main worry was how it would affect Rose and the Kwantlen if natives became embroiled in a war between America and Britain. His heart went out to the Indians. It wouldn't matter who won, Britain or America, they would lose. The Indians would suffer most from restructuring the land. Hawaii was proof of that. It would be the end of one way of life, and birth of another. And birth was always painful.

He had a restless night, waking several times to pound his pallet. At one point, he sensed his grandfather's presence, but when he turned, the old one had gone. He always thought of his kupuna as being just across the ocean, alive yet in the ohana, for there were times his spirit still called to him. He tried a silent chant to call the old one back, but couldn't, so he lay, watching the moonlight slip under the doorway, a thin sliver lighting the floor.

He rose, dressed and left the room to its snoring occupants. The air outside smelled sweet. It was cool and clear, the kind of morning Mrs. Finlay called "crisp." The sun was rising, flaring across the mountaintops, firing them with an orange glow. Golden Ears, even in May, wore a cover of snow on its higher peaks, as if someone had dusted them with sugar. Mountains stretched gloriously, as far as the eye could see. They took your breath away. Not just the first time you set eyes on them, but every time, for they were ever-changing, depending on the light and movement of the sun and clouds across the sky. At some point, he'd come to imagine them as guardians, sentries, giant watchers over the land, a blanket enfolding the people, holding the rivers and valleys securely in place.

The Kwantlen said some erupted from time to time, especially the huge dome-shaped peak to the south always covered in snow. They spewed lava and ash for weeks on end, and he thought of Mauna Loa, on Hawaii's Big Island. But mighty Mauna Loa stood alone in her grandeur. Here, wave after wave of Mauna Loas guarded the land, shoulder to shoulder, the length of the country. They were awesome in their power, and majestic. He'd miss them, if he left.

Not the rain, though. No. He'd not miss the rain that fell on the coast in so many different ways — in morning mists, in gray drizzles, in falling rods, and wind-driven, slanting sheets. Langley rain would depress Hopoo's Noah, himself. It could fall gently in even descent then whip into a tempest that soaked you through in seconds, and in winter, could pour for days on end. Yet, rain made the place. Things grew tall and strong because of it — those giant firs and cedar and hemlock that covered the landscape, giving shelter and food to men and animals. The soil never dried up and produced food readily. Nor did the rivers, with their endless supply of fish. But summers were good, long and hot enough to make you forget the winter rains. Just not as hot as summers at home, of course. He started across the compound, bunching his shoulders in the cool morning air.

Why is it, he wondered, that home is always where you were born, and not where you come to live? At home, his ohana, his mother and kupuna had loved him of course, and he them. But as long as he could remember, he'd felt out of step, somehow outside of life, looking in. And at the Mission school, as Hawaiian values bowed to European, he'd felt secure with neither. He'd always felt fractured, trapped in an ill-fitting life, not quite at home in his own skin. Dislocated. Alone.

Crossing the compound, he stopped and lifted his eyes to the hills, as if they should tell him something. And it came to him with sudden insight that he didn't feel that sense of isolation any more. It had gone, that crippling sense of not belonging. Now he felt strong, secure in his worth as a Kanaka. And, more importantly, as a man. The realization washed over him, hitting him suddenly like a west-coast squall.

When had it happened? He didn't know, but it had. He felt whole, content with himself. He measured himself by the men of the fort, hard men of strength and character, and he could stand with the best of them. Three years in the wilderness had forged him. He felt he could face any challenge, any obstacle that came his way. It was odd, at the fort, how men split into two camps. Some struggled wretchedly, counting the days till their contracts expired and they could return to the comfort of hearth and home. But others embraced the wilderness life. Tough, self-reliant souls, they breathed life from the forest, rivers and mountains. Clearly the land spoke to their souls, and they lived in harmony with it. They fit. The thought rose again, like a cork in a milk pail. *He fit, too.*

He walked to the river and sat on a rotted log near the water's edge, savouring the light breeze. A haze of mosquitoes, newly hatched, danced in swirls above the water, throwing shadows many times their size on the surface. A solid shadow emerged among them suddenly, and grew large and dark. Curious, he raised his head, squinting through the sunlight. A raven, he thought, circling high, but as it soared, he sat upright. No raven, but an eagle, spiraling upwards towards the sun, spinning higher and higher. His throat tightened, and he fought back the tears pooling in his eyes from the glare of the sun. And maybe, just maybe, from the thought of leaving this terrifyingly beautiful land. The bird stopped its upward spiral and hung, wings spread, suspended in mid-air for a long time, then swooped sharply in a great arc in the sky to dive at breakneck speed towards the river. It swept headlong, with no pulling back, along a great length of the river then dropped like a stone, cutting the surface of the water on an angle with his legs. Directly in front of Kimo, only yards from where he sat on the stump, the bird rose with a silver fish caught in its talons, thrashing and jerking from side to side, sparkling silver in the sunlight as the eagle soared upwards.

Moments later, from a great height, the struggling fish escaped the bird's talons and fell, thrashing still, back into the river with a splash. The eagle, in awesome flight, continued to soar downriver, till it shrank to a black speck then disappeared. The fish appeared dead, suspended in the water. But then it moved slightly, just one fin, then the other, and jerked to life with a sudden swish of its tail, and swam swiftly away. It had gained itself a second life, and Kimo rejoiced in its freedom.

There was a gentle breeze, just enough to move the leaves on the cedars and sway the willows, and when it blew his way, it carried the scents of the forest and he breathed deeply. Surely nothing smelled as clean and sharp as cedar and pine intermingled. It was then he saw it drift towards him on the downdraft, flipping gently, rising and falling. He rose to meet it, hair prickling the back of his neck and caught it before it touched the ground. He cradled it gently in his open palms then raised the feather to the sky.

The first, by Work's river — men called it the Stave now — that had been an omen, one he didn't comprehend. But this, this he understood. The gods had spoken. Like the fish, he was being given another life. Now he knew what he would do. He rose, chanted a soft, low melé of thanks then returned to his quarters and laid the feather carefully in his drawer between his shirts.

He made his way to the fort's dining hall. He'd already eaten but his stomach rumbled, triggered by the aroma of smoked bacon and beans escaping from the hall when men opened the door. He climbed the steps, and found Peopeo inside. He reached him in two steps and grasped him by the shoulder.

"I'm not going back," he said and Peopeo rose to his feet and gripped him in a great bear hug.

"What changed your mind?"

He didn't tell him about the eagle feather. Not yet. It was too soon to share, even with such a friend.

"I fit here, Peopeo. My family's well. My mother's healthy and happy, so I don't need to worry on her account. The place here has taken hold of me, the life, the land. It suits me. I belong."

"I know. It gets under your skin. Like a bad rash," he laughed, then grew serious. "Or a good woman. You know we could be in for trouble if Britain and America go to war."

"At least in Langley, we'll be able to help the Kwantlen if war comes."

"You mean the Fanon girl. What're you going to do about her?"

"Take out a marriage contract, if she'll have me. Though she always said she wouldn't be a country wife."

"Well, ask her anyway. Women change their minds. Though don't act as if you're making a big sacrifice on her account, bestowing some grand favour on her. Remember you're not the only one to risk something. Signing a contract is one thing. Promising to stay and make a life together, that's something else. You've seen men here drop wives and children like used boots. I made promises to my wife I intend to keep. What have you promised Rose?"

Nothing. Because he hadn't truly been able to give up Hawaii, till now. Till the moment the eagle spoke to him. Then, and only then, did he reverse his thinking — like Hopoo's Paul on the long road to Damascus. He suddenly felt jubilant and laughed out loud so that Peopeo thought he'd gone lolo. He left then to speak with the Chief Clerk, and returned shortly, bounding down the Big House steps, with a signed renewal agreement with the Company.

He borrowed a pen and ink from the clerk, and wrote Hopoo to say he was staying in the Pacific Northwest and described the life he planned with Rose, in this new land of mountains and rivers and trees. He would deliver the news to his mother for him. It hurt that he would never see her again, but her marriage to Pikoi had turned out well, and for that he was grateful. She was happy. She would cry, but in time would be content that he was happy too. He would always love her. Distance could not alter that. In his heart, his mother would always embody what was good and beautiful about Hawaii. Just as Rose embodied what was good and beautiful about Langley.

He felt calm, as after a storm. The gods had brought him here to these mountains and to the mighty Fraser. Whether they were Keaka's old gods or the haoles' new God didn't seem to matter. As time passed, they had rolled themselves into one in his mind anyway. Now he looked to the future. He understood others would follow. The mountains would call them, the rivers and the forests, to discover not just this great land, but themselves, as he had done. It didn't need discovering of course, for the land had always been here, but people were discovering it anew. He was part of the great changes happening in this land. Part of the future. He would serve the Company for another term. Perhaps after that he might join the free traders. Even own his own land. Meantime, he and Rose could move to Kanaka Creek with the others. He'd break new ground, cut some trees, grow potatoes, plant an orchard. Maybe even build a chicken coop! Strange he'd always dreamed of possessing land, yet in the end, this land came to possess him.

He returned to his hut, rummaged in his drawer and took out the white eagle's feather from between his folded shirts. It lay flat, its spine and feathers intact. He riffled the dark edges with his thumb then stuck it in his pocket. He'd need it now for what he still had to do.

The Sunday sun shone overhead and the air felt crisp and clear as he strode to the wharf. Along the path, bracken bushes and waist-high sword fern broke open in a sudden flurry of wings as a family of blue grouse heaved up from the ground and beat skyward. The faint sweet scent of ground dogwood reached his nose, and its fragrance lingered till he reached the river. He untied one of the Company canoes and paddled across to McMillan Island. The distant mountains felt close, awash with shades of mottled green. He breathed the fresh river air, feeling his muscles stretch as he pulled against the current. A wind picked up, shaking the trees along the shore and forming whitecaps on the river, but it was at his back — a good wind.

He paddled, knowing he'd chosen well. Here, good men would thrive. Men like Yale and Allard and Annance, equally at home in the wilderness with a book or a gun. And the wise Kwantlen Chief, Whattlekainem, seeking peace and drawing knowledge from the whites.

He hoped the natives would survive the waves of change washing across the land. They assimilated newcomers into the tribes, and clung to their culture, and this he judged their strength. If only they would rid themselves of wars and slavery. As for the haoles, he rued their will to prevail in all things, and over all men, no matter the cost. The Kanakas would find their fit. They were explorers too, with ambitions grown too large for their Island home to contain again. He saw himself as such a one, part of the new breed of men to embrace this great land.

When he reached shore, he hauled the canoe onto high ground and made for Neetlum's house. He walked the dirt path beneath his feet with bold strides, while his heart sledged in his chest. He felt he was passing through invisible gates beyond which lay a new future. He rapped on the hut wall sharply, then rustled the layered skins covering the doorway.

"Rose Fanon! Rose!" He heard the jangle of copper ankle bracelets as feet approached the door. She pulled aside the pelts, a half-finished basket dangling from her wrist and stepped out into the sunshine. She wore her haole style dress with the white shawl collar that set off the bronze of her skin. Long earrings hung from her small lobes, tiny pierced shells. She didn't speak immediately. He'd always liked that about her. Her right hand lifted as if by instinct to touch the dolphin at her throat.

"Aloha, Rose."

She dropped the basket and a smile began, a smile that would sprout pansies mid-winter. Again her fingers rested on the charm at her neck, Keaka's dolphin, no parting gift after all.

"Aloha, Kimo." Her smile widened, lit up her face and he felt ten feet tall. He didn't know how to say what he felt. He needed to get it right. English was the language of those men at the fort with their hungry pencils. It was the language of commerce, of money, not much good for exchanging intimacies between people who cared for each other. But he didn't know enough French or Kwantlen. So he spoke haltingly, like a man throwing a rope across a chasm he wasn't sure could be crossed.

"I'm staying, Rose. I can't go. The land here speaks to me. It's taken hold of me. And Fort Vancouver's buzzing with talk of splitting the Columbia. If that happens, it may mean war between Britain and America. That means the tribes may have to take sides as well. This land's worth fighting for, Rose, and if war does come, I'll stand with Britain and the Kwantlen. So I'm staying in Langley, that's a promise, and I'm asking you to marry me. Will you have me?"

He raised the eagle feather upright, level with his heart, so she would know he spoke the truth. She stared down at the feather and he thought for a long moment that she would say no, but she looked up and smiled. Histrionics he didn't expect. It wasn't her way. Later in private, it would be different. He waited patiently till she reached up and touched his cheek.

"You certainly used your short paddle to get here."

He laughed, way down deep in his belly somewhere. She had a way of surprising him sometimes that delighted him. In her presence, he felt as though he'd come home after a storm, to a place that was safe from the arrows of the outside world. He couldn't afford what Nicamous offered, but he'd produce some sort of bride price for her. Lower class Indians simply made verbal marriage arrangements but Rose was *smela:lh,* high status. He'd use the contract money he'd just received to buy goods from the store for that.

Surprisingly her parents offered no objection. They invited him into their home to arrange plans for the wedding — after the marriage agreement, a ceremony in the Kwantlen Village followed by a luau at Kanaka Creek. Rose walked with him to the canoe and the two hauled it to the river's edge. A silver fish leapt from the water, sparkling in the sunlight, splashing and sinking deeply into the river, leaving ripples across the water. He thought of his fish, dropped from the sky by the eagle, and wished it long life. When they reached shore, two bearded Canadiens whittling on the dock called to them in French. The day's wind caught their words, rustling them in with the leaves that scampered at their feet.

"What're they saying, Rose?"

"They're saying 'Welcome home, Kanaka.'"

Yes, it would be now, for Langley was his chosen place, and here his soul would bide. But Hawaii was home too, the place his soul had found its being. He halted then, for Keaka's voice came faintly on the wind. Or maybe it was his imagination. He strained to hear the old one's message, knowing somehow it would be the last, and his heart contracted with sudden understanding. Leaving one shore for another but never truly arriving was the road to despair.

He raised his head to the wind so it would catch and lift his words. He touched his lips and threw "Aloha!" upward with an out-stretched palm, towards the west, reaching as far as he could with his fingers, holding till his arm ached. It was no farewell to Hawaii, for that would never leave him. It was love he sent there now on the wind, and thanks.

"Aloha!" he called again, touching his lips and reaching his brown palm towards the broad blue river. The wind picked up his greeting and skipped along the whitecaps the length of the Fraser towards the tree-covered, soaring mountains beyond, bearing all his hopes and dreams.

He'd reached shore a long time ago. At last he had arrived.

ABOUT THE AUTHOR

SUSAN DOBBIE was born in Edinburgh, Scotland and educated at James Gillespie's High School for Girls. She immigrated to Canada in 1957. Married with three children, she is her husband's business partner in Dowco Consultants Ltd., with offices in Burnaby, Maple Ridge and Toronto. She has written newspaper and magazine articles, and edited various publications for groups she has been associated with over the years. She received a B.A. (English) from Simon Fraser University as a mature student. For ten years she has worked as a docent at Langley Centennial Museum, where she developed her interest in early Pacific Northwest history and, in particular, the Hawaiians who signed on with the Hudson's Bay Company for work at its forts on the west coast in the early nineteenth century. Now semi-retired, she lives in Langley and at Harrison Lake. This is her first novel. She is at work on a sequel.